OSLG

W9-BJK-988

DEC 2007

MR. MONK AND THE
TWO ASSISTANTS

MR. MONK AND THE TWO ASSISTANTS

LEE GOLDBERG

BASED ON THE USA NETWORK
TELEVISION SERIES
CREATED BY ANDY BRECKMAN

THORNDIKE
CHIVERS

This Large Print edition is published by Thorndike Press, Waterville, Maine, USA and by BBC Audiobooks Ltd, Bath, England.

Thorndike Press is an imprint of The Gale Group

Thorndike is a trademark and used herein under license.

The moral right of the author has been asserted.

Copyright © 2007 Universal Studios Licensing LLLP. Monk © USA Cable Entertainment LLC.

Thomson Gale is part of The Thomson Corporation.

Thomson and Star Logo and Thorndike are trademarks and Gale is a registered trademark used herein under license.

ALL RIGHTS RESERVED

This is a work of fiction. Names, characters, places, and incidents either are the product of the author's imagination or are used fictitiously, and any resemblance to actual persons, living or dead, business establishments, events or locales is entirely coincidental. The publisher does not have any control over and does not assume any responsibility for author or third-party Web sites or their content.

Thorndike Press® Large Print Laugh Lines.

The text of this Large Print edition is unabridged.

Other aspects of the book may vary from the original edition.

Set in 16 pt. Plantin.

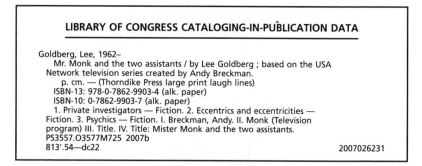

LIBRARY OF CONGRESS CATALOGING-IN-PUBLICATION DATA

Goldberg, Lee, 1962–
    Mr. Monk and the two assistants / by Lee Goldberg ; based on the USA Network television series created by Andy Breckman.
      p. cm. — (Thorndike Press large print laugh lines)
    ISBN-13: 978-0-7862-9903-4 (alk. paper)
    ISBN-10: 0-7862-9903-7 (alk. paper)
    1. Private investigators — Fiction. 2. Eccentrics and eccentricities — Fiction. 3. Psychics — Fiction. I. Breckman, Andy. II. Monk (Television program) III. Title. IV. Title: Mister Monk and the two assistants.
PS3557.O3577M725 2007b
813'.54—dc22   2007026231

BRITISH LIBRARY CATALOGUING-IN-PUBLICATION DATA AVAILABLE

Published in 2007 by arrangement with NAL Signet, a member of Penguin Group (USA) Inc.
Published in 2008 in the U.K. by arrangement with NAL Signet, a division of Penguin Group (USA) Inc.

U.K. Hardcover: 978 1 405 64294 1 (Chivers Large Print)
U.K. Softcover: 978 1 405 64295 8 (Camden Large Print)

Printed in the United States of America on permanent paper
10 9 8 7 6 5 4 3 2 1

Mystery
Goldberg, Lee, 1962-
Mr. Monk and the two
assistants [large print]

To Valerie and Madison, who keep me
(relatively) sane

ACKNOWLEDGMENTS AND AUTHOR'S NOTE

I would like to thank Dr. D. P. Lyle, William Rabkin, Pat Tierney, Sarah Bewley, Ivan Van Laningham, Rhys Bowen, Bob Morris, William Tapply, Carol Schmidt, Peggy Burdick, Mark Murphy, Annette Mahon, Mary Ellen Hughes, Alex Brett, Jack Quick, Robert Thompson and Anne Tomlin for their technical assistance on a variety of murderous topics. Any mistakes or factual liberties are my fault and not theirs, though I suppose they could be accused of aiding and abetting my crimes.

Special thanks to Kerry Donovan, Gina Maccoby, Stefanie Preston and most of all Andy Breckman, the creator of Adrian Monk, for their incredible support and encouragement.

While I try as best I can to stay true to the continuity of the TV series, it's not always possible, given the long lead time between when my books are written and when they are published. During that period, new episodes may air that contradict details or situations referred to in my books. If you come across any such continuity mismatches, your understanding is appreciated.

I would love to hear from you. Stop by www.leegoldberg.com and say hello. Remember to floss twenty times daily.

CHAPTER ONE:
MR. MONK GETS
HIS KICKS

My name is Natalie Teeger. I'm an honest-to-goodness soccer mom and proud of it. My twelve-year-old daughter, Julie, plays defense on the Slammers in the all-girl league. The kids get together at Dolores Park for practices on Saturdays and games on Sundays.

On this particular Sunday, my boss, Adrian Monk, the legendary detective, was with us at the game. He was too restless to stay at home. For the past couple days, he'd been investigating the brutal beating death of the reviled E. L. Lancaster, who ran the mortgage division of a San Francisco bank.

Lancaster was disliked by just about everyone he'd ever met. He'd even fore-closed on his parents' home when his father, slipping into senility, missed a couple mortgage payments.

I'm not kidding. Lancaster was that lovable.

9

The only clue Monk had to work with was a confusing cluster of overlapping bloody footprints belonging to the murderer.

Captain Leland Stottlemeyer's theory on the footprints was that the victim must have delivered a blow in self-defense that left his attacker reeling and dizzy.

Lieutenant Randy Disher, the captain's right-hand man, was checking area hospitals for anyone who might have come in with a head wound.

I've seen Monk solve a homicide within a few minutes of arriving at the crime scene. But this case had too many suspects and too few clues. The investigation was making Monk even more nuts than usual.

Monk's basic problem is that he's obsessed with imposing order on a world that is, by nature, disordered. It's a problem he's never going to solve. But he's not alone in his futile pursuit. We've all got the same problem, only not to his degree.

Look at me, for example. My job is to make Monk's life as orderly as possible so he can focus on bringing order to disorder, which is the method he uses to solve murders, which is how he makes a living, which is how he's able to pay me.

When I'm not with Monk, I'm trying to maintain some kind of order in my own life

10

and to create a consistent, safe and nurturing environment for my daughter.

So I scramble to pay the bills, to do the laundry, to keep the house clean, to get Julie to school on time, to make sure she gets all her work done, to coordinate all her activities, playdates, to — Well, you get the point, because you're probably doing it, too.

I can never get ahead of it all. I can never get everything under control. And I never will. I know that, but I keep trying to anyway.

That's Monk, too.

But I don't obsess about my failure to get my life under control.

And because I'm unlike Monk, the act of trying to put things in order doesn't give me a unique perspective on the world around me — one that allows me to see things that others don't and solve complex mysteries.

I've learned to accept that there's always going to be chaos, that things can never, ever be brought under control and that it's the unpredictable, disorderly, uncontrollable nature of things that *is* life.

Disorder is the unexpected. It's discovery. It's change. And as hard as we try to bring order to our lives, deep down we all know that it's that little bit of disorder that makes life exciting.

So why do we constantly keep working to put our lives in order anyway? Why do I?

I don't know.

But sometimes I wonder if Monk does, because restoring order in all things is his obsession.

I knew the disorder that the Lancaster case represented had to be eating away at Monk. And I was worried about what he'd do to compensate for that anxiety.

So on that Sunday afternoon, I had decided to stop by Monk's place on our way to the soccer game just to see how he was doing. Julie begged me not to, but I was worried about him.

It turns out I had good reason to be.

I found Monk on his hands and knees cleaning his carpet strand by strand, using a magnifying glass and a toothbrush.

I couldn't leave him like that, so I made him come along with us, despite Julie's fervent protests. I couldn't blame her for objecting. Monk once helped me coach her basketball team, and it was a disaster.

I tried to console Julie by assuring her that this time Monk was going to be merely a spectator in the stands. How much harm could he do?

Little did I know.

We were playing at Dolores Park on a clear, sunny day, with barely a wisp of fog in the air. The park was on the steep hill that divided the Noe Valley neighborhood where we live from the urban bustle of the Civic Center. The spectators not only had a great view of the field, but of the downtown San Francisco skyline as well.

The Slammers were up against the Killer Cleats, the number-one team in the league — also the meanest. The Killer Cleats played soccer as a contact sport, mowing down any kid who got in their way. They were way too rough, and their coach, a big, angry man named Harv Felder, drove them hard, brutally berating any player who didn't come off the field with an opposing team member's flesh between her teeth.

The coaches and families of both teams were on the same side of the field, but each on their own set of four-row, metal bleachers.

Early in the first quarter, one of the Killer Cleats got hit in the back of the head with the ball, allowing one of the Slammers to get past her and score a goal.

The ref blew his whistle, calling a brief time-out to give the injured player, a girl named Katie, an opportunity to leave the field.

Katie staggered to the sidelines, trying not to cry, and another Killer Cleat went out to replace her.

"Good defense, Katie. Way to play," Raul Mendez, our coach, said sincerely to Katie as she passed him. He was the father of four girls and a real sweet guy. The player glanced at him but didn't acknowledge his comment.

"You call that playing?" Felder screamed at her, getting his face right in hers, close enough so Katie could probably feel his spittle spraying her from between his clenched teeth. "You're a loser, Katie, a sniveling little worm. You sicken me."

Katie burst into tears and Felder mimicked her as she lumbered back to her embarrassed parents.

"Boo-hoo-hoo. And you're a crybaby too," Felder added. "Get out of my sight before I puke."

Raul shook his head in disgust. "Hey, man, don't you think you're being a little hard on her? They're just kids. It's only a game."

Felder sneered at Raul. "That's what the losers always say."

The game resumed and almost immediately one of the Killer Cleats plowed into a Slammer, knocking her on her back and actually running over her to make a goal.

Felder thrust his fist into the air and did a little victory dance.

"I hate that man," I hissed to Monk.

But Monk wasn't at my side anymore. He was up in the bleachers trying to convince people to move to different spots so there would be an even number of people on each row. I got up and dragged him back down.

"Please stop harassing the parents," I said.

"Look at them," Monk said. "Three sitting in one row, five in another. Only one sitting up top. It's irresponsible. They should set an example for their kids."

The Killer Cleats elbowed, kicked and tackled their way through the Slammers to score another goal. The ref never called a single penalty against them. I figured he was either blind or a buddy of Felder's.

"What about the example *he* sets?" I said, motioning to Felder, who was doing another one of his victory dances.

"Make 'em bleed," Felder yelled to his team.

"Our team is getting murdered," I said.

Monk stared at Felder. "Call the captain."

"I didn't mean that comment literally," I said.

"Call him." Monk shifted his shoulders and rolled his head. "Tell him to bring handcuffs."

By the time Captain Stottlemeyer showed up, it was the second half, the score was seven to one, and Monk had nagged all the parents on our team to sit on a single row in the middle of the bleachers.

"You'll thank me later," he told them.

I doubted it. In fact, they might even ban me from attending future games. I could feel them glaring at me, but I pretended not to notice.

Stottlemeyer had the same look on his face as the parents. He was wearing a T-shirt, a Windbreaker, and a pair of faded jeans. The captain clearly wasn't thrilled at being dragged out of his apartment on his day off.

"You better have a good reason for this, Monk," Stottlemeyer said.

"We need to have a talk with them." Monk motioned to the parents on the Killer Cleat bleachers. "They aren't going to listen to me."

"You called me down here to rearrange the people on the bleachers?"

"It's a safety issue," Monk said.

"Uh-huh." Stottlemeyer turned his back on Monk, so the captain missed seeing the Slammer goalie get pummeled by the ball and the Killer Cleats score another goal. "I'm leaving."

"Wait," Monk said. "You can't go without arresting the coach."

"For disorderly seating?"

"For murder," Monk said.

Stottlemeyer stopped walking and turned around slowly to face Monk again. "I can't arrest him for winning the game."

"How about for killing the banker?" Monk said.

Stottlemeyer gave him a look. "You've got to be kidding."

Monk pointed to Felder, who was doing his little victory dance. "That explains the footprints."

"It does?"

"It's his ritual. He does it whenever he wins," Monk said. "Those steps match the sequence of bloody footprints at the bank."

Stottlemeyer and Monk stepped closer to Felder, staring at his feet as he danced.

"I'll be damned," Stottlemeyer said, rubbing his bushy mustache.

Felder spun around and glowered at them. "What the hell do you think you're doing?"

Stottlemeyer flashed his badge at Felder. "SFPD homicide. You're under arrest for the murder of E. L. Lancaster, manager of Golden State Bank."

Felder's jaw dropped in astonishment. So did mine. Jaws were dropping everywhere.

Stottlemeyer cuffed Felder, read him his rights and started to lead him away.

Monk cleared his throat. "Aren't you forgetting something?"

Stottlemeyer groaned, turned around and held up his badge so the parents in the Killer Cleat bleachers could see it.

"Hey, everybody, listen up," the captain said. "You have two choices. Either sit in even numbers on even-numbered rows, or all of you have to sit together on one row."

"Why?" one parent asked.

"It's a safety issue," Stottlemeyer said. "If you want to avoid a citation, I suggest you listen to him." Stottlemeyer tipped his head toward Monk and then led Felder off the field.

The Slammers and their parents began to applaud. We were cheering about Harv Felder getting taken away in handcuffs, but that's not how Monk saw it.

"See?" Monk said to me. "Everybody appreciates balanced seating."

CHAPTER TWO:
MR. MONK AND THE
UNLUCKY BREAK

I don't think there's anything in the soccer rule book that covers what to do when the coach of a team is arrested for murder during a game. The ref didn't know how to deal with it. The parents of the Killer Cleats wanted to call it quits and take their kids home. Raul was glad to oblige — if the Killer Cleats agreed to forfeit the game. The Killer Cleats weren't willing to take a loss, so the game went on.

Raul probably figured that the trauma of seeing their coach dragged off to jail would undermine the morale of the Killer Cleats to such a massive degree that we actually might have a chance to beat them. Instead, it just pissed them off. They returned to the field seething like a pack of rabid wolves.

Christy Clark, the Cleats' forward, drove the ball right down the center of the field. She was as wide as two girls and plowed through everything, and everyone, in her path like a runaway bulldozer.

Most of the Slammers had the good sense to get the hell out of Christy's way, the game be damned, except my dear, sweet, stubborn daughter.

Julie was not going to let that ball get past her. She grimaced and charged Christy.

I think I even heard Julie growl.

Christy and Julie bashed into each other like raging elk, kicking the ball between them as they butted against each other. Somehow Christy managed to kick the ball past Julie and knock her down.

My daughter hit the ground hard and let out an anguished cry that was equal parts pain and fury.

Christy and the Killer Cleats surged past Julie and made another goal, the whole team erupting in cheers.

At least they didn't trample Julie, which I took as an act of rare mercy on their part. I stood up and waited for Julie to get to her feet.

Monk tugged at my shirt.

"You're standing," he said.

"I know that, Mr. Monk."

"But everyone else is sitting," Monk said. "You're making a scene."

"I'm concerned about my daughter."

"What if another person stands up? Then

it's *two* people standing and everyone else sitting, and before you know it, the whole world collapses into anarchy."

At that moment, my whole world was one twelve-year-old girl and she wasn't standing up. I ran out onto the field. Raul joined me.

Monk stood and waved everyone else in the bleachers to follow, which they did, presumably cowed into obedience by Captain Stottlemeyer's speech.

When Raul and I reached Julie, she was sitting up, cradling her right arm and trying very hard not to cry.

"Are you okay, honey?" I asked.

She shook her head. "I think my arm is broken."

"It's probably just a sprain," Raul said.

He was accustomed to kids overreacting to the sudden pain of an unexpected fall. But he didn't know Julie the way I did. When she was a baby, she once managed to wriggle out of her high chair and fell on the kitchen floor. Any other baby would have been wailing, but Julie sat there, fighting the urge to cry and furious with herself for not being able to succeed.

Julie was a fighter, like her dad.

So seeing her now, eyes filled with tears, told me more than any X-ray ever could. If she said her arm was broken, it was.

I looked up and saw Monk organizing the reluctant parents into a circle around us. According to Monk-think, if one spectator was on the field, then *all* the spectators had to be out there. Monk had a pained expression on his face, even more so than Julie. He leaned down and whispered in my ear.

"Get ahold of yourself, woman," Monk said. "This is no way to behave in public."

"We're going to the hospital, Mr. Monk," I said.

"Why would you want to do a crazy thing like that?" he said, exasperated, as Raul and I gently lifted Julie to her feet.

"Can't you see that Julie has hurt herself?" I said as we led Julie toward the parking lot. Even though I was pretty sure she'd broken her arm, I didn't want to confirm her fears by saying it aloud.

"You can't take her to a hospital," he said, trailing after us, insistently waving the other parents to follow. "They're full of sick people!"

"That's where we're going," I said. "If you want to take a taxi home, be my guest."

He groaned. "That's like giving me a choice between slitting my own throat and shooting myself."

But he came with us anyway.

■ ■ ■ ■

The doctor had already given Julie a preliminary exam and she'd just returned from having her arm x-rayed when Monk finally joined us. He opened the curtain surrounding Julie's bed in the ER as if he was stepping out onto a stage.

Ladies and gentlemen, give it up for Adrian Monk!

He'd managed to find a hospital patient gown to put over his clothes, rubber gloves for his hands and a surgical mask to cover his nose and mouth.

It was quite a sight and well worth the wait. He brought a smile to Julie's face when she needed it the most — not that he meant to.

"What?" Monk asked us, totally oblivious to his clownish appearance.

"Don't take this the wrong way, Mr. Monk," Julie said, "but you look silly."

"I think what you mean is 'sensibly dressed.' "

"You're right," she said, sharing a glance with me. "That's exactly what I meant."

"I'm relieved to hear you say that," he said as he wheeled in a cart containing gowns, gloves and masks for us both. "It may not be too late to save you, too."

"From what?" I said.

"You name it," he said. "The black death, Ebola, scurvy."

"You can't catch scurvy," Julie said. "You get it from not eating enough oranges."

"That's an old wives' tale," Monk said, handing out our garments, "from wives who later died of scurvy."

That's when the doctor came in. He had such a grim expression on his youthful face, I was afraid he was going to tell us Julie had a brain tumor.

"I'm afraid you have a broken wrist," the doctor said. "The good news is that it's a clean break. You'll only have to wear a cast for a couple weeks."

If that was all, why did he have to look so serious? Maybe he thought it made him appear more learned and mature so he wouldn't get a lot of flack from patients for being so young.

Actually, it made him look like he'd eaten something for lunch that decided to fight back.

"Do I get to pick the color for my cast?" Julie asked.

"Absolutely," he said and waved over an ER nurse.

She walked behind Monk and held up a

chart with a dozen sample plaster colors for Julie to see. There was something vaguely familiar about the nurse, but I couldn't place her.

She had thick, curly brown hair with blond highlights and stood with attitude. By that, I mean she had a certain rough confidence about her, the kind that's like a scar. It's a toughness you can only get on the streets, and not the ones you find in suburban housing tracts. Growing up in suburbia, you end up with a pampered confidence that comes from knowing you have mutual funds earning money for you.

"We have a wide selection of colors to choose from," the doctor said. "Or you can go with white and rent your arm out for advertising."

"Really?" Julie replied. "What does that pay?"

I was taken aback by the question. When had Julie become so entrepreneurial?

"I'm kidding," the doctor said.

"But it's not a bad idea." Julie looked at me. "We could go around to local businesses, like the pizza parlor or the bike shop, and see if they'd be interested in using my arm as a walking billboard."

This broken wrist was revealing a whole new side of my daughter to me.

"You have a deal," I said.

"You could offer them a special rate to advertise on both arms," Monk added.

"But I don't have a cast on my left arm," Julie said.

"You will," he said, nodding.

"No, I won't," she said.

"It's what they do in these situations."

The nurse was starting to fidget, tapping her foot on the floor in frustration.

"But my left wrist isn't broken," Julie said.

"It doesn't matter," he said. "It's standard medical procedure."

"You want me to put a cast on her left wrist?" the doctor asked Monk incredulously.

"Doesn't that go without saying?"

"No," the doctor said, "it doesn't."

"You can't put a cast on only one wrist," Monk said. "She'll be off-balance."

"The cast isn't that heavy," the doctor said. "I can assure you that her balance will be just fine."

"It will if she has a cast on both arms." Monk turned to me. "Where did this guy go to medical school? If I were you, I'd get a second opinion."

The nurse's face was growing tense and a flush was rising on her cheeks. She looked like she might hit Monk with that display board she was holding.

I knew what she was feeling all too well. I had to bring this ridiculous debate to an end before Monk needed medical attention.

"Julie is not getting a cast on her left wrist, Mr. Monk," I said, "because it's not broken."

"You aren't thinking rationally. You're clearly in shock over Julie's injury. You ought to have a doctor look at you." Monk glanced dismissively at the doctor. "A *real* one."

"I don't want a cast on both wrists," Julie said to me.

"Don't worry, honey," I said. "It's not going to happen."

"Of course it is," Monk said. "She can't leave here imbalanced."

"You mean unbalanced," the doctor said, "not imbalanced."

"What do you know?" Monk said.

"I know you're imbalanced for thinking she's unbalanced," he said, smiling at his own cleverness.

Monk was not amused. "You're under arrest."

"For what?" the doctor asked.

"Impersonating a doctor."

"Are you a police officer?"

"I'm a consultant to the police," Monk said. "I investigate homicides."

"I haven't killed anyone," the doctor said.

"Not yet," Monk said. "But if you keep practicing medicine like this, you will."

The nurse suddenly threw the display card against the wall in a fit of anger, startling us all.

"That's enough, Adrian," she said. "Believe it or not, the whole world doesn't revolve around you and your special needs. This poor girl has been through enough today without having to deal with you, too. So shut up and let us do our jobs."

Monk jerked at the sound of her voice, his eyes going wide with shock.

The nurse took a deep, calming breath and then looked at me. "I'm sorry about that, but this is an argument you can't win. Trust me. The only way any of us is going to get any peace is if we put a cast on Julie's left wrist."

Before I could object, the nurse stepped up to Julie. "Don't worry, honey. After the cast dries, I'm going to cut it off, put some Velcro straps on it and give it to you. That way, you can put it on whenever Adrian is around and take it off the instant he leaves. Problem solved."

Adrian? Hearing Monk addressed that way by a person I assumed was a complete stranger to him startled me a bit. I'd never heard anyone but Monk's brother and his shrink refer to him by his first name. I assumed that familiarity was simply a calming and controlling technique nurses and other medical professionals used to deal with emotionally or psychologically disturbed individuals.

"Or I could have this guy committed," the doctor said, narrowing his eyes at Monk. "That would solve the problem, too."

"I appreciate the offer, but I think we'll go with the second cast," I said, turning to Julie. "If that's okay with you."

"Yeah," Julie said. "I just want to go home."

The nurse smiled. "Don't we all. I'll be right back."

She left to get whatever she needed to make the cast. Monk hadn't moved since she'd spoken. I don't think he'd even blinked. I was impressed with the decisive way she'd handled the situation, and I appreciated it, but I couldn't figure out why her speaking up shocked Monk into silence.

The doctor said something about us coming back in a couple weeks, gave me a prescription for painkillers for Julie and then he left to treat another patient.

I looked at Monk. He seemed frozen in place.

"Would you mind staying with Julie for a minute?" I asked him.

Monk nodded ever so slightly. He wasn't going anywhere.

I caught up with the nurse at the supply cabinet.

"Excuse me," I said. "I just wanted to say thank you for helping out. Sometimes my friend can be difficult to handle."

"I'm used to it," she said, her back to me as she scrounged around for her things.

"You must meet a lot of people like Mr. Monk."

She sighed wearily. "There's nobody like Adrian."

She'd done it again. She'd called him Adrian. There was something about the way she said it, with her strong New Jersey accent, that gave me a pang of anxiety in the pit of my stomach. I suddenly had an ominous inkling what the explanation for her familiarity with him might be.

"You've obviously had some experience with him before," I said, fishing.

"That's one way of putting it," she said, turning to look at him again, almost affectionately. "I used to have your job."

And that's when I saw the ID badge clipped to her uniform and my suspicions were confirmed.

Sharona was back.

CHAPTER THREE:
MR. MONK AND THE
REUNION

From what I've been told, Monk has always had obsessive-compulsive tendencies, but after his wife, Trudy, was killed by a car bomb, they completely overwhelmed him. He couldn't function at all. The police department forced him into taking an unpaid leave of absence and going into intensive, outpatient psychiatric care.

It became so bad for Monk that, in order to avoid institutionalization, he required a private nurse to administer his medication and help him put his life back together.

Sharona Fleming was that nurse.

She was a divorced mother who was raising a boy who was the same age as Julie. I know from personal experience that it couldn't have been easy taking care of Monk at his worst and her kid at the same time. She must have reserves of strength that Arnold Schwarzenegger would envy.

Sharona not only got Monk off the meds

and out of the house again, but she even coaxed him into consulting for the police on their trickiest homicide cases. Thanks to her, Monk gradually overcame his crippling grief and got a good-enough grip on his phobias that it seemed possible that he might get his job back again.

And then one Monday morning, without any advance warning, Sharona didn't show up for work. She left a note informing Monk that she'd moved back to New Jersey and remarried her ex-husband, Trevor.

In Monk's desperation to find a new assistant, he stumbled on me, a woman with no nursing experience whatsoever. I was a widowed mother working as a bartender in a real dive. But, for some reason, we got along.

Monk didn't care that I wasn't qualified, so I didn't, either. All that mattered to me was that it was a better job than the one I had, I'd be home to put my daughter to bed each night and no more drunks would be vomiting on me.

At first, I felt like an actress brought in to replace a beloved character on a hit TV show. For months, it seemed as if I was constantly being compared by Monk, and everyone else in his life, to Sharona, and falling short.

But somehow Monk and I made it work.

It was hard, and it took time and effort, but Monk, Stottlemeyer and Disher eventually accepted me for who I was instead of expecting me to be a Sharona clone. I was even picking up a few things about detective work.

I finally had a job I was comfortable with, even competent at, and things were going more smoothly than ever.

And now Sharona was back, damn her.

I turned to Monk. He still hadn't moved. She followed my gaze.

"He's handling it much better than I thought he would," Sharona said.

"He's catatonic," I said.

"He'll snap out of it eventually," she said. "Enjoy the quiet while you can."

"I like Mr. Monk when he's lively," I said.

"Yeah, I noticed." She gave me a look and carried her supplies over to Julie.

I followed along behind her. I was pissed off and couldn't tell you exactly why. Maybe I could if I had her medical and psychological training. I looked at Monk. He was still staring, wide-eyed, at something none of us could see.

"Julie," I said, "this is Sharona."

My daughter's eyebrows shot up. "*That* Sharona?"

Sharona smiled. "I'm infamous. I guess I should be flattered."

"Don't be," I said.

Julie looked at me, making me feel self-conscious about my hostility. Sharona had never done anything to hurt me, at least not yet. But she'd certainly hurt Monk.

"You won't feel a thing," Sharona said to Julie. "Just keep your arm still and let me do all the work."

She began to wrap Julie's broken wrist with gauze.

"You never even said good-bye," Monk mumbled. It was barely more than a whisper.

"Excuse me?" Sharona said, glancing at him. "You'll have to speak up."

"Good-bye," Monk said, clearing his throat and rolling his shoulders. "You didn't say it."

Sharona kept her eyes on her work, running the gauze in the space between Julie's thumb and index finger and around her wrist. "It was for your own good, Adrian. If I'd told you I was going to leave, you never would have let me go. You would have fallen apart."

"I did," Monk said.

"It could have been worse," she said.

"No," Monk said, "it couldn't."

"Adrian, we both know that isn't true," Sharona said. "You were ready for more independence and I had my own life to lead. I was doing us both a favor."

"You lied to him," I said.

"No, I didn't," she said and began applying strips of moist gauzy material over Julie's wrapped-up wrist.

"You're still in San Francisco," I said. "You didn't go to New Jersey."

"I went," Sharona said.

"Then what are you doing here now?" I said.

She gave me a cold look. "Not that it's any of your business, but things didn't go the way I planned. We were only back in New Jersey for a few months when a friend of Trevor's in LA offered to sell him his little landscaping business: mowing lawns, trimming hedges, that kind of thing. Trevor wanted us to buy it. That meant using almost all our savings."

Sharona finished with Julie's right arm and began applying gauze to her left.

"But it seemed like a good business to me and I thought it could be a fresh start for all of us. So we bought the business and moved. Things went well for a while and then they didn't. Trevor and I split up again. Benji and I moved back here."

"Why San Francisco?" I asked. "Why not go back to New Jersey?"

"Because I knew I couldn't hold down a job and raise Benji alone. I needed help and my sister lives here."

"I do, too," Monk said.

"I know that, Adrian," Sharona said. "But you need more help than you're capable of giving."

"You were there for me," Monk said. "I would have been there for you. I still can be."

I wanted to grab him and shake him hard.

Why was he mewling like that? Sharona walked out on *him*. Where was his anger? He sounded like it was all his fault that she left. And then it hit me that he probably thought that it was.

"I was going to call you, Adrian. Honestly I was. But I just wasn't ready for you in my life again. Things are too complicated as it is."

I took some comfort in that.

"What drove you and Trevor apart this time?" Monk asked.

She took a deep breath and let it out slowly. "He murdered someone," Sharona said.

Everyone within earshot who wasn't Sharona gasped at once. That would be me,

37

Monk, Julie, and an orderly who happened to be walking by.

I don't know what was more astonishing: that Sharona's husband was involved with a murder or that she didn't call Monk, the world's best homicide investigator, about it the day Trevor was arrested.

Sharona gave the orderly a look and he hurried along to spread the gossip to the rest of the hospital staff.

"Your husband is accused of murder," I said, "and you *still* didn't call Mr. Monk?"

Sharona turned to him. "You couldn't have helped me."

He nodded.

Why did he nod? He couldn't possibly have agreed with her. Monk was insecure about everything *except* his detective skills. On that point, he was in complete agreement with everyone else that he was the best of the best at solving homicides.

She had to know that, too. But I decided to rub it in anyway, if only to get a rise out of Monk.

"Solving murders is what Mr. Monk does," I said. "It's like a superpower."

"He found out who killed the firehouse dog for me," Julie said. "He's a great detective."

"I know he is, honey, but it wouldn't make

any difference this time," Sharona said to Julie, beginning to apply the wet strips to her left arm, "because my husband is guilty."

"Did he confess?" I said.

"Of course not," Sharona said. "Trevor says he's innocent. He always says that and he never is. That's why I divorced him before."

"Maybe he's telling the truth this time and you've abandoned him when he needs you the most," I said. "You seem to be pretty good at that."

"Maybe," Sharona said, ignoring my cheap shot. "But I've run out of trust where he's concerned. I won't put myself or Benji through the ordeal of a trial. I'm done. I never should have remarried him."

"So now you're living in San Francisco again and working in a hospital," Monk said, finally speaking up to state the obvious. "How can you stand it?"

"It's a job," Sharona said.

"Is it better than the one you had?" he said.

"You mean with you?"

"Don't you miss it?" he asked.

"My life has changed, Adrian." Sharona glanced at me, and then back at him. "And so has yours."

That was the end of the conversation, at

least between us adults.

Sharona made some small talk with Julie about school as she completed the casts and let them dry. Then Sharona cut the left cast off with a plaster saw and fitted it on her arm again with Velcro tabs. She put Julie's arms into slings, adjusted the straps and then admired her handiwork.

"How's that look to you, Adrian?" Sharona asked.

"Balanced," Monk said.

"Wow, there's no higher praise than that in your book," Sharona said. "That may just be the nicest compliment you've ever given me."

I resented Monk for making my daughter even more uncomfortable than she had to be and I resented Sharona for just being there.

"Can I play soccer next weekend?" Julie asked.

"With your arm in the cast?" Sharona said.

"Arms," Monk corrected.

"Why not?" Julie said. "You're only supposed to use your feet, not your hands."

"I don't think that's a very good idea," Sharona said. "But I like your attitude. You're tough."

"I'm a Teeger," Julie said. "We don't give up."

I don't know whether Julie was sending a message to Sharona on my behalf, but I loved her for it anyway.

"I believe you." Sharona looked at me. "It was really nice meeting you both. I'm just sorry it was under these circumstances."

"Me, too," I said.

Sharona turned to Monk. "It was good to see you, Adrian. You seem to be doing just great."

"I was," Monk said forlornly.

I was so angry with Monk that I was tempted to leave him at the hospital. Let Sharona take him home if he missed her so much.

But in the end, I just walked out with Julie and he followed along with us to the car, like nothing had ever happened. Like we hadn't just run into his former assistant and he hadn't practically offered her *my* job in front of *my* face.

How could he be so insensitive? So selfish?

So *Monk?*

We rode in silence. Nobody said a word.

I dropped him off at his house and sped off, not even waiting to see if he got to his door. He was a grown man; if he couldn't handle the journey from the sidewalk to his living room, too bad for him.

"Are you angry?" Julie said.

"What makes you say that?" I snapped.

"You're grimacing and your face is red," she said. "Is it because of me? Because of the medical bills?"

"No, dear, of course not," I said, consciously willing the edge out of my voice. "I'm not mad at you at all. You've been amazing. I am so proud of you."

"What for? It's no big accomplishment to break your wrist."

"For being so brave and strong and mature. You were very considerate with Mr. Monk when he wasn't very considerate with you."

"That's not true, Mom. Mr. Monk is scared of hospitals but he came with us anyway," she said. "He must really care about me."

"He does," I said.

"Now he knows that I care about him, too."

"That's why I'm so proud of you," I said. "You're worrying about how other people feel at a time when you should only be worrying about yourself."

"There is no such time," she said.

"Who says?" I asked.

"I do," she said. "It's something I decided."

I'd spent so many years teaching my daughter how to think, but I'd missed the moment when she'd started thinking for herself. My little girl was growing up into someone with her own beliefs and opinions about life.

When had *that* happened? And why was it bringing tears to my eyes? I was turning into an emotional wreck.

"You still haven't told me what you're mad about," Julie said.

"I'm mad at the Killer Cleats for playing so rough. I'm mad that you got hurt. And I'm mad that both of your arms are in casts when only one of them needs to be."

"And you're mad that Sharona came back."

"Yeah," I admitted, "that, too."

"If you lose your job," Julie asked, "will Mr. Monk still come to see us?"

"I hope so," I said.

CHAPTER FOUR:
MR. MONK CAN'T
DECIDE

When we got home, I took the extra cast off Julie's left arm, made us both grilled cheese sandwiches and gave her a couple painkillers. She went to bed early that night and was asleep within a minute. I went to bed early, too, but sleep didn't come as easily for me.

I was really troubled about Sharona coming back into Monk's life. I won't lie to you, I felt threatened.

Monk wasn't an easy man to work with. I was hired to take care of him, to be his caretaker, his driver, his shopper, his secretary and his companion. It was a real struggle at first.

Over time, though, that relationship had changed and things got easier for both of us. I wasn't just taking care of him anymore — he was taking care of me, too. I had come to rely on Monk, and he on me, in ways that went beyond employer and employee.

If you set aside Monk's phobias and hang-ups, we had a lot in common. We'd both lost a spouse to a violent death — my husband, Mitch, was a Navy pilot shot down in Kosovo. I never found out exactly what happened to Mitch and Monk is still haunted by his wife Trudy's unsolved murder.

When Monk and I met, we were both reeling from our losses and trying to cope. We still were, but at least we had each other to lean on. We understood each other's pain without having to explain a thing. It was nice to know that *someone* did and that meant a lot to me. It made me feel less alone and I think it did for him, too.

Monk had also become the only dependable, constant man in my daughter's life since Mitch was killed. Sure, I'd dated some men, but there hadn't been any real romances (though I almost fell for a firefighter once, a guy named Joe Cochran, who still pursues me. Sometimes I wish I'd let myself get caught, but I was afraid I'd lose him to a fire the way I lost Mitch to a war). I didn't introduce Julie to many of the men and I never brought any of them home to spend the night. I didn't want Julie to get attached to a man only to have her heart broken when he left.

I never thought that she'd see Monk as anything but my strange boss or that she would come to care for him so much. I guess that, despite all his eccentricities, Julie knew she could count on him.

Monk was the ultimate creature of habit and a man who strenuously resisted change. Sometimes, where kids are concerned, that can be a good thing.

The three of us spent a lot of time together doing mundane, domestic things that had nothing to do with my job. It was comfortable, and it was safe, and I didn't want to lose it.

And I knew that I would if Monk fired me and gave Sharona her old job back.

But Sharona had a big edge over me. She was the one who'd saved Monk and she always would be. No matter how long I worked for him, or how close we became, I couldn't beat that. He'd forgive her for just about anything. I would always be in second position.

It scared me.

But like Julie said, I'm a Teeger. I wasn't going down without a fight. And I'd pretty much decided at the hospital that my relationship with Adrian Monk was something worth fighting for.

■ ■ ■ ■

I would have gladly let Julie stay home from school on Monday but she insisted on going anyway. I think she wanted to show off her cast and prove how tough she was, which was fine by me. I promised to take her around our bohemian Noe Valley neighborhood that night to offer the merchants along Twenty-fourth Street the chance to advertise on her arm. In the meantime, Julie was going to give some thought to the advertising rates she wanted to charge.

I thought she had a pretty good chance of finding some takers. We were living in San Francisco, after all, where people enthusiastically embraced the weird, the radical and the crazy. It was no wonder that Monk was so comfortable here and found so much around him that needed straightening, balancing and organizing.

San Francisco. Home of the crookedest street in the world *and* Adrian Monk. Somehow that just seemed right to me and was proof that God has a terrific sense of humor.

I dropped Julie off at school and headed straight to Monk's apartment on Pine. There was an old, beat-up Volvo station wagon in my spot with a hospital-employee parking permit stuck to the windshield.

I found the symbolic value of that very unnerving. Sharona certainly hadn't wasted any time moving in on me. This was going to be war. I could see that now.

I flung open Monk's front door and marched in like a jealous wife hoping to catch her husband cheating on her.

The two of them were sitting at Monk's dining room table, eating bowls of Wheat Chex, without milk, of course. Monk was afraid of milk, even when it was in someone else's bowl.

"Perfect timing, Natalie," Monk said. "Sharona just stopped by with breakfast. She brought Chex!"

"How nice," I said, meaning, of course, *How terrible.*

"I was on my way home from work and thought I'd drop in and say hello," Sharona said. "I know Adrian can always use more Chex."

"You just finished work?" Monk asked. "But it's nine a.m."

"The Sunday hell shift was the only one I could get," Sharona said. "All the good ones were already taken by nurses with more seniority than I have. But what could I do? I needed the job."

Which I was sure was her oh so subtle way of saying she wanted her old one back. It was bad enough she was bribing Monk with Chex.

"So who got Benji off to school?" Monk asked.

"My sister. We're living with her until I can get on my feet again," Sharona said. "But with Trevor's legal problems, that could be a while."

"I thought you'd turned your back on him," I said.

"I did, but we still have a joint bank account and he's already taken what little we had left in our savings to pay his defense lawyer."

"I'm sure Mr. Monk could help," I said.

"I couldn't borrow money from Adrian," Sharona said.

"No," Monk said, "you couldn't."

"What I meant was that you wouldn't have to live with your sister, or pay any legal fees, if Mr. Monk gets Trevor out of prison," I said, turning to Monk. "You don't have any cases right now anyway."

"If Sharona says he's guilty," Monk said, "then I'm sure he is."

"How do you know?" I said.

"Because the police arrested him and he's in jail," Monk said. "That means he's guilty until proven innocent."

"It's the other way around," I said.

"Not in this case," Monk said.

"You haven't even looked at the evidence," I said.

"Nobody has asked him to," Sharona said.

"Maybe somebody should," I said.

"Maybe somebody should butt out of things that are none of her business," Sharona said.

"Mr. Monk has figured out murders that everyone else thought would be impossible to solve."

"I know," Sharona said tightly, "because I was at his side for most of them."

"You were there for the early, less interesting cases before he really hit his stride," I said. "I've worked closely with him on the classic mysteries that have made him famous. They even tried to make a movie out of one of them — the one with the astronaut whose alibi for the murder of his lover was that he was orbiting the earth in the space shuttle."

"I heard about that," Sharona said. "But wasn't Adrian's assistant in the movie going to be an Asian-American hottie with incredible martial-arts skills?"

I like Chinese food, I'm easy on the eyes and I can throw a mean punch, so it wasn't *that* big of a change for the movie. But even so, screw her for mentioning it.

"The point I'm trying to make is that solving your husband's case would be a no-brainer for Monk," I said. "Why don't you want your husband to be freed?"

"You don't know the first thing about me or Trevor," she said.

"I know he's in jail and you want to keep him there," I said.

"So do I," Monk said. "He's a threat to society."

He was a threat to Monk. If Trevor got out of prison, it would mean Sharona would leave Monk again. Monk was so selfish, he'd rather let an innocent man rot in prison than jeopardize his own comfort.

"His whole life Trevor has been a scammer and a petty thief, always looking for the scheme that would make him rich," Sharona said. "He'd take advantage of anyone, even his own family, to do it. I told you he had this landscaping business, right? Well, he'd go back to the houses when no one was there, break in and steal stuff. Then he'd sell the stolen goods on eBay — under his own name."

"If he's such a dimwit," I said, "what did you see in him?"

"He's not stupid. He just doesn't think,"

she said. "There's a difference. The problem with Trevor is that he lives entirely in the moment. He never considers the consequences. That's also part of his charm. I certainly fell for it. Twice."

"She has terrible taste in men," Monk said. "She once dated someone in the Syndicate."

"The Syndicate?" I said.

"It's how we law enforcement professionals refer to organized crime," Monk said.

"If you were a cop in 1975," Sharona said.

"Trevor doesn't sound very dangerous to me," I said. "What makes you think he's a killer?"

"Because he killed someone," Sharona replied testily. "A woman he worked for came home early and caught him in her house. He panicked, grabbed a lamp and hit her with it. I'm sure he didn't mean to kill her. But that doesn't excuse what he did."

"What he did was unforgivable," Monk said. "Luring you away to New Jersey with his smooth talk and false promises, forcing you to abandon the people who needed you most, plunging them into the impenetrable darkness and despair that lies in the pitiful depths of their tormented souls."

Monk noticed us both staring at him and

then hastily added, "And Trevor murdered someone, which is also very bad."

Sharona glanced at me. "You know what? It's a lot later than I thought. I'd better be going."

She was right about that.

"What's the rush?" Monk said. "We could measure my ice cubes to be sure they are perfectly square. Remember how you loved to do that every morning?"

"You loved it, Adrian," Sharona said. "For me, it was a chore."

"And what's the definition of a chore?" Monk said, like he was asking everyone to sing along. "Something you love to do."

"I don't think so," Sharona said.

"It's in the dictionary," Monk said. "Look it up."

"Okay, let's do that," Sharona said. "Go get your dictionary. I'll wait."

Monk grinned at me. "Isn't she a kidder? This was our thing, this witty repartee. We've fallen right back into it as if she'd never thoughtlessly abandoned me. We fit like a comfortable pair of new shoes."

"Don't you mean old shoes?" she said.

"Who would want to put on *old* shoes?" Monk said, shaking his head and looking at me. "See what I mean? This is gold. You should really be writing this down."

Maybe I should just have fallen to my knees and genuflected in front of her, too. I didn't say that of course, but the gist of my thoughts must have been evident on my face, at least to Sharona. She picked up her handbag and headed quickly for the door.

"I've really got to go," Sharona said. "If I don't leave now, I'll fall asleep at the wheel."

"You need to get a new job," Monk said.

"Like what?" Sharona asked, pausing at the door. "Supermodel? Chef? International spy? This is all I know how to do."

"You could go back to being a private nurse," Monk said. "You could devote yourself to the simple needs of a single, disinfected person as opposed to dozens of unwashed strangers who spew germs and bodily fluids all over you."

I stared at him in disbelief. Did he really just say what I thought he said? Didn't he see me standing there? Didn't he care at all about my feelings?

Obviously, the answers were yes, no and no.

If those were the questions on a test measuring sensitivity and basic decency, Monk would have just flunked.

"That's a big responsibility, one I'm not sure I can handle right now," Sharona said. "But I'll think about it, Adrian. See you around."

And then she left.

See you around? What did she mean by that?

It's not like they lived in the same neighborhood or moved in the same social circles. They weren't going to just bump into each other at the grocery store while Monk was reorganizing every bottle of wine by date and shape.

The only way she was going to see him was if she planned it. And yet, less than twenty-four hours earlier, she was hiding from Monk. Now she was promising to be a regular character in his life again. What had changed?

I'll tell you what changed. She discovered that, contrary to her fears, Monk didn't hate her for abandoning him. And that fact opened up all kinds of possibilities she hadn't considered before, like re-creating her old life in San Francisco as if the last few years hadn't happened . . . as if I hadn't happened.

"Isn't it great that she's back?" Monk said.

"I'm overcome with joy."

"I'm sensing a little resentment from you," he said.

"Really?" I said. "You must be a detective."

"What do you have to be upset about on such a happy, happy day?"

"That," I said, pointing at him. "You're absolutely giddy."

"You don't like to see me happy?"

"Of course I do, Mr. Monk. I just don't like what this burst of joy implies."

"That I'm not sad?"

I couldn't believe how dense he was. "Has your life been that miserable with me as your assistant?"

"No more miserable than usual," he said.

"Then why do you want to fire me?"

"I don't," he said.

"Twice now, right in front of me, you've not so subtly offered Sharona my job."

"How can you say that? I couldn't possibly fire you," he said. "Not after everything we've been through together."

I felt tears welling up in my eyes. "Really?"

"I need you in my life, Natalie. Don't you know that by now?"

"You don't know what a relief that is to me and how much I needed to hear you say that," I said, feeling embarrassed, ashamed and stupid. How could I have so seriously misjudged him? "When I saw how thrilled you were that Sharona was back, I was sure that you were going to give her my job."

"Don't be silly," Monk said. "There's

plenty of me for both of you."

My heart skipped a beat. "What do you mean by that?"

"You can share me," Monk said. "I've always needed more time and attention than one person can give. This is the perfect solution."

"You want to hire us *both* as your assistants?"

"Isn't that wonderful? You could alternate days. Or days and nights. Or weeks. I'm a flexible guy. I'm sure you two gals will work it out."

I wiped the tears from my eyes and felt my cheeks flushing with anger.

"Are you going to pay each of us 'gals' a full salary?"

"Why would I pay you a *full* salary for only doing *half* the work? Get real."

"Okay, here's the reality. I can barely live on what I get paid now working full-time for you," I said. "I can't live on half of that."

"You could get a second job," Monk said.

"I don't want a second job," I said.

"Then you can use all of that free time to get your house in order," Monk said. "God knows there's plenty of organizing you can do."

"I'm not going to share my job, Mr. Monk."

"She came back, Natalie. The people who leave me almost never do. I can't let her go now."

Emotionally, I could sympathize with his feelings. His father had abandoned him when Monk was a child and only recently reappeared. Monk lost his wife and was never going to get her back. And then Sharona, someone he relied on every day just to survive, abruptly left him. I'm no shrink, but it was obvious to me that he needed to bury his anger and accept her back in order to ease his own insecurities.

Pretty perceptive, huh? Call me Dr. Natalie and give me my own TV show.

But on a practical level, I had to face facts and so did he.

"You're not listening to me, Mr. Monk," I said. "I can't afford a fifty percent pay cut and I'm not going to juggle two jobs just to accommodate you."

"Then what am I supposed to do?"

"Make a choice," I said. "Sharona or me."

"That's not fair," Monk said.

"Fair?" I said. "How can you stand there and talk to me about fair?"

"Because I'm being rational and you're not?"

I wish I could say that I responded with a brilliant rejoinder that put him in his place and made him confront his own insensitivity. Instead, I totally reinforced his point of view by marching out of his house and slamming the door behind me.

CHAPTER FIVE:
MR. MONK'S
ASSISTANT TAKES A
TRIP

I was fairly certain that I had a much closer relationship with Captain Stottlemeyer than Sharona had. I can't say that was much of a consolation.

Our mutual concern for Monk was what initially drew Stottlemeyer and me closer together. But what really changed things between us was his divorce. We didn't date or anything — he just started to open up to me about his troubles.

I guess there wasn't anybody else he could unload on. He couldn't turn to Lieutenant Disher, as that would have irreparably undermined Stottlemeyer's authority in their professional relationship. And outside of Monk, he didn't seem to have that many friends, at least not that I knew of.

I was flattered that Stottlemeyer trusted me with his problems but, until Sharona showed up in Monk's life again, I didn't feel equally comfortable sharing my woes with him.

But that day I went straight from Monk's house to the captain's office and told him everything that happened. I didn't even mind that Disher listened in.

"I've got to say, I never expected her to come back," Stottlemeyer said, leaning back in his desk chair.

"Sharona and I had this erotic tension between us," Disher said, standing in the doorway. "A hot 'will they/won't they' thing."

"More like a 'will never happen' thing," Stottlemeyer said.

"It was palpable," Disher said.

"It sure was," Stottlemeyer said.

"So it was sort of like the relationship that we have," I said to Disher.

"It is?" he said.

"A 'will never happen' thing," I said.

"Right," he said. "But it's searing. People can feel the heat."

"I sympathize with your situation, Natalie," Stottlemeyer said. "But I don't know what to tell you. It's Monk's decision and it's going to be a hard one for him."

"You can help me," I said.

"I'm not going to choose sides," Stottlemeyer said. "I've got a lot of respect for

Sharona. She went through hell with Monk."

"I know that, and I don't want you to get in the middle of this," I said.

"Then what do you want from me?"

"I'd like you to find out the details of the murder that Trevor is accused of committing down in Los Angeles."

"I can do that," Stottlemeyer said, then glanced at Disher. "Take care of it, Randy."

"You just said that you were."

"I am," he said, "through you. It's one of the privileges of being captain."

"So you should have said, 'I'll ask Randy if he can do that,'" Disher said. "And I would have checked my calendar."

Stottlemeyer just stared at him.

"Which happens to be wide-open at the present moment," Disher said and went to his desk.

Stottlemeyer turned to me. "Can I buy you a cup of coffee?"

"That would be great," I said.

We went to a coffeehouse across the street, chatted a bit about his kids and how things were going with his girlfriend, a successful Realtor I'd inadvertently introduced him to in my disastrous attempt to turn Monk into a private eye, but that's a long story.

Stottlemeyer's sons were doing well, the relationship with his girlfriend was moving comfortably along and he was happy and relaxed for the first time in ages.

"Life is good," he said.

I was pleased for him. He'd had a rough year or two and deserved a little peace, at least as much as a guy who looks at dead bodies every day can have.

When we returned to Stottlemeyer's office, there were some faxes from the LAPD waiting for him on his desk. Stottlemeyer flipped through the pages while Disher and I sat and waited. After a moment or two, Stottlemeyer sighed and leaned back in his chair.

"They've got a strong case here, Natalie."

"What does that mean?" I said.

"They found Trevor's fingerprints all over the house," Stottlemeyer said.

"Of course they did," I said. "He worked there."

"He worked outside," Stottlemeyer said. "Why would the mow-and-blow guy's fingerprints be *inside* the house?"

Oh. Right. So much for my detective skills.

"Maybe he was one of those full-service landscapers," Disher said, "and was also watering her houseplants."

"That's possible," I said.

63

"No, it's not," Stottlemeyer said. "The police also found jewelry belonging to the victim hidden in his truck."

"So you're telling me he gets caught by the lady as he's stealing her jewelry, he kills her and, instead of getting the hell out of there, he sticks around to gather up the bling?" I asked. "Doesn't that seem odd to you?"

"Not really," Stottlemeyer said. "That's why he was in the house to start with."

"But then he leaves the incriminating evidence in his truck instead of ditching it the first chance he got?" I said. "How stupid is this guy?"

"The jewelry was too valuable to throw away," Stottlemeyer said. "He couldn't bring himself to do it, especially after what it cost him to get. He was only holding on to it until he could sell it on eBay."

"Did Trevor have an alibi?" I asked.

"He claims he was parked in his truck on the side of a road somewhere, having burgers with a couple members of his crew at the time of the murder."

"There you go," I said. "He has witnesses who can prove he's innocent."

"His crew was usually day laborers he'd pick up on Sepulveda Boulevard and pay in cash. He didn't know any of them. They were all Hector and Jésus to him, if you know what I mean."

"They were illegal aliens," I said.

Stottlemeyer nodded. "If these corroborating witnesses exist, which I sincerely doubt, they're in another state or back over the border by now. The last thing they'd want to do is get involved in a murder investigation."

"So that's it?" I said.

"Until the trial and the likely conviction, yeah, that's it," he said. "What's it to you?"

"I don't know Sharona at all, but if she's the woman you've all told me that she is, I have to believe that as bad as her taste in men might be, she wouldn't marry a guy, have a child with him, divorce him, then remarry him if he was capable of murder."

"I have to agree with Natalie on that, Captain," Disher said.

"How can you agree with something that doesn't make any sense at all?" Stottlemeyer said to him.

"I have faith in Sharona's instincts," Disher said, "even if she may not have it herself."

Stottlemeyer looked at Disher as if he was seeing him for the first time. "I'll be damned."

65

"Could you arrange for me to see Trevor?" I asked.

Stottlemeyer shifted his gaze to me. "Why would you want to do that?"

"I want to hear his side of the story."

He studied me for a long moment. "Okay, I suppose I can do that."

"You mean that I can," Disher said.

"I meant that I could," Stottlemeyer said.

"So how am I supposed to know when you say, 'I can do that,' whether you really mean that I can do that, as in me not you?" Disher said.

"Have faith in your instincts," Stottlemeyer said; then he turned to me. "I've never met Trevor, but judging by his rap sheet, he's done a lot of stupid things. Sometimes you mix stupid and bad luck and you get murder. Do you really think that he's innocent and that Monk can help him, or are you just afraid of losing your job?"

"I'm exercising my right to remain silent," I said, "to avoid self-incrimination."

"You haven't been arrested," Disher said, "or charged with a crime."

"That's true," Stottlemeyer said, reaching for his phone. "But she's guilty."

He was right.

■ ■ ■ ■

It only takes about an hour to fly down to LA and you can get cheap flights leaving out of Oakland Airport all day long. So I arranged for the mother of one of Julie's friends to pick up her up after school and take care of her until I got back that night.

Julie was going to be upset that I was reneging on my promise to take her out to look for advertising clients, but I'd make it up to her.

I drove over the Bay Bridge to Oakland, stowed my car in short-term parking and took a Southwest Airlines flight to the Burbank airport, which was closer to downtown LA than LAX was.

On the plane, I thought about what I wanted to ask Trevor and couldn't come up with anything. I was somewhere over San Jose when I realized that this was a pointless trip, but it was too late to turn back.

So I thought instead about the real reason I was going. About my relationship with Monk. And, for some reason, my mind kept wandering to the Cement Ship.

In the 1970s, my parents bought a painting of the Cement Ship at a gallery in Capitola, a quaint seaside village not far from where I grew up in Monterey. They hung the painting in the living room over the fireplace and I've spent countless hours just sitting and staring at it.

On those rare occasions when I visited my parents, I'd curl up in front of the painting with a hot cup of coffee and gaze at the ship like it was the view out of a window.

The Cement Ship was actually a ship-wreck at the end of a fishing pier in Aptos, a beach town between Monterey and Capitola. The real name of the ship was the *Palo Alto,* one of two concrete tankers constructed in San Francisco during World War One.

I've often wondered whose brilliant idea it was to build a cement ship.

Why not one made of bricks, too?

How could they have been surprised when the thing didn't float?

Okay, that's not entirely true.

It floated. *Once.*

The *Palo Alto* made one short voyage before she was towed down to the Monterey Bay seventy-five years ago and deliberately beached to become a dance hall.

A couple years later, the ship was torn apart by a big storm, and the wreckage has been left there to rot ever since.

The Cement Ship on the canvas above my

parents' fireplace was a broken hulk, fading into the mist like a lost memory.

It enthralled me.

Monk couldn't look at it. For one thing, just looking at the ocean, even in a painting, made him seasick. But I think what bothered him the most was that it was a shipwreck. It was something that needed to be put back together but was instead forever captured in the painting in a state of disorder.

For Monk that image was like what Kryptonite is for Superman, or what a crucifix is to a vampire.

It was a painting of a mess that could never be cleaned up, a thought Monk simply could not reconcile himself with. We had to cover the painting with a sheet whenever he visited the house.

For me, I found peace in the Cement Ship. It relaxed me and centered me somehow. Sure, the painting was creepy, and a little bit sad, but there was a beauty in it, too.

The *Peralta,* the sister ship of the *Palo Alto,* was also a wreck. It was one of ten rotting ships strung together to form a breakwater on the Powell River in British Columbia. I've never seen it, but I wonder sometimes if anyone has ever done a painting of it.

If so, I'd like to have it.

There's something I find beautiful, captivating, and scary about shipwrecks. But the Cement Ship wasn't just any shipwreck. It was my shipwreck.

Sometimes, it felt like my life was a cement ship and that I was constantly battling not to end up beached.

Maybe Monk's life was a cement ship, too.

We were the *Palo Alto* and the *Peralta,* leaving port together in San Francisco.

And I believed that if we were separated now, we'd both become grounded somewhere and end up slowly eroded by the relentless surf.

I arrived in Burbank in time for lunch, but I didn't have time to go out to eat, so I bought an overpriced bag of potato chips and a Diet Coke in the terminal. It's a good thing I don't gain weight easily. I wolfed down that healthy snack on my way outside of the airport, where I snagged a taxi and told the driver to take me to the jail downtown. Between the plane ticket and the taxi fare, I'd burned through most of my personal fortune.

Captain Stottlemeyer had called ahead and arranged everything for me, so things went very smoothly. The security staff was expecting me and my pass was ready. So after I went through security, which was almost as tight as what I'd gone through at the Oakland airport, I was led directly to the visiting room.

It was just like what you've seen on TV. The room was divided by a Plexiglas wall with cubicles on either side. Each cubicle had a telephone receiver attached to a long cord. It could have been 1967. You'd think they'd have come up with something more sleek and high-tech since then, something like those force fields they used in the brig on *Star Trek.* I was lost in big thoughts like that when Trevor sat down on the other side of the Plexiglas, startling me.

I knew he was about my age, but he looked to me like a frightened child with his arched eyebrows, ruffled hair and pouty lips.

There was something undeniably East Coast about his features and bearing, though if you asked me to pick out something specific, I couldn't tell you. He had the same look as all those guys on *The Sopranos,* though without any of the subdued malevolence. What I saw in his face was sadness, fear and confusion.

We picked up our phones and openly stared at each other. He was studying my face as if searching for landmarks. I was scrutinizing his for glaring signs of guilt.

"Do I know you?" he asked.

"I'm Natalie Teeger," I said. "I work for Adrian Monk."

"Monk?" He seemed to inflate with hope and relief. "That's terrific. Whew. I knew Sharona wouldn't let me down. Is he going to help me?"

"You have to convince me first," I said.

"Why? I'm Sharona's husband. Isn't that enough? Besides, Monk owes her plenty for —" He stopped, seeing the answer on my face. "She didn't ask Monk to help me, did she? She really thinks I did it, that I could kill somebody."

I nodded. And then he began to cry.

Chapter Six:
Mr. Monk's Assistant Makes a Discovery

There's something about seeing a man cry that makes me feel like I should avert my eyes. But I couldn't bring myself to do it this time.

I stared at Trevor and openly studied each stinging tear on his face, each pained grimace, each tortured heave of his chest. I haven't seen many men cry, but when they do, there's a nakedness about it that I think is even more intimate and revealing than sex.

I've only seen my father cry once. I was nine years old when it happened. I was heading to his study to show him a drawing I'd done of our dog. The doors weren't closed all the way, and something made me stop and peek through the crack before I went in.

He was alone at his desk, his face in his hands, his shoulders shaking. At one point, he dropped his hands and I saw his tear-streaked cheeks. But I saw much more. I saw vulnerability. I saw fear. And I saw shame.

He didn't see me and I never said a word about it to him. I didn't know then, and I still don't know now, what he was crying about. But I've never forgotten that moment or what it felt like. The only thing that comes close to it is the uncertainty and fear that I feel whenever there's an earthquake and the once-solid ground below my feet turns to Jell-O.

As I sat in that visitors' room, I wondered if that was what Dad felt like and if that was what Trevor was feeling now.

When I looked into Trevor's face, I saw everything that I saw in my dad's face that night. Try faking that. It isn't easy to do unless you're somebody with an Oscar or an Emmy statuette on your mantel.

Trevor's tears lasted two minutes, maybe three, but I could see that they startled and humiliated him. He got control of himself with two big, deep breaths and a grimace. Then he looked around to see if anyone else witnessed the momentary crack in his masculine shell, but there were only me and the guard in the room, and if the guard saw anything, he didn't acknowledge it.

I didn't bother pretending that I hadn't

seen him cry or the vulnerability that it exposed. I'm not that good an actress, anyway.

He wiped his eyes on the sleeve of his denim jailhouse shirt. "I didn't kill Ellen Cole," he said.

It was the first time anyone had mentioned the poor woman's name to me.

"Then why was her stuff in your truck?" I asked.

"Someone is framing me," Trevor replied.

"Who would want to do that?"

"Whoever caved her head in with a table lamp," he said. "That's who."

"Can you think of anyone who might have wanted her dead?" Of course he couldn't. If he could, he would have told someone by now. It was a stupid question, but I didn't know what else to ask. I was just fumbling along.

"I don't know. I mowed her lawn, pulled her weeds and trimmed her shrubs," Trevor said. "That's as deep as our relationship went."

"Then why were your fingerprints all over her house?"

"She was always asking me in to do little tasks for her," he said. " 'Could you reach this? Change this bulb? Help me move this dresser?' "

"Was she an old woman?"

He gave me a look. "Don't you know anything about this case?"

"Frankly, no," I said. "I'm not even sure what I'm supposed to ask."

"She was in her thirties, but she was short, kind of slight. Plus she was flirting, not that I'd ever act on it. I'm a happily married man." He winced, as if feeling real pain. "At least I was. Or thought I was. What do you do for Monk?"

"What Sharona used to do," I said, "only not as well."

"How do you know?"

"Because he wants her back," I said. I owed Trevor something real from me for his tears. "So why doesn't Sharona believe you?"

"That's the worst thing about this, worse even than being in here," Trevor said. "I'm a screwup. I know that. I've lied to people. I've used people. I've disappointed everyone in my life, especially her. But this isn't me. I couldn't kill anybody."

"If you were such a screwup," I asked, "how did you and Sharona get back together?"

"A few years ago, I came out to San Francisco to make a play to get Sharona back," he said. "But it was just so I could show my rich uncle Jack that I was domesticated again. He'd cut me off when Sharona walked out on me. Problem was, I'd accumulated some gambling debts and needed him to bail me out."

"Which he wouldn't have done unless he thought the money was going to your wife and kid," I said. "You were just using them as props."

"Yep. Sharona figured that out the day we were supposed to move back east. She sent Benji to her sister's place, and when I showed up with the moving truck, she really gave it to me. Then she asked me if I wanted to give Benji a call and tell him how I'd manipulated them or if I was gonna leave that to her, too. You want to guess what I chose?"

"You made her do it," I said.

He nodded, ashamed. "That night, and every day after that for the next few weeks, I kept imagining their conversation, and the look of disappointment on my son's face, and it made me sick. I couldn't stop puking. I couldn't even look at myself in the mirror no more. So I decided to change."

"What did you do?"

"I got a job in New Jersey waiting tables, and another one dry-cleaning, and paid off my debt. And after that, I sent every cent I could back to Sharona," he said. "It was only a few bucks, but I wanted her to see the cash flowing the other way for once. I finally got some guts and called Benji. He didn't hang up on me, so I copped to what I did and apologized. I called back every week and then twice a week. And then one day, Sharona and I started talking again, too."

"And one thing led to another," I said, letting my voice trail off.

"I really wanted us to work this time, more than anything else in the world. And I really thought that it was working and that Sharona knew that I wasn't the same guy anymore. Then Ellen Cole got killed and I found out I was wrong. It was all a lie. Sharona never had any faith in me, never really trusted me again. She doesn't know who I am. She doesn't want to know. That's worse than giving me the needle, you know?"

I knew.

I got back to the Bay Area in time to take Julie around to a few places in the neighborhood that night after all.

When we got home, she had a check for thirty dollars from Sorrento's Pizza in her pocket and an advertisement to glue to her cast. Anyone who ordered a pizza and said they had heard about the restaurant from Julie's cast would get a ten percent discount. If the sales were good, Sorrento's would pay for a second week of cast-vertising (a term my daughter coined and that we've trademarked).

That deal wasn't good enough for my daughter. She stunned me by negotiating an escalator clause. If Sorrento's made five hundred dollars in sales as a result of the advertisement, her rate would go up to fifty dollars for week two.

"Where did you learn to negotiate like that?" I asked her as we were leaving the restaurant. She'd even managed to finagle two slices of pizza for us to nibble on during our walk home.

"Deal or No Deal," she said.

"The game show with the bald guy and the briefcases full of money?"

"It's quality TV," Julie said.

She now had a strong incentive to do more than just walk around, showing off her cast. I had a feeling she'd be aggressively drumming up business for Sorrento's all over campus. I just hoped that she wouldn't provoke the principal into shutting down her business before it even got started.

After all, if Sharona got my job, we'd have to live on those pizza slices and the advertising dollars.

CHAPTER SEVEN:
MR. MONK TAKES
THE CASE

It was my neighbor's day to carpool the kids to school, so that meant I could get a few extra minutes of sleep and that I didn't have to get dressed right away. I could even laze around in my bathrobe and pajamas for a half hour after Julie left and before going to work.

Which is exactly what I did, enjoying a second cup of coffee and reading the *San Francisco Chronicle* in peace. I was about to go take a shower when there was an insistent knock at the door.

It's surprising just how much personality and character a knock can have. Without even going to the door, I knew that whoever owned those knuckles was irritated, impatient and in a hurry. So just to piss off whoever it was even more, I took my time getting to the door. I walked around the couch twice and the coffee table once just to drag things out.

I peered through the peephole and was surprised to see Sharona standing on my front step. I didn't have to open the door to know why she was at my door the first thing in the morning. There was no sense avoiding her and pretending I wasn't home or was already in the shower. She knew where I'd be going later anyway and I figured this was a confrontation I'd rather not have in front of Monk.

So I opened the door wide and invited her in without even saying hello.

"Yes, I went down to LA and I talked to your husband in jail," I said.

She marched right past me. "What the hell were you thinking?"

"I was thinking that he might be innocent," I said, slamming the door. "I'm surprised the thought hasn't occurred to you, too."

"You don't know him and you don't know me," she said. "Stay out of my life."

"Stay out of mine," I said.

"I'm not in it," she said.

"You are when you start messing with my livelihood," I said.

She stared at me. "I'm sorry. I didn't realize that no one was allowed to see Adrian Monk without clearing it with you first. Should I have given you my references, my fingerprints and a urine sample, too?"

"Don't play innocent with me," I said. "You didn't just 'happen' to be in Mr. Monk's neighborhood yesterday. We both know what's really going on here."

"You are seriously nuts," she said. "I have known Adrian for years. I was visiting a dear friend."

"So dear that you've been hiding from him since you returned to San Francisco. But then we showed up in your ER and you discovered that Mr. Monk isn't pissed at you anymore. And lo and behold, the next morning, you're at his door with breakfast and whining about how long your hours are and how you wish you had a better job. *My* job."

"Don't make me laugh," Sharona said. "You aren't the least bit qualified to be caring for Adrian. Do you have any medical training? How about psychiatric experience?"

I got right up into her face, though it's hard to be intimidating in a pink bathrobe and bunny rabbit slippers.

"You're right. I am totally unqualified. That just goes to show you how desperate he was for help after you abandoned him," I said. "I'm the one he leaned on and I didn't have any experience dealing with someone with his problems. If you think that was easy for me, you're deluding yourself. But here's what I've learned from it. He doesn't need a professional nurse anymore. All he needs is someone who cares about him, which clearly you don't."

"I will not apologize for choosing to have a life," she said. "I know I hurt Adrian and I want to make it up to him."

"By taking my job," I said.

"He offered it to me," she said.

"Because you manipulated him into it by telling him your sob story."

"I told him what's happening in my life," she said. "It happens to suck right now. That's the way it is. But that doesn't matter. He knows as well as I do that I can take better care of him than you can."

"This isn't about helping Mr. Monk," I said. "You're looking out for yourself. It's all about you."

"You think you're any different? You didn't go see Trevor because you think he's innocent. You're trying to save your precious job," Sharona said. "You're hoping that Adrian can prove Trevor didn't do it so that I'll reunite with my husband and go away again."

"You're right. That's exactly what I want," I said. "What I don't get is why you don't want the same thing."

"Trevor is a liar," she said. "He always has been."

"He's your husband. He's the father of your child. Now you're abandoning him when he needs you the most," I said. "But then, abandoning people who need you is your specialty."

"Trevor did this to himself," Sharona said.

"You can save him," I said. "You don't have to lose him."

"I've done it before," Sharona said. "I'm not doing it again."

"You have no idea how lucky you are," I said. "I would have given anything for the chance to save Mitch."

I burst into tears. And I mean burst, shocking myself and probably Sharona, too.

The next thing I knew, Sharona was holding me, my face was pressed against her shoulder, and I was heaving with sobs. I was overcome with grief as sharp as the day I got the news that Mitch was dead.

I don't know how long we stood there like that with me crying my guts out, but when I finally stopped, and all the tears were gone, I didn't give a damn anymore. Let her have Monk. Let her have my job. I didn't have the strength to fight. I was weak from a sorrow I thought I'd finally managed to bury.

"I'm sorry," I said and I went to the kitchen to look for some tissues.

I couldn't even find a napkin. I ended up having to settle for a Brawny paper towel.

Sharona followed me into the kitchen. Oddly enough, the fight seemed to have gone out of her, too.

Without asking, she sat down at the table and I poured us both cups of coffee. I took a seat across from her. There was a long, strangely comfortable silence that lasted for a few minutes.

She asked me how Mitch died. I told her how the navy fighter plane he was flying was shot down over Kosovo and how he'd been killed on the ground afterward.

"Trevor isn't a hero," she said.

"Mitch wasn't either, except to me and Julie. The official story is that he was a coward, that he ran away from the crash scene, leaving his injured crew behind. I don't believe that. I think his instinct would have been to save his men, and if he ran, it was to draw the Serb patrol away from his men. I'll never know the truth about my husband. But you can know the truth about yours. Mr. Monk can find it for you."

Sharona chewed on her lower lip. "You

believe Trevor, don't you?"

I nodded.

"Sap," she said. "I used to be just like you."

Sharona finished her coffee. I finished mine.

"I guess I still am," she said with a sigh. "I'll ask Adrian to look into it as a favor to me. If Adrian thinks something is screwy about the case, then I'll help him investigate and I won't ever give up. But if he thinks Trevor is guilty, then I'm dropping it and so are you."

"Fair enough," I said. "And I won't make it difficult for you if Mr. Monk decides he wants you back."

"I never said I'd take the job if he offered it," she said.

"He did," I said. "And you would."

When Sharona and I showed up together at Monk's door, he smiled with delight and relief and beckoned us in.

"I knew you two would work it out," Monk said. "You're going to be great co-assistants."

"Co-assistants?" Sharona said.

I'd forgotten to tell her about Monk's brilliant plan for us to share the bliss of taking care of him.

"You can divide up the responsibilities however you see fit," Monk said. "For instance, when you work together, you could alternate who carries my water and who carries my wipes. It will be fun for you. Maybe even liberating."

"How about you liberate my husband from jail instead?" Sharona said.

"You want me to plan a prison break?" he said.

"I want you to prove he's innocent," Sharona said.

"But he's not," Monk said.

"We don't know that," I said.

"She does," Monk said, gesturing to Sharona. "And I have enormous faith in her instincts."

"I'm not so sure anymore, Adrian," she said.

"I am," Monk said. "He's guilty as sin. No, he's even guiltier than that. He's guilty as dirt."

"You don't know anything about the case," I said.

"I have no doubt the police did a very thorough job. They should lock Trevor up, throw away the key and then forget where they threw it," he said, "for the sake of humanity."

"You mean for *your* sake," Sharona said,

narrowing her eyes at him and putting her hands on her hips. "You want him locked up just so I can work for you again."

"That's one way of looking at it," he said.

"What's another way?" she said.

He rolled his shoulders as if that act would put him and the rest of the world back into proper alignment.

"That it would be really great if he stayed in jail and you worked for me again."

"That doesn't sound any better, Adrian."

"Somehow it does to me," he said.

"We're going to Los Angeles today, Mr. Monk. Sharona's sister has agreed to watch Julie and Benji for us," I said. "Captain Stottlemeyer talked Lieutenant Sam Dozier, the cop on the case, into meeting with us and going over the evidence."

"Los Angeles is hundreds of miles away from here," Monk said.

"Yes, Adrian, it's going to require some travel," Sharona said.

"The flight is less than an hour," I said.

"I'm not getting on an airplane," Monk said.

"You had no problem getting on a plane and following me to Hawaii," I said.

"He followed you to Hawaii?" Sharona asked.

"I was under the influence of mind-altering drugs at the time," Monk said. "I won't do that again. I don't want that monkey on my back. I don't even want to imagine a monkey on my back. Or any monkey anywhere. But it's too late. There he is. I can see him. Now the filthy animal is in my head, and who knows where he's been? Look what you've done and we haven't even left the house."

Sharona sighed and looked at me. "Maybe I can take those drugs instead."

"We'll drive," I said.

"Does anyone have a wipe?" Monk said.

"What do you need a wipe for?"

"My brain," Monk said.

Chapter Eight:
Mr. Monk and the
Long Drive

Interstate 5 is a straight shot down the San Joaquin Valley in central California. It is so straight, you could almost take your hands off the wheel and drive with your feet.

The scenery, like the drive itself, is monotonous and unchanging, nothing but flat stretches of baked farmland as far as you can see. There aren't even any interesting towns or tourist attractions to visit. The only signs of civilization are the gas stations and fast-food outlets that are spaced about every thirty or forty miles.

I've always wondered where the people come from who work in those desolate, out-of-the-way rest stops. When I was a kid, my dad told me they weren't people at all, but zombies, living dead who chose to serve hamburgers for eternity rather than go to hell.

I believed him. It's not that I was a gullible kid. If you've seen the glassy look in the

91

eyes of those cashiers, you'd be convinced, too. To tell you the truth, I'm not so sure he was joking.

If you obey the speed limit and only stop for gas, it's about a six-hour drive down to Los Angeles from San Francisco. But it's easy to shave an hour off that by speeding. The good thing about a straight drive across a 250-mile valley is that there aren't a lot of places for the California Highway Patrol to hide, and if the drive hasn't lulled you into a zombielike stupor yourself, you can usually see the CHP plane circling the highway long before you get into the range of their radar.

But speeding was out of the question with Monk in the car. Thank God for cruise control. I could keep the speedometer set at exactly sixty-four miles per hour. Yes, I know the speed limit is sixty-five, but it's an uneven number and sixty-six would have made me a felon in Monk's eyes.

Sharona and I were in the front seat of my Jeep Cherokee. Monk sat in the back, directly in the middle. That may seem like a small detail to you, but it was a big thing for Monk. Before we left San Francisco, he'd insisted that we bring a fourth person along just to make the seating even and balanced.

I refused.

"Okay," Monk said. "We'll just have to pick up a hitchhiker on the way."

"I'm not going to pick up a complete stranger just so you can have an even number of people in the car," I said. "He could be an ax murderer."

"Hitchhikers provide a valuable service to society."

"You really think they're riding along with you just so you have an even number of passengers?" Sharona asked.

"Of course not," Monk said. "They're doing it to get from one place to another."

"It's nice to know you aren't completely disconnected from reality," Sharona said.

"And in return for the ride, they balance your car," Monk said. "That's the social contract. It really took off in the sixties. All the peaceniks were doing it."

"The peaceniks," I said.

"You know, give peace a chance. Make love not war. Gather in even numbers," Monk said. "Those were some wild times."

"If you can get Trevor out of jail, then we'll have four people in the car on the way back," Sharona said. "Think of it as an incentive."

Monk insisted on bringing along enough food and water for a two-week stay, along with all the clothes, bedding, dishes and silverware he'd need.

It was a good thing I had a big car.

Sharona and I each brought one overnight bag, a couple bottles of water, and a big bag of Cheese Doodles for us to share. I'm a firm believer that no road trip is complete without Cheese Doodles.

The drive was going pretty well, everything considered, until we were within a few miles of Harris Ranch, seven hundred acres of feedlots teeming with a hundred thousand cows, all of them eating and crapping and waiting to die right alongside the north-bound lanes of the interstate.

You can smell the cows long before you see them. Monk began to squirm and gag the instant he caught his first whiff of those mountains of manure. It was as if all the oxygen had suddenly been sucked out of the car and he was suffocating.

"What is that?" he croaked.

"It's a cattle ranch," I said. "We'll be past it in five or ten minutes."

"I'll be dead by then," Monk said. "We all will."

"Breathe through your mouth," Sharona said.

"What difference is *that* going to make?" Monk said with as much exasperation as he could manage while trying to speak without inhaling.

"You won't smell it," Sharona said.

"Get real, woman. You can't smell radiation and it will fry you anyway," Monk said. "Even if we survive today, our hair will start falling off in clumps tomorrow. Pull over. I have to get my gas mask out of my suitcase."

"Forget it," I said. "In the time it would take us to pull over, rummage through your suitcase and get your gas mask, we could be ten miles away from here."

Monk took a handful of antiseptic wipes from Sharona and covered his nose and mouth with them. He closed his eyes, too, to protect himself from the sight of all those cows and all that manure. I wasn't wild about the sight either, but as straight as the road was, I still couldn't drive with my eyes closed.

Once we were past the ranch and the smell, Monk drank about six bottles of Sierra Springs water to cleanse himself of the toxins, which soon created a new problem for him.

"We have to turn around and go back to San Francisco immediately," he said.

"Why?" Sharona asked.

Monk didn't want to say. He rolled his shoulders. He shifted his weight. He squirmed.

"I have to go to someplace private," Monk whispered, ashamed, "to do something private."

"You have to go to the bathroom?" Sharona said.

I glanced in the rearview mirror. Monk was blushing.

"Great," Monk said. "Now everyone in the car knows."

"I'm the driver," I said. "I kind of have to know."

"Okay," Monk said. "But that's as far as it goes. It remains between us."

"We'll stop at the next gas station," I said. "There's one coming up in five miles."

"You've got to be kidding," Monk said.

"What were you planning to do, Adrian?" Sharona said. "Hold it the whole time we're in Los Angeles?"

"That was one option," Monk said.

"Even if we did turn around, you couldn't hold it all the way back to San Francisco," Sharona said. "Face it, Adrian. You have no choice but to use a restroom. Or a tree."

"This is a living hell," he said.

I was beginning to agree with him.

Before going in the gas station restroom, Monk donned a hazardous-materials suit, complete with its own fan and air-filtration system. I'm not kidding. It was the kind of suit that the people from the National Institutes of Health wear when they're dealing with an Ebola outbreak. He usually wears it to clean dog crap off his front lawn.

Monk secured the area outside the men's room with crime-scene tape and then began scouring the lavatory with the industrial-strength cleaning supplies he'd brought along.

Usually, in a situation like this, I feel incredibly embarrassed and alone. And unless we happen to be with Captain Stottlemeyer, I also end up having to deal with all the people who are either pissed off or inconvenienced by whatever outrageous, bizarre or outrageously selfish thing Monk is doing.

But not this time. With Sharona there, I finally had some support.

Sharona treated the situation as if it was completely normal, and if anyone gave Monk a funny look, she gave them a hard stare right back, scaring them off.

When the bewildered manager of the gas station came out to complain about Monk shutting down his men's room and terrifying customers with his hazmat suit, Sharona handled the man beautifully.

"Think about this a minute," Sharona said. "The guy is cleaning your restroom for you and it isn't costing you a cent. Do you really have a problem with that? Is it a job that *you* would rather be doing?"

That was all the owner had to hear. He went back to his register and didn't say another word to us.

With the owner appeased, and Monk busy cleaning, disinfecting and presumably relieving himself somewhere in the midst of all that, Sharona and I got a hamburger at the Carl's Jr. across the street.

I couldn't help wondering if my Super Star with Cheese used to be one of the cows up the road. But I was so hungry, I didn't care.

While we ate, Sharona and I talked about the difficulties of being a single parent and trying to take care of Monk at the same time.

"It's like being a single parent with *two* children," I said.

"At least this one cleans his room," Sharona said.

"And yours," I said.

I discovered that we had a lot more in common than I thought. It was getting difficult for me to keep disliking the woman, even if she was out to ruin my life.

It took Monk about an hour and a half to do his thing and then we got back on the road. We got into Los Angeles around six p.m., and even though it was the height of evening rush hour, the traffic wasn't too bad until we hit the Sepulveda Pass. That's where the San Diego Freeway goes over the Santa Monica Mountains and down into the LA basin. Even with six lanes on each side, the freeway still wasn't wide enough to handle all the cars. I've crawled faster than these cars were moving.

Perhaps that was why everyone seemed to be driving an SUV the size of a house. They spent so much time on the freeway, it was like they lived there, so they figured that they might as well have all the comforts of home in their cars.

The SUV in front of us had TV screens in the rear of the front-seat headrests for the viewing pleasure of the passengers in the backseat. Sharona and I were able to watch *Entertainment Tonight* and catch up on the latest important news.

When we reached the top of the pass, we had a clear view of the LA basin and what we were breathing.

Monk took one look at the thick brown layer of smog and put on his gas mask, which he must have taken out of his suitcase when he unpacked his hazmat suit.

I couldn't blame him for wearing the gas mask. I found myself wishing I had one, too.

Sharona called Lieutenant Sam Dozier. He was working a homicide at an antiques store in Brentwood, which happened to be pretty close to where we were, so we decided to meet him there.

I was surprised that Dozier was okay with that. I figured that maybe he wanted to see what made Monk so special.

Well, the lieutenant was about to find out. Big-time.

CHAPTER NINE:
MR. MONK AND THE
FLY

It's never easy finding a parking spot at a crime scene, but it was even worse this time because there was a lot of roadwork being done. The traffic was bottlenecked. The street was clogged with bulldozers, pipes, and construction materials.

We ended up having to park two blocks away and make our way through the crowd of construction workers and lookee-loos to the police line around the antiques store.

Monk doesn't like crowds. It significantly raises the possibility that he may brush against another human being, which would mean he'd have to rush home and take three showers.

We didn't have time for that today.

Sharona and I both knew what had to be done. All it took was a shared glance between us and we ran interference for Monk so he could walk in a brush-free zone of his own.

I hated to admit it, but having a co-assistant definitely had some advantages.

We were met at the police line by a plain-clothes cop who was chewing on a drool-soaked, unlit cigar. He had bags under his rummy eyes, jowls only a hound dog could love and a gut that reminded me of what I looked like when I was eight months pregnant.

"Lieutenant Sam Dozier," he said, lifting the police tape for us to duck under and offering Monk his chubby hand.

Monk shook hands with Dozier.

Out of habit, Sharona and I simultaneously offered Monk a disinfectant wipe. He took one from each of us, wisely not playing favorites, and cleaned his hand.

"I'm Adrian Monk and these are my co-assistants, Natalie Teeger and Sharona Fleming, though I believe you and Sharona have already met," Monk said, sounding like Darth Vader with that mask on.

Dozier shook my hand, then turned to Sharona.

"I'm sorry about what you and your son have been through, but as far as I'm concerned, this is a waste of time," he said. "The Ellen Cole murder case is closed and your husband killed her. I'm only meeting with you as a professional courtesy to the SFPD."

"I appreciate it," Sharona said.

"What's with the gas mask?" Dozier asked.

"Allergies," Monk said.

"What are you allergic to?"

"Los Angeles," Monk said. "I'd like you to take us to Ellen Cole's house and walk us through the crime scene."

Monk held his hand up in front of his face, as if shielding his eyes from the glare of the sun.

But there was no glare.

"It's going to have to wait until tomorrow or maybe the day after," Dozier said. "As you can see, I'm a little busy right now."

"It has to be today," Monk said, squinting at Dozier over the top of his hand.

I tried to guess what Monk didn't want to see, but there were so many possibilities. It could have been the torn-up asphalt or the Dumpster in front of the store or the Porta Potti down the street or the soggy cigar between Dozier's teeth.

"Maybe you haven't noticed," Dozier said, "but I'm in the middle of working a homicide here."

"So wrap it up and let's go," Monk said.

"It's not that easy," Dozier said.

"Maybe not for you," Sharona said. "But

it is for him."

Dozier gave Monk a look. "Is that so?"

"Show him, Adrian," Sharona said.

"I may be a little rusty," Monk said. "It's been a day or two since I solved a murder."

"If you can close this case for me," Dozier said, "then you've got my full attention for as long as you're here."

"Tell me what happened," Monk said.

"It's not too complicated." Dozier turned his back to us and led us toward a charming storefront in the style of a Victorian house. "It's a simple holdup gone bad."

Monk lowered his hand from in front of his face and followed Dozier. We followed Monk.

"A guy barged into the store about an hour ago, took the cash from the register, then shot the owner and left."

"Sounds simple enough." Monk recoiled from the construction Dumpster on the street as if it might attack him. "What did the witnesses tell you?"

"There weren't any," Dozier said, turning to face Monk, who immediately raised his hand in front of his eyes again and averted his gaze. "The Dumpster behind you blocked the front door from view and the jackhammers muffled the sound of the gunshot. The owner's wife didn't even hear it and she was in the back room. It doesn't matter, though, because we've got the whole thing on video."

"Then what's the mystery?" Sharona asked.

"We know what happened but we don't know who the killer is. His face was hidden under a ski mask." Dozier stood in the doorway of the antiques store, staring at Monk. "You got a problem with me?"

"What makes you say that?" Monk said.

"You're shielding your eyes," Dozier said, "like I repulse you."

Dozier was right. So I checked him out again and that's when I saw it. Dozier's fly was open.

Monk could calmly scrutinize the gory bodies of people who'd suffered incredibly violent deaths but he couldn't look at a guy wearing unzipped pants and showing a hint of boxer shorts.

"I have sensitive eyes," Monk said.

"Your fly is open," I said to Dozier.

"There isn't any equipment there he hasn't seen since the day he was born," Dozier said, glancing down at himself.

"It's the open zipper itself that bothers him," Sharona said. "If you'd missed a button on your shirt, he'd be reacting the same way."

"I heard you were odd," Dozier said to Monk.

"Actually, I'm even," Monk said, still shielding himself. "You will be, too, once you zip up."

"I used that Porta Potti earlier and I guess I was in a hurry to get out." Dozier reached down, yanked up his zipper and strode into the store. "Big deal."

As soon as Dozier's back was turned, I reached into my purse for a wipe.

For me, not for Monk. I'd just remembered I'd shaken Dozier's hand, too. I scrubbed my hands and tossed the wipe in the Dumpster and followed everyone into the antiques store.

Nowadays people call anything more than a week old an antique. I think if you call something an antique, it should be at least twice as old as me and have some artistic value. Otherwise it's a collectible.

This place was definitely full of antiques. You wouldn't find any *Knightrider* lunch boxes here. There were pottery, furniture, paintings and knickknacks everywhere, mostly from Europe, with price tags from three to four figures.

Although the store was small, there was nothing dusty or dingy about it — a fact that I'm sure Monk appreciated. All the items were thoughtfully laid out and illuminated by pinpoint halogens, as if on museum display.

The cash register was on a carved wooden desk in the front of the store to the left of the door. There was a bloodstain on the carpet and blood spatter on the wall.

Monk glanced up at the security camera, rocked his head from side to side, then glanced at the open register.

"Why did he hold up the store?" Monk asked.

"Why does anybody rob a place?" Dozier said. "For the money."

"But this isn't really a cash business. These are high-priced antiques," Monk said. "People usually pay for them with credit cards."

"The only thing the perp saw was the expensive stuff and didn't think it through," Dozier said. "We aren't dealing with Professor Moriarty here. We're talking about some hophead looking for cash to buy his next fix."

"But he was smart enough to hit a store that was obscured from view," Monk said, "and to shoot the owner when the jackhammers were going."

"Trust me. You're overthinking this," Dozier said. "I've seen a hundred homicides just like it. Let me show you the video."

Dozier led us into the back room, a windowless, cramped space dominated by a large table covered with packing materials: UPS mailing labels, scissors, tape guns and rolls of bubble wrap. Suspended over the table were enormous bags of Styrofoam popcorn with funnels at the ends for filling the empty spaces in cardboard boxes.

The bits of popcorn were all over the floor and tabletops, and charged with static electricity. As soon as we walked in, we had pieces of Styrofoam clinging to our ankles.

There was a woman sitting on a stool. Her eyes were bloodshot, her nose was red and her cheeks were moist from the tears. She was obviously the wife — a short, thin woman in her thirties. But even in her grief, she somehow managed to project refinement and intelligence. Perhaps it was the way she sat with her back perfectly straight, her chin up and her eyes focused on the African-American detective taking her statement. I had an almost uncontrollable urge to swipe away the two bits of Styrofoam that clung to her leg.

In fact, I was surprised Monk hadn't beaten me to it, but he was busy trying to shake off the popcorn that was clinging to him. Judging by Monk's reaction, you'd think they were bloodsucking leeches instead of bits of Styrofoam.

"You might want to step outside, Mrs. Davidoff," Dozier said, nodding toward a VCR and monitor on a shelf. "We need to view the tape again."

Mrs. Davidoff stood up and regarded Monk. "Why are you wearing that mask?"

"My sinuses," Monk said. "I'd like to keep them."

That was when Monk collided with a stack of boxes piled up by the door to the alley for the UPS man. His peripheral vision wasn't great with that mask on.

Mrs. Davidoff caught the boxes before the stack could topple over. "Be careful," she said. "These are fragile antiques awaiting shipment."

"I'm sorry," Monk said.

Mrs. Davidoff turned to Dozier. "The UPS man should be arriving soon. Will you allow him to pick up these boxes? If they don't go today, they may never go. I don't think I can ever come back to this store again."

"No problem," Dozier said. "I'll personally make sure they're sent."

"Thank you," she said and walked out with the other detective.

"Classy lady," Dozier said. "She's holding

up well now but she's going to have a hard fall. I've seen it before."

Dozier turned on the TV and hit PLAY on the VCR. The video, taken from above and behind the front desk, was in crisp, clear color. There was no audio. We saw a man every bit as elegant as Mrs. Davidoff sitting at the desk, doing some paperwork. He had a bald spot on the top of his head that he tried to hide with a comb-over.

Monk wasn't paying much attention to the video; he was busy restacking the boxes according to size. At least it temporarily distracted him from the Styrofoam clinging to his ankles.

I looked back at the monitor just as the robber stepped into the frame. He was tall, with big shoulders, a barrel chest and a ski mask over his face. His turtleneck sweater, ski mask and gloves were all black. Because of where the desk was situated, he was only visible from above the waist.

Mr. Davidoff looked up. The robber held the gun sideways, the way gang members do in the movies, and motioned to the register. Mr. Davidoff opened the register and scooped out the few bills that were inside. The robber kept motioning to the register. The owner lifted out the cash tray, presumably to prove there was no more money there. And that was when the robber shot him. It was startling even without the sound.

I looked back at Monk, who glanced up at the monitor just as the robber was running out of the store.

"It's a good thing Mrs. Davidoff hasn't seen this," Dozier said. "Imagine seeing your own spouse getting killed."

I could. And I have imagined that. If there's a tape that exists of Mitch getting killed, I hope I never find out about it.

Dozier fast-forwarded the video to the point where Mrs. Davidoff came out. According to the time code, it was five minutes after her husband was killed. She ran to her husband's side and screamed, which was even more creepy and powerful in silence.

"Freeze it," Monk said.

Dozier did. Mrs. Davidoff's frozen, anguished image on the screen reminded me of Edvard Munch's famous painting *The Scream*. Hands on her cheeks, eyes wide, mouth open in a wail from the depths of her soul.

I knew exactly how she felt.

Monk stepped up, stared at the screen and cocked his head one way and then the other.

He'd solved the murder.

I knew it and one glance at the smile on

Sharona's face told me that she knew it, too.

"I know where you can find the man who shot Mr. Davidoff," Monk said.

"You do?" Dozier said, incredulous.

"Follow me," Monk said.

He walked out into the store and led us directly to Mrs. Davidoff, who was sitting on a couch, trying hard not to look at the desk where her husband was killed.

"Mrs. Davidoff, you have Styrofoam on your ankle," Monk said.

She glanced at her ankle. "It's the least of my problems."

"You are so wrong," Monk said. "It's the worst thing that's ever happened to you."

Mrs. Davidoff reared back as if reacting to a foul stench. "My husband was killed today. You honestly think that it's of less importance to me than some piece of boxing material on my pants? What kind of lunatic are you?"

"He's Adrian Monk, a homicide consultant for the San Francisco police," Dozier said, then looked at Monk. "You've got Styrofoam on your pants."

Monk let out a little shriek and started hopping around, wiggling his leg, trying to shake off the Styrofoam.

"He's a little messed up," Dozier said.

"So I see," she said.

At that moment, I hated them both. Who were they to pass judgment on Adrian Monk? Dozier was grotesque and Mrs. Davidoff, despite her terrible loss, was a snooty bitch. They were hardly superior to him.

Then again, Monk was in a gas mask hopping around on one foot. It hardly put him in the best light.

"Arrest her," Monk said as he hopped around. "She's the man who shot her husband."

It was a strange way of saying that she was the shooter, but he made his point. It made me feel justified in hating Mrs. Davidoff.

"That's insane," she said. "I was in the back room when he was killed."

"You saw the surveillance video," Dozier said. "He was shot by a broad-shouldered man who is at least a foot taller than she is."

"That doesn't mean a thing," Monk said.

He accidentally kicked the coffee table in his hopping frenzy and knocked over a six-hundred-dollar vase. I caught the vase before it could hit the floor and he managed to shake the Styrofoam off his leg.

Monk straightened himself, tugged on his sleeves and faced us. I knew what was coming. He was going to deliver his account of how the murder had actually occurred.

It was a necessary ritual for him.

He didn't do it to show off or to humiliate anyone. He did it for himself.

It was the one moment when he could feel that he'd set everything right and brought order to the universe. It was the only time he was truly free of his anxieties and his sorrows. It made him whole, at least for a moment or two.

But then he'd notice something out of place, or realize he was vulnerable to a germ, or remember that he hadn't solved his wife's murder, and all his anxieties would come back in full force. And once again, he'd be struggling to restore order in a world that defied it.

"Here's what happened," Monk said.

He explained that Mrs. Davidoff waited in the back room until the construction workers started using their jackhammers. Then she strapped down her breasts with Ace bandages, put on a set of shoulder pads and slipped her feet into shoes with lifts. This hid her femininity, gave her broad shoulders and added height. She covered her hair with a ski mask and wore a turtleneck sweater to cover her throat. Otherwise her Adam's apple would have been a telltale giveaway of her sex. She left the store through the alley, pulled down the ski mask over her face when she came in the front door and shot her husband. She ran outside again, returned to the back room, removed her disguise and then came out to wail for the camera.

Dozier stared at Monk once he finished his summation. "That is the most preposterous story I've ever heard," Dozier said.

"That was nothing," Sharona said. "Adrian once accused a guy of murder who was in a coma at the time of the killing."

"And people still take him seriously?" Dozier said.

"He was right," Sharona said.

"He was?" Dozier said.

"It's irrelevant," Mrs. Davidoff said. "I find his accusations insensitive, outrageous and thoroughly despicable."

"Murderers usually do," I said.

"You're out of line," Dozier said to me and then turned to Monk. "And so are you. There isn't a shred of evidence to back up what you said."

"There's that." Monk pointed to the Styrofoam on Mrs. Davidoff's leg.

"That?" Dozier said.

"This?" Mrs. Davidoff said.

"The Styrofoam is charged with static

electricity. It's sticking to everyone and everything that passes through the back room," Monk said. "You should have watched the security camera video before the police got here."

"I never want to see it," Mrs. Davidoff said.

"That was your big mistake. If you'd watched it, you would have noticed a piece of Styrofoam sticking to the shooter's sweater. That meant that the killer came from the back room. And you were the only one back there. So the video you thought would exonerate you as a suspect is practically a confession."

"I've walked back and forth to the showroom all day," she said. "I probably tracked the Styrofoam out with me before, just like I have now, and that's how it stuck to the monster that shot my husband."

"Makes sense to me," Dozier said to Monk. "It's what we in the detective trade call the 'commonsense explanation.' And even if you were right, which you're not, where's the disguise and the murder weapon?"

"Packed up and ready to go to Madison, Wisconsin. That's what's in those boxes that UPS is coming to pick up," Monk said. "That's why Mrs. Davidoff was so insistent about those packages getting out of here today."

Dozier turned to look at Mrs. Davidoff, who was glaring at Monk with such hatred that I was afraid she might launch herself at his throat.

"Shall we open the boxes and prove him wrong?" Dozier asked.

She didn't say a word. She just glared.

"Mrs. Davidoff?" Dozier insisted.

She blinked hard and looked at Dozier. "You can address any further questions to my lawyer. We're done talking."

Dozier's jaw dropped. Really. His mouth just hung open in slack-jawed shock. It took him a moment, but he managed to regain his composure. He waved over the other detective.

"Read this lady her rights. Then call Judge Mooney," Dozier said. "We're going to need a search warrant to open up those boxes in the back room. And make damn sure the UPS guy doesn't take them first."

Sharona put her arm around Monk's shoulder. He cringed all over at her touch, but she didn't seem to care.

"It's been so long since I've seen you nail a murderer that I'd forgotten how much I liked it."

"What's not to like?" Monk said.

"I can think of a couple of things," Mrs. Davidoff muttered.

CHAPTER TEN:
MR. MONK HAD A LITTLE LAMB

It was getting dark by the time we got to Ellen Cole's house in Santa Monica, just a couple miles west of the antiques store.

Ellen lived in a tiny Spanish-revival bungalow with white stucco walls, arched windows and a gabled, red-tiled roof. Decorative tiles with a flower pattern lined the arched front doorway. The bungalow was adorable.

The front yard had become wild and rangy since her gardener was sent to jail, but it didn't take much imagination to envision how nice it must have looked when everything was trimmed.

"It's a crime." Monk stood on the sidewalk, facing the house and shaking his head. The gas mask was so tight on his head, it was a miracle any blood was getting to his brain.

"That's why we're here," Dozier said.

"He's referring to the grass," Sharona said.

"Why hasn't anyone done something

119

about this?" Monk said. "It's an affront to human decency."

"The ownership of the house is in dispute," Dozier said. "Ellen Cole willed it to her lover, but her parents are contesting it, since the couple had an acrimonious split and were fighting over this house and custody of their two-year-old kid at the time of her murder."

Monk, Sharona and I stared at Dozier. He looked back at us.

"What?" Dozier said.

"You never said anything before about Ellen Cole being in the middle of an ugly breakup," Sharona said.

"Why should I?" he said.

"Because her lover had a much better motive to kill her than Trevor did," Sharona said.

"But she didn't kill her," Dozier said.

"She?" Monk said.

"Ellen Cole was a lesbian," Dozier said. "She and her lover, Sally Jenkins, lived together in this house with their kid before the breakup."

"So Sally would have known the alarm code," I said.

"Unless Ellen changed it," Dozier said.

"Did you check?" Sharona asked.

He didn't reply, which meant the answer was no.

"Maybe Ellen came home early and caught Sally in the house," Sharona said. "They fought and Sally hit her with the lamp during the struggle."

"There's just one problem with that theory," Dozier said.

"It would mean you screwed up," Sharona said.

Dozier let that remark go. "Sally Jenkins couldn't have done it. At the time of Ellen Cole's murder, Sally was in Sacramento testifying in front of a state senate committee that's considering a bill to legalize gay marriage. That's what we in the detective trade call 'an airtight alibi.'"

"Mr. Monk has broken better alibis than that," I said, and turned to Monk, only to find him on his knees, measuring blades of grass with his finger and cutting them individually with a pair of nail clippers.

"Adrian," Sharona said, "what are you doing?"

"Mowing the lawn," he said, though it was hard to hear him mumbling from inside that mask.

"At the rate you're going, it's going to take you a month," I said. "And by the time you're done, everything that you've already cut will need to be trimmed again. You could be cutting this lawn for the rest of your life."

"I can live with that," he said, clipping another blade.

Sharona groaned, grabbed Monk by the strap of the gas mask and forced him to his feet. "We're investigating a murder here, Adrian. Pay attention."

She snatched the nail clippers from him and dropped them in her purse. "You'll get these back when we're done here," she said and gave me a hard look. "You're way too soft on him."

"I try to be sensitive and understanding," I said. "I think it's more effective in the long run."

"Where did you get that idea? If I treated him the way you do, he'd still be wearing a gas mask every time he left the house."

It took Sharona a moment to realize the absurdity of what she'd just said. "As opposed to just occasionally," she added.

"Big improvement," Dozier said.

Monk walked up the path to the front door of the house with his hands on either side of his face to make sure that he wouldn't see the overgrown lawn.

We joined Monk at the front porch, where he was scrutinizing the door.

"There's no sign of forced entry," Monk said.

"He came in through an unlocked window," Dozier said.

"Didn't she have an alarm system?" I asked.

"Yes, so he must have known the code," Dozier said.

"How?" Sharona said.

"It's easy," Monk said.

"It is?" she said.

"Is the alarm activated now?" Monk asked.

Dozier nodded.

"Open the door but don't type in the code," Monk said. "Let me do it."

"Sure." Dozier unlocked the door and opened it, immediately triggering the alarm.

The loud, electronic wail sounded like a red alert on the Starship *Enterprise.*

Yeah, I know that's my second comparison to *Star Trek,* but so much of what was on that show is now part of our daily lives. Take a look at your flip phone or all the people walking around with those Bluetooth things in their ears like Lieutenant Uhura and tell me I'm wrong.

Monk stepped in and scrutinized the keypad. "The code is 1212333."

I was stunned. "How did you know?"

"The one, two and three on the keypad are dirtier than the rest," Monk said, stepping into the living room, holding his hands out in front of him like a director framing a shot.

The house was only about fourteen hundred square feet and very cozy, with lots of fluffy pillows on the furniture and plenty of paintings, mostly landscapes, on the walls.

"But how did you know the order of the numbers?" I said. "There must be thousands of possible combinations."

"Monk figured it out the same way Trevor did," Dozier said and punched in the code. The tones formed a familiar tune, "Mary Had a Little Lamb." The alarm went off. "Trevor must have heard her deactivate the alarm one of the times when he was here gardening."

"Over the sound of the mowers, the blowers and the ringing alarm?" Sharona said.

Monk seemed to be swaying to a rhythm only he was hearing as he moved through the living room. It was his observational dance, his method of picking up the details in the room and feeling the karmic traces of what had occurred.

"Maybe he wasn't mowing or blowing," Dozier said. "Maybe he was standing here, talking to her at the time."

124

"That would make her awfully stupid," Sharona said.

"That's why she's dead," Dozier said.

I was still impressed that Monk figured out the security code thing and was surprised that nobody else was, especially Dozier.

"Aren't you amazed that Monk guessed the security code?" I asked him.

"Not really," Dozier said. "Ian Ludlow figured it out, too."

"Ian Ludlow the author?" Sharona said, clearly surprised. "He was here?"

"Ludlow has helped me out on some tricky cases. He's like our Adrian Monk," Dozier said, then lowered his voice to a whisper. "Only sane."

I knew who Ludlow was. It was impossible not to. You couldn't step on an airplane without seeing one of his Detective Marshak novels in just about everybody's hands. It made me wonder if there was some FAA regulation requiring airline passengers to read Ludlow's books.

Ludlow must have had elves cranking out his books for him because there seemed to be a new title every month in the grocery store checkout line, in the place of honor and prestige, right next to the *National Enquirer* and the *Star*.

Lieutenant Disher, who took a UC Berkeley extension class from Ludlow, once referred to the author as the "Tolstoy of the Mean Streets."

I glanced at Monk, who was still examining everything, pausing to align pillows by size, straighten crooked pictures or alphabetize a bookshelf. It was his process and I didn't dare intrude.

"I've been Ludlow's technical adviser on his last couple of books, which were inspired by some of my cases," Dozier said. "He creates the excitement. I provide the gripping realism."

"So I guess in Ludlow's next book Detective Marshak's fly will be open the whole time," Sharona said. "And he'll send the killer's murder weapon to Wisconsin."

"What was Ludlow doing here?" I asked quickly, hoping to distract Dozier from gunning Sharona down for that remark.

"He was intrigued by the case," Dozier said. "All we had at the time was a UCLA professor of gender studies found dead in her home. We looked at her lover and her students but we didn't have any suspects. Ludlow helped us develop the leads that led us to *her husband*."

Although Dozier was answering my question, he delivered those last two words directly at Sharona as if they were physical blows.

And that was exactly how she took them, but she probably deserved it for her crack about his technical advice.

"Was this where you found the body?" Monk asked from afar.

I'd been so caught up in my conversation with Dozier that I'd completely lost track of Monk. He'd wandered down the hall into the master bedroom.

There was a big four-poster bed in the center of the room that was covered with pillows and a fluffy, frilly comforter. I wanted to climb into that bed with a good book and never get out.

There were matching nightstands on either side of the bed. One had a lamp on it; the other didn't. Now I knew where the murder weapon came from.

Before I met Monk, I never noticed details like that. Then again, before I met Monk, I never imagined anybody ran their doorknobs through the dishwasher every week.

The bed faced a flat-screen TV mounted on the wall above a waist-high entertainment center.

On one side of the room was a set of French doors that opened out onto a backyard patio. On the other was a wall lined with a dresser and vanity.

Monk stood by Ellen Cole's dresser, studying the bloodstained carpet at his feet.

"We found her laying right there," Dozier said. "The back of her head was a bloody mess."

"Could you show me exactly what her position was on the floor?" Monk said.

Dozier hiked up his pants and curled up on the floor, facing the dresser, careful not to actually lay his head on the bloodstain.

Monk crouched beside Dozier and studied the detective's position. Then he got up. He held his hands out in front of him, palms up, as if warming himself by a fire, and did a little pirouette, coming to a stop facing the closet.

He went over to the closet and opened the double doors.

The clothes that were hanging on the wooden bar had been pushed aside. Behind the clothes, there were several file boxes stacked against the back wall. On the floor, there were shoes, which had been cleared away to make room for one of the boxes.

Monk shook his head and groaned.

"What's wrong, Adrian?" Sharona asked.

"Everything," Monk said sadly. "Trevor didn't kill Ellen Cole."

CHAPTER ELEVEN:
MR. MONK TAKES
THE CASE

I was glad that I was right about Trevor and relieved that my job might no longer be in jeopardy. But at the same time I felt terrible for Sharona, who sat down on the edge of Ellen's bed and hugged herself.

"Oh my God," she said softly, "what have I done?"

Dozier scrambled to his feet. "He's wrong."

Sharona shook her head. "He's never wrong about murder. Never."

"There's no Styrofoam in this case," Dozier said. "Trevor killed her. All the evidence points right to him."

"Only if you don't see all the evidence that points somewhere else," Monk said.

"Like what?" Dozier said.

"Your theory is that Ellen came home early and caught Trevor in the act of stealing her things. So he hit her with the lamp and fled."

129

"That's how it went down," Dozier said.

"Why didn't Trevor run out into the backyard when he heard her coming in?"

"Maybe he didn't hear her," Dozier said. "Or he didn't think he could escape from the backyard without her seeing him. So he hid in the closet."

"That's impossible," Monk said.

"Why?" Dozier said. "The closet was right behind him."

"Why didn't he just wait in there until she left again?" I asked.

"Maybe he panicked. Or maybe she opened the closet and caught him," Dozier said. "She ran to the phone to call the police, so he grabbed the lamp and hit her."

"All you have are 'maybes,' " I said.

"That's because Trevor won't talk," Dozier said. "But the evidence clearly shows what happened."

"Yes, it does," Monk said. "Have you thought about getting your eyes checked?"

"Someone was obviously hiding in the closet," Dozier said.

"Yes, that's true," Monk said. "But look at how the boxes are arranged. Someone moved the clothes aside and put a box down on the floor to give him something to sit on. That means the killer was taking his time. He was waiting for her to show up long before she got here and he wanted to be comfortable."

"Or the boxes were already like that," Dozier said. "And Trevor moved the clothes to make space for himself when he hid."

"But she was hit on the back of the head and fell forward. If he'd jumped out of the closet and then grabbed the lamp off the nightstand by the bed, she would have had time to turn around and face him. That means she should have been hit on the side of her head, not the back," Monk said. "If he hit her as she was running out of the room, her body would have been in the doorway or the hall, not in front of the dresser. The fact that she was hit from behind proves that whoever killed her already had the lamp in his hands when he went into the closet. We aren't talking about a man doing a desperate act. This is what we in the detective trade call 'premeditated murder.' "

I had to smile at that last, patronizing comment. Monk had obviously been paying a lot more attention than I thought to what Dozier had been saying before.

"I'm the most horrible wife in wife history," Sharona said. "I wouldn't blame Trevor if he never wanted me back."

I sat down next to her and took her hand.

"Don't be so hard on yourself, Sharona. Trevor is partly to blame for the way you reacted. If he hadn't misled you so many times before, you wouldn't have had any reason not to believe him this time."

"Instead I believed the worst about him, the absolute worst," Sharona said. "It's as if I wanted him to be guilty."

"He *is* guilty," Dozier said.

"I know how you feel," Monk said to Dozier. "I wish he was, too."

"That's an awful thing to say," I said. "Why would you wish that?"

"He's a bad influence," Monk said.

"What terrible thing has he ever made me do?" Sharona said.

"He made you marry him again and move back to New Jersey," Monk said.

"You are the most selfish man I have ever met," Sharona said. "You should be ashamed of yourself, Adrian."

"Not only that — he's wrong," Dozier said. "We found Ellen Cole's jewelry in Trevor's truck. He was stealing jewelry from his landscaping clients and auctioning it off on eBay. The payments for those sales went directly into his personal checking account. If he's innocent, how do you explain that?"

"I didn't say he wasn't a thief," Monk said. "But he didn't kill Ellen Cole."

"He didn't steal those things, either," Sharona said. "This whole thing is a setup."

"Who would want to set up your husband?" Dozier said. "He's a nobody."

"I don't know who, but it wouldn't have been too hard to pull off," Sharona said. "Anybody could have created an e-mail account for him on Yahoo!, got his checking account number somehow and used it to open an account in his name on eBay. Give me your name and one of your checks and I could do it in ten minutes."

"Was it the eBay auction of stolen goods that led you to Trevor?" I asked Dozier.

"We found out about the auction after we got the lead on Trevor," Dozier said. "It was Ian Ludlow who put the clues together. It made sense to me then and it still does now."

"Even after everything Monk just told you?" I said.

"It's all speculation," Dozier said. "I see the evidence one way and he sees it another. Nothing he's said makes me think we arrested the wrong guy."

"You did and we're going to prove it," Sharona said, standing up. "Aren't we, Adrian?"

"Yes," Monk said mournfully, "we are."

Whodunit Books was located in a storefront underneath a large parking structure in the middle of Westwood Village, right on the edge of the UCLA campus.

There was a casket outside filled with bargain paperbacks. The front windows were cluttered with poster-sized blowups of book covers advertising the upcoming signings of various mystery authors, all of whom seemed to have shopped at Leather Jackets R Us before having their author photos taken.

The first thing we saw when we came in the store was a large table filled with stacks of Ian Ludlow's previous books in hardcover and paperback and a pile of his newest one, *Death Is the Last Word.*

"What's with him?" asked the woman behind the counter. Her name tag read LORINDA.

I guess she didn't get many customers wearing gas masks.

"Asthma," Sharona said.

Lorinda was a thin brunette in a low-cut tank top who had a safety pin in one nostril.

Yeah, just one nostril.

I could see the trouble ahead.

Monk immediately started to organize Ludlow's books on the table into even stacks. He opened each book to check the copyright date so he could arrange them in chronological order. I only know this because he did the same thing to my bookcase.

I looked over his shoulder and saw that the books were signed and dated by Ludlow on the title page. This seemed to stump Monk for a moment, but then he came to a decision and continued his arranging.

There were about twenty people there to meet Ian Ludlow, who sat at a desk in the back corner of the store, signing books with surprising speed.

The Tolstoy of the Mean Streets was in his early thirties, with buzz-cut hair and a day's worth of stubble on his cheeks. He was dressed in a black leather jacket, a black T-shirt, faded jeans and a Dodger baseball cap that I suspected was hiding a prematurely receding hairline. I don't know who men think they're fooling with those caps.

At the front of the line was a man with a rolling suitcase full of books for Ludlow to sign. He had dandruff and his breast pocket was bulging with pens, papers and business cards.

"I've got every book you've ever written," the man said, presenting a stack to Ludlow.

"Even those Jack Bludd paperbacks you wrote under a pseudonym."

"It's nice to know my mother isn't the only one with a complete collection," Ludlow said as he signed the books. "You ought to hold on to them. They might be worth their cover prices again someday."

"I don't know how you keep churning them out," the man said, shaking his head.

"I'm a natural storyteller," Ludlow said. "It's what I was born to do. It's all I know how to do."

"But you write four books a year," a large woman said, clutching Ludlow's latest mystery protectively to her bountiful bosom as if someone might try to snatch it away from her. "Aren't you ever afraid that you're going to run out of stories?"

"Perhaps I would be if all I had to rely on was my imagination," Ludlow said. "But the world around me gives me endless material. There are millions of people out there, each with a story to inspire me. And my deadlines are a great motivator. If I don't deliver, I have to give back my advance."

Sharona gave Ludlow the once-over from a distance and frowned. "He looks a lot taller and a lot tougher in his author photo."

"They always do," said Lorinda. "They take those moody photos and try to look mysterious and rugged so readers will think they prowl the dark streets looking for stories," Lorinda said. "The only place Ludlow prowls is bookstores to sign his stock and hit on women."

"You don't sound like a fan," I said.

"We've supported him from the start, before he was anybody, but after he leaves here today, he's going to head down the street to sign stock at Borders," she said. "They sell his books at thirty percent off, which we can't afford to do, so he's undercutting us when he does that. But he can't help himself. He can't pass a bookstore without signing his books. It's like a compulsion."

"Someone should tell him to get a grip," Monk said, busily rearranging the books on the table. "He doesn't have to sign every book that has his name on it. How hard could it be to just ignore the unsigned books?"

Sharona and I turned and looked at him.

"It's as easy as walking past a crooked painting without straightening it," Sharona said.

"That's different," Monk said. "That's a public safety issue."

There was no way Sharona or I was going to convince Monk that a crooked painting didn't pose a danger to humanity, so I turned back to Lorinda.

"If Ludlow is working against you by signing down the street," I asked, "why do you keep inviting him back?"

She shrugged. "He's a big name in mystery. Our customers expect us to have his books, though it's getting to the point that an unsigned Marshak is harder to find and more valuable than a signed one."

The whole store rumbled. My first thought was an earthquake, but I quickly realized it was just a car driving into the parking structure overhead. I hoped the rent was cheap.

"Voilà," Monk said, stepping back from the table. It looked pretty much as it had before, except every stack was even. "Done."

"What did you do?" Lorinda asked.

"Someone completely messed up the books on this table. I put them back into their original order."

"Original order?"

"The way you had them before," Monk said. "Arranged by copyright, the number of printings, and the date they were signed, with the most recent book on top and the oldest on the bottom."

"Right," Lorinda said. "The original order. Thanks."

Monk seemed to notice her for the first time and was troubled by what he saw. Sharona and I shared a weary look. We both knew what was coming. It was inevitable.

"You're missing a safety pin," he said, gesturing to her nose.

"No, I'm not," she said.

"You've lost the one in your other nostril," Monk said.

"My other nostril isn't pierced," she said.

"It should be," Monk said.

"One is cool," she said. "Two would look ridiculous."

I didn't see the distinction myself. I think anybody with a paper clip, a nose ring, a bone or anything else in their nose looks stupid.

"Faces are symmetrical. It's a law of nature. You don't want to break a law of nature." Monk nodded toward Sharona. "She's a nurse. She'd be glad to stick another safety pin in your nose for you."

"No, I wouldn't," Sharona said.

While they argued, the last of the readers who'd come to have their books signed by Ian Ludlow filed out of the store with their purchases. The man with the rolling suitcase was so distracted by Monk's gas mask that he nearly ran over my feet.

"You took the Hippocratic oath," Monk

said. "It's your duty as a nurse to save this poor woman."

"There's no medical reason to stick a safety pin in her nostril, Adrian."

"Have you taken a good look at her face?" Monk said. "It's hideous."

"Hideous?" Lorinda said.

"You better be careful, Monk. They keep a shotgun behind the counter," Ian Ludlow said, a cocky grin on his face as he strode up to us. "And Lorinda has been looking for an excuse to use it."

"You know Mr. Monk?" I asked.

"Of course I do. I'm a huge fan of his work. I was teaching a creative writing course up in Berkeley during the police strike six months ago when Monk solved the Golden Gate Strangler case," Ludlow said. "I toyed with turning it into a book, but the serial killer genre is getting stale."

"As opposed to police detectives who solve murders," Lorinda said. "That never gets old."

"Cute, isn't she?" Ludlow said.

"Not with only one safety pin in her nose," Monk said. "Her face is an asymmetrical nightmare."

"I'll take my safety pin out if you take off your gas mask," she said.

It was a draw.

"I'm Sharona Fleming and this is Natalie Teeger," Sharona said to Ludlow. "We're his associates. Lieutenant Dozier said we could find you here. We're investigating the murder of Ellen Cole."

"Your husband did it," Ludlow said. "Case solved. Can I autograph a book for you?"

"I don't think so," Sharona said.

"It makes a great gift for a loved one in prison," Ludlow said.

"He's not guilty," Sharona said.

"That's not what the evidence says," Ludlow said.

"But it's what *he* says." Sharona gestured at Monk.

"Well, that changes everything," Ludlow said.

CHAPTER TWELVE:
MR. MONK AND THE
BROOCH

"Are you being sarcastic?" I asked Ludlow because I honestly couldn't tell.

"Not at all. I have enormous respect for Monk's abilities," Ludlow said. "Who am I, a mere scribbler, to argue with a legend in homicide investigation? May I sign a book for you?"

"Sure." I picked up one for myself, then two more to give as Christmas gifts. I handed them to Lorinda along with my credit card. She rang up my purchase.

"How did you get involved in this case?" Monk asked Ludlow.

"As soon as I finish writing a book, I hang out with Lieutenant Dozier for a couple of days until a murder comes along that intrigues me."

"But this wasn't a bizarre or unusual case," I said. "It almost seems mundane."

"That's exactly what drew me to it," he said. "I have found that what may seem simple or ordinary on the surface can turn out to be more compelling and complex than you ever imagined. That's a trademark of my books."

"That and every description of a female character begins with her breasts," Lorinda said, handing me my receipt to sign.

"I like to give my books a little sizzle," Ludlow said. "What's the crime in that?"

"What's the sizzle in the Ellen Cole story?" Sharona asked.

"Are you kidding me?" Ludlow said. "You start with a lady conked on the head by an intruder, but you dig just a little bit and you get warring lesbian lovers, a heart-wrenching child-custody battle, a political battle in the capitol over gay marriage, academic backstabbing at a major university and a steamy affair with a married man. I couldn't make up anything that good. It has enough sizzle for *two* Detective Marshak novels. And the gardener did it, the ultimate surprise ending."

"But he didn't," Sharona said. "Someone else did."

"Another shocking twist," Ludlow said. "This story keeps getting better and better."

"I'd read it," Lorinda said, putting my copy of the receipt in one of the books and handing them to me.

"See?" Ludlow said. "It's a grabber."

"Where does adultery fit in?" I asked as I handed my books to him to sign.

"That's what broke up the relationship. Sally cheated on Ellen," Ludlow said as he signed and dated my books, "with a *man*. Dr. Christian Bayliss. And if you think that's a twist, get this: He was their secret sperm donor. And he's married, or at least he was until this story broke."

"And you still thought my husband was the most likely suspect?" Sharona said. "These two have a million reasons to want to kill Ellen Cole."

"That's the thing. Sally and her lover were the obvious suspects. Bor-ring," Ludlow said. "So while Dozier was banging his head against a wall trying to nail them, I looked in another direction."

"The least likely suspect," Monk said.

"You got it. The guy nobody was looking at for this. Trevor had means and opportunity," Ludlow said. "All that was missing was a motive. Dozier did some checking and found out Trevor was known back east as a two-bit hustler always looking to make a quick buck. I stumbled on his eBay account and it all fell into place."

"Except you were wrong," Sharona said.

"So I've been told," Ludlow said, turning

to Monk. "What's your theory?"

"That Trevor didn't do it," Monk said. "And someone else did."

"Well, when you figure it out, let me know," Ludlow said. "It's going to make a hell of a book."

We stayed at the Holiday Inn at the foot of Santa Monica Pier that Tuesday night. We had rooms 204 and 206. Monk stayed in one room and Sharona and I shared another.

Monk put his own sheets and pillows on the bed and had some of the food he brought with him for dinner. I'm not sure, but I think he spent the rest of the night cleaning the bathroom. I don't know how he ate with the gas mask or if he slept with it on. I didn't ask.

Sharona and I had a pizza delivered and ate out on the deck, overlooking the parking structure of a shopping mall. But if we leaned over the railing and craned our necks, we got a nice view of the pier and the glittering Ferris wheel at the end.

The pier was a pleasant sight, if you were in the dark and looking at it from a distance. Up close, the decaying midway, loud arcades and shabby rides resembled one of those scummy traveling carnivals that show up for a weekend in shopping center parking lots.

The darkness also hid the homeless who congregated in the long, cliffside park that overlooked the bay and that ran parallel to Ocean Avenue. They probably had the best view of any homeless encampment in America.

Sharona went inside the room to try to call Trevor at the jail. She told me that she wanted to tell him that she believed him and was fighting for him, but they wouldn't put her call through. So we decided that I'd drive her downtown in the morning to visit him and then we'd go have a talk with Sally Jenkins, Ellen Cole's ex-girlfriend.

Yesterday, Sharona was my mortal enemy. But my feelings toward her had changed. I realized that it was more than just fear about losing my job that drove me. It was also jealousy.

She was like me in so many ways. We both had twelve-year-old kids and raised them, more or less, on our own. And we'd both worked for Monk, an experience that no one, with the possible exception of Captain Stottlemeyer, could truly appreciate.

But there were some significant differences.

She would always be in first position with Monk. No matter how long I remained with him, I would still be the replacement, the consolation prize.

She had a profession, and I didn't. I had never found my true calling, though until Sharona came along, I was beginning to think it was being an assistant to a detective.

And she had her husband. If we weren't so much alike, maybe that fact, out of all the others, wouldn't have made me so jealous. But it did.

I was thinking about these things as I nibbled on the last cold slice of pizza and Sharona leaned over the rail again to look at the ocean and the pier.

"All it would take is one shove and you wouldn't have to worry about me taking your job ever again," Sharona said.

"It occurred to me," I said. "But if I tried to make it look like an accident, Mr. Monk would see right through it."

"He might let you get away with it anyway," Sharona said, standing up straight again. "Because if I'm dead, and you go to prison, who is going to take care of him? He is, after all, the most selfish man alive."

"Good point," I said. "Take another look at the view."

We both smiled.

"You're good for him," Sharona said. "I

see that now. I was wrong about some of the things I said about you."

"Just some?"

"This is where you're supposed to say how wrong you were about me," Sharona said. "It's a bonding moment."

"I know," I said. "But now if I say that, it will seem like I'm doing it because it's expected of me. It won't feel sincere."

"Would it be sincere?"

"Probably not," I said. "But I like you now, if that means anything to you."

"It does," she said.

During the hour that Sharona spent in the jail visiting her husband early Wednesday morning, Monk and I stayed in the car. I tried to start reading one of the three signed Ludlow books that I'd bought, but Monk wouldn't give me any peace. He nagged me to help him write letters to members of Congress urging them to pass a law that all the M&Ms in a package must be the same color.

"If we want to win the war on terror," he said, "we have to start at home."

"Multicolored M and Ms aren't an act of terrorism," I said.

"They've got you fooled, too. It's sugar-coated anarchy," he said. "It's insidiously ingenious. It makes the idea of anarchy acceptable, even tasty. Left unchecked, it could eventually topple our society and our entire system of government."

Somehow, I just couldn't picture terrorists plotting to destroy America by hooking the populace on multicolored candies.

Sharona returned with bloodshot eyes and tear-streaked cheeks. She got into the car without saying a word to either of us. She didn't speak until nearly twenty minutes later, during which time we'd managed to travel maybe two miles on the traffic-clogged, westbound Santa Monica Freeway.

"He still loves me," she said, sniffling. "Can you believe that?"

"Yes," Monk said, "I can."

I could, too.

It took us another hour to make our way back to Santa Monica, where Sally Jenkins ran Funky Junk, a small boutique that sold "fashion accessories with an edge." That was what the advertisement in the *LA Weekly* said and I had no idea what it meant.

But I was about to find out.

Funky Junk was a tiny shop wedged between a florist shop and a Starbucks. As we passed the Starbucks, the patrons at the tables outside looked up from their laptops, and the spec screenplays they were writing, to stare at the strange man in the gas mask.

Monk didn't mind. The only time I'd ever seen him embarrassed was when he inadvertently went out in public with his shirt open at the collar. When he realized his button was undone, he was mortified by his show of "public nakedness."

Funky Junk was an eclectic mess, full of couture belts, scarves, hats and accessories that were designed to look as if they were scavenged from a vintage-clothing store. I didn't get it. I'd rather buy the real thing for a lot cheaper.

A young woman with shocking white hair and radiant blue eyes greeted us. She wore a starburst-style brooch with a tiny gold chain attached to it that disappeared over the shoulder of her white blouse.

"May I help you?" she said with a smile.

"Sally Jenkins?" Sharona asked.

"Yes?"

"I think Lieutenant Dozier called you this morning and told you we'd be coming by," Sharona said. "This is Adrian Monk. He's investigating the murder of your girlfriend."

"Ex-girlfriend," she said. "Ex as in 'we broke up,' not as in 'she's dead,' of course. That would be callous and cruel, and I'm neither of those things."

That was when the biggest cockroach I've

ever seen in my life crawled over her shoulder and hissed at us.

Sharona and I both instinctively jerked away.

Monk instinctively ran out the door and back to the car.

It took me a moment to realize that the four-inch-long cockroach was leashed by the gold chain to Sally's brooch and that his body was adorned with glimmering Swarovski glass crystals.

"I see you've noticed my roach brooch," Sally said.

"It's hard not to," I said, appalled.

"It's a real eye-catcher and our biggest-selling item," Sally said. "It's a Madagascar hissing cockroach."

"Who would want to wear a cockroach?" Sharona said.

"Anybody who wants to make a powerful fashion statement by defying convention, by turning the ugly and the repulsive into art," Sally said. "I can't keep them in the store."

"Because they keep running away?" Sharona said.

"They're affordable, live a long time and require very little care," Sally said.

"That's hardly a selling point for jewelry," I said.

"Would you like to try one on?" Sally asked.

"No, thanks," I said.

My cell phone rang. I could tell from the caller ID readout that it was Monk calling from the car on Sharona's phone.

"I can't believe you're still in there," Monk said.

"We haven't talked to Sally yet," I said.

"There's a cockroach the size of a dog on her," Monk yelled.

"It's jewelry," I said.

"Run," he said. "Run for your lives."

"Not until we're done," I said.

I switched the phone to speaker mode and held it up so Monk could listen as we spoke to Sally and so he could ask her questions, too. I asked the first one and it was quite blunt, but the lady was wearing a cockroach, so I figured she was tough enough to handle it.

"Ellen's murder makes your life a lot easier, doesn't it?"

"We may have broken up, but we had a deep and everlasting bond," Sally said. "Her death has devastated me."

"You mean her murder," Sharona corrected her.

"But now that she's gone, you don't have to fight her for custody of your daughter," I said. "No more legal bills, no more uncertainty."

"There was never any doubt that I'd win custody," Sally said. "I gave birth to her. She was my biological child. The court wasn't going to acknowledge that a woman in a lesbian relationship has any parental rights to her lover's biological child."

"And yet, at the time of her murder, you were at a hearing at the state capitol arguing in favor of gay marriage," Sharona said.

"So?" Sally said. "Just because my relationship with Ellen ended doesn't mean I've stopped believing that gays and lesbians should have the same rights as heterosexual couples."

"As long as it doesn't happen until after you win custody of your child over your lesbian lover," Sharona said. "Of course, now that she's dead, it's a moot point."

"That's a vile thing to say," Sally said, which struck me as a bizarre statement coming from a woman with an enormous cockroach on her shoulder.

"What's really odd is that you were arguing for gay marriage after you'd left your lesbian lover for a man, Dr. Christian Bayliss," I said. "So it wasn't even an issue that affected you anymore."

"Inequality affects us all as a society," she

said. "My testimony before the state senate, especially given my personal circumstances, only demonstrates how strongly I believe in the principles of fairness. I see nothing unusual about that."

"Then you probably don't think it's unusual that you ran off with the same man who provided the sperm for your artificial insemination," I said.

"How stupid was that?" Sharona said. "If you'd left Ellen for the guy earlier, you could have saved a bundle by inseminating yourself the old-fashioned way."

"Don't be grotesque," she said.

Once more, I'd like to point out that she had a cockroach crawling on her at the time.

"And on top of that, he's a married man," I said. "So, if I have this right, shortly after you left your lesbian lover for the married man who artificially impregnated you, you went up to Sacramento to argue that it was time we liberalized our notions of marriage."

Her face turned dark red. She was flushed with anger, not embarrassment. I'm sure she saw nothing wrong with her behavior.

"I don't see what any of this gay bashing and character assassination has to do with Ellen's murder," Sally said.

"Considering all the hypocrisy and contradictions in your story," Sharona said, "a cynical person might argue that you went to that hearing in Sacramento just so you'd have an alibi while your ex-girlfriend was murdered."

"Do you really think I've benefited from any of this?" Sally said. "Whoever killed Ellen has made my life a living hell. My private life is now public and Christian's marriage has crumbled."

"Freeing him to be with you," Sharona said. "Another win."

"His kids hate him now," Sally said. "And although he's got tenure, this has probably ruined any chance he has of being the new chairman of the university's gender-studies department."

"Isn't that where Ellen worked?" I said.

"They were colleagues," Sally said. "That's how she knew him well enough to ask for his sperm."

"That must have been an interesting conversation," Sharona said. "Why him?"

"Christian was married and fertile," Sally said. "He wasn't likely to try to assert any parental rights and Ellen liked his kids. They were bright and attractive."

"So why wasn't she the one who was inseminated?" I said.

"Medical problems," Sally said. "She

couldn't have children."

"This chairmanship position," Sharona asked, "was that something Ellen wanted, too?"

Sally's face was so red now, she looked like a tomato being devoured by the king of cockroaches.

"Yes," Sally said.

"So you've got the kid, you've got the man, you're probably going to get the house," Sharona said, "and if things really go well, your man will get the chairmanship, too. Yeah, this murder certainly was a big tragedy for you."

"Where was Dr. Bayliss when the murder happened?" I asked.

This question seemed to brighten Sally's mood considerably. She gave me a smug smile. "He was delivering a lecture in front of fifty students."

So there.

I was tapped out. I think Sharona was, too.

"Do you have any questions, Mr. Monk?" I said into the phone.

"Yes," said Monk over the telephone speaker, "when can we get the hell out of this godforsaken city?"

CHAPTER THIRTEEN: MR. MONK FINDS THE HOLES

Dr. Christian Bayliss' office was on the first floor of Haines Hall, one of UCLA's original four redbrick buildings on either side of Dickson Plaza. They were built in that Romanesque style that screams education and pricey tuition.

His office had none of the imposing grandeur promised by the exterior of the building. It was just plain white walls, scuffed linoleum floors, acoustic tile ceilings and a sliver of a window. There was barely enough room for his desk, a small sagging bookcase and the man himself.

I've been in roomier elevators.

Sharona and I squeezed in, brushing against the spare sport jacket, shirt and slacks he had hanging on the coatrack.

Dr. Bayliss had the perfect teeth of a television anchorman, a chin prominent enough to merit landmark status and the beginnings of a potbelly, which was pulling his shirttails out of his pleated slacks.

We introduced ourselves, reminded him that Lieutenant Dozier had sent us and then told him why we were there. He took it all in surprising good humor.

"I'm glad to help. While I was waiting for you, I Googled Mr. Monk," Dr. Bayliss said. "He's quite a remarkable man. What I can't figure out is why he's taken an interest in this case."

"The gardener accused of killing Ellen Cole is my husband," Sharona said. "And I used to be Adrian's assistant."

"I see," Dr. Bayliss said. "So actually the police don't really have any doubt about who is guilty."

"They do now," Sharona said.

That wasn't true, but I wasn't going to correct her. It was better for our interview if Dr. Bayliss was a little uncertain of his standing.

"Is Mr. Monk going to be joining us?" he asked. "Or are you investigating under his imprimatur?"

Wow. "Imprimatur." I guess he wanted to remind us he was the only professor in the room. It was a shame that I'd left my thesaurus at home.

"He's out in the hall," I said.

"Why doesn't he come in?"

"He wanted us to check to see if you were covered with insects first," I said.

"We met your girlfriend. Adrian was afraid she might have given you a live cockroach tie clip for Christmas." Sharona leaned out the door and waved Monk over. "It's okay, Adrian. The guy is bug-free."

Monk still seemed hesitant to enter and stood with one foot in the office and one in the hallway. It wasn't entirely by choice. The office wasn't big enough for the four of us anyway. To make room, Sharona almost had to stand in the garbage can, which contained the latest issue of the *Daily Bruin*.

"Why are you wearing a gas mask?" Dr. Bayliss asked.

"Why isn't everyone?" Monk said.

"I don't see any smoke," Dr. Bayliss said. "And as far as I know, the air in this room is safe to breathe."

Monk stared at him in shock. Or at least I think he did. It wasn't too easy to see his face through that mask.

"Have you looked outside lately?" Monk said. "There's a toxic cloud hanging over the city."

"That's just the smog," Dr. Bayliss said, tucking in his shirttails, which showed a hint of blue ink.

"Calling it by another name doesn't

change the facts," Monk said.

"But let's change the subject," I said. "We didn't come here to talk about air quality. We want to ask you about your relationship with Ellen Cole."

"We were simply colleagues in the gender-studies department," Dr. Bayliss said.

"Do you give all your colleagues your sperm?" Sharona asked.

"I'd be happy to," Dr. Bayliss said.

"Let's change the subject again," Monk said, "to one that doesn't involve that, um, stuff."

"You mean sperm?" Dr. Bayliss said — deliberately, I think, for the pleasure of seeing Monk squirm.

Monk motioned to me for a wipe. Just the word seemed to make him feel dirty. I gave him one.

"How did your wife feel about your 'donation'?" Sharona asked.

"I didn't tell her," he said. "Isabel didn't find out until Lieutenant Dozier and Ian Ludlow came to our door."

"What was Ludlow doing there?" Monk looked up from the headline he was reading off the *Daily Bruin* in the garbage can. It was something about shoplifting problems at the student store.

"He was some kind of consultant or

160

observer or something," he said. "Frankly, I'm surprised at all the third parties involved with the police in this investigation."

"How did your wife take the news?" I asked.

"Not well," he said. "But, to be honest, our relationship has been troubled for some time. She's become less and less flexible when it comes to my sexual availability."

I glanced at Monk. He seemed more interested in a hole in the coattail of the sport jacket hanging on the coatrack than in our discussion. But I knew better than to assume Monk wasn't hearing, absorbing and at least subconsciously analyzing every word. I would have to watch him carefully, though, to make sure he didn't poke a hole in the other coattail just to make the jacket even.

"You mean she didn't like you cheating on her," Sharona said.

"She's not as tolerant of a humanity-embracing lifestyle as she used to be. She felt that impregnating another woman, even artificially, crossed some kind of line." He shrugged and shook his head, as if to suggest her point was absurd. "But the so-called infidelity in and of itself didn't bother her. I've always been actively multisexual."

"Excuse me?" Monk said.

"I could have sex with anyone in this room," Dr. Bayliss said, "including myself."

"Uh-huh," Monk said.

And immediately left the room. And the building.

Sharona glowered after him and continued glowering for some time. I think the way she saw it, Monk was abandoning her as opposed to, say, fleeing from a potbellied pervert who consorted with cockroach-covered lesbians.

Not that I was being judgmental.

"He seems awfully uptight," Dr. Bayliss said.

"And you seem awfully loose," I said.

"Thank you," Dr. Bayliss said. "It's what I strive for. It's the essence of multisexuality."

"Don't you mean bisexuality?" Sharona said.

"That term is rigid and inadequate, particularly when describing me," he said. "I am currently in an erotic relationship with a lesbian."

He said it as if he expected us to applaud his accomplishment.

"She's not a lesbian anymore if she's sleeping with you," I said.

"Sally didn't renounce her lesbian self to get involved with me," Dr. Bayliss said.

"She's simply attracted to my lesbian qualities."

"You're a man," Sharona said.

"Who is in touch with his inner lesbian," he said. "I relate to her from a female rather than male perspective. I make love to her like a woman. It's not a male-female coupling in the conventional heterosexual sense at all."

"Whatever you call it, I'm sure Ellen Cole was furious," I said. "She came to you to help her and her partner start a family. But instead, you ultimately destroyed her family. You took away her lover and their child."

"I bet she didn't take that well," Sharona said. "What did Ellen do, Doc? Did she threaten to expose your lifestyle? Did she threaten to go to your wife? To the faculty? To the media?"

"If she did, then killing her would have been a foolish move, since it has resulted in my private life becoming public, hasn't it?"

"People don't always think straight when they're angry," Sharona said.

"Which is clearly the case here," Dr. Bayliss said. "You're angry that your husband killed Ellen Cole. And rather than accept it, you are lashing out at innocent people like me and Sally. You seem to have forgotten that both Sally and I were in front of not one, not two, but dozens of people at the time Ellen was murdered. Neither one of us could be responsible for this."

"They're great alibis," Sharona said. "Almost too good to be true."

"And what about your husband's alibi?" he asked. "How good is it?"

Before Sharona could answer, we were distracted by the sound of footsteps approaching in the hallway.

I turned, expecting to see Monk. Instead, I saw two uniformed campus police officers coming our way. They were both men, one Asian, the other Hispanic. No one could accuse the campus police of not being multiethnic in their hiring practices.

Sharona and I had to practically climb up on the bookshelf and the desk to let the two officers in. Their name tags identified them as Officers Tran and Dempsey.

"Dr. Bayliss?" Officer Tran asked.

"Yes?" he responded.

"We're here because of a tip from Adrian Monk," Officer Tran said.

Dr. Bayliss grinned. "I didn't know that multisexuality was a crime."

Officer Tran shared a look with his partner. "Multisexuality?"

"He could have sex with anyone in this room," Sharona said.

"The hell he can," Officer Dempsey said, absentmindedly putting a hand on his holster.

"We're not here about your sexual activities," Officer Tran said. "We're investigating the shoplifting from the student store."

My cell phone rang. I answered it. It was Monk, who said he was calling from a pay phone in Ackerman Union, which housed the student store.

"The man you're talking to is a freak," Monk said. "A kleptomaniac freak."

"You better do the talking," I said to him as I put the phone on speaker and held it up for everyone to hear. "It's Mr. Monk."

"Dr. Bayliss has been stealing clothes and other items from the student store," Monk said. "He removes the security tags later, but he does a bad job of it. That's why he's got holes or ink stains on all his clothing."

"You're mistaking the work of moths and leaky pens for criminal behavior," Dr. Bayliss said. "I need to buy mothballs but I simply refuse to wear pocket protectors."

"Nice try," Monk said. "The problem is your holes and ink stains are mostly on shirttails that you try to hide by tucking them into your pants. Or they're on the coattails of your jackets, where they won't be as easily noticed. Moths aren't nearly so selective. Besides that, the ink is a unique dye used by security devices."

The officers looked at the sport jacket and shirt hanging on the coatrack and at the clothing Dr. Bayliss was wearing.

Beads of sweat started to form on the doctor's upper lip.

"Surely you don't believe any of this," Dr. Bayliss said to the officers. "It's craziness."

"If you look at the glasses he's wearing, as well as the two others on his desk, you'll notice the frames all have broken arms that were glued back together," Monk said. "That's because he snapped the arms when he clumsily removed the security tags. And the clothes and frames are brands sold at the student store."

I was convinced.

Sharona was convinced.

The officers were convinced.

And so was Dr. Bayliss.

"You better come to the station with us," Officer Tran said sternly. "The detectives will want to talk with you."

Dr. Bayliss swallowed hard. "Perhaps I should call my lawyer first."

"Perhaps you should," the officer said.

We didn't get Dr. Bayliss for murder, at least not yet, but it felt satisfying to nail him for something anyway since there was so much he was doing in his life that was just plain wrong. Unfortunately, this might have been the only thing that was punishable by law.

"I'm going to start walking back to San Francisco now," Monk said. "You can pick me up on your way."

CHAPTER FOURTEEN: MR. MONK GOES HOME

True to his word, we found Monk walking down Westwood Boulevard toward Wilshire, where the on-ramp to the northbound San Diego Freeway was.

Los Angelenos are a jaded bunch, but even they were distracted by the sight of a man strolling down the street in a gas mask. When we pulled up in my car, Monk was attracting the kind of stares usually reserved for movie stars and half-naked women.

He was either oblivious to the attention or simply didn't care. Monk got into the backseat of the car, slammed the door and locked it.

"Are we home yet?" he said.

"It's a six-hour drive," I said as we went through the center of Westwood Village down toward Wilshire Boulevard.

"We can't go home yet," Sharona said. "You haven't found Ellen Cole's murderer."

"I can't do it here," Monk said.

"But this is where the murder occurred," she said.

"Look at what the toxic air has done to the people who live here. They inject themselves with Botox, walk around with their pants hanging open and cockroaches crawling all over their bodies, and mate with anything," Monk said. "If we stay here much longer, breathing this air, we're going to turn out just like them."

"But you aren't breathing their air," I said.

"Mark my words, in another five years, everybody in Los Angeles will have three eyes, tails and webbed feet," Monk said. "They ought to quarantine the entire city."

"Trudy grew up here," Sharona said.

I thought that was a very low blow, but Sharona was a desperate woman and her husband was in prison for a crime he didn't commit, so I was willing to be forgiving. I hoped that Monk was, too.

"She got out in the nick of time," Monk said. "But God help her parents."

"You need to investigate Sally Jenkins and Dr. Bayliss some more," Sharona said.

"They didn't do it," Monk said.

"You nailed a guy for murder whose alibi was that he was in the space shuttle orbiting the Earth at the time of the killing," Sharona said. "Don't tell me you're intimidated by a woman who has the entire California State Senate as witnesses that she wasn't in LA at the time of the murder. That's a pitiful alibi by comparison."

"I believe her," Monk said.

"She could have hired someone," she said.

"Then why bother framing Trevor for it?" Monk said.

"What about Dr. Bayliss?" Sharona said. "He only has a lecture hall full of students to back him up. You can figure out how he was able to be in two places at once if you put your mind to it."

"He's a sicko freak," Monk said. "But he's right. He had nothing to gain and everything to lose from killing Ellen Cole."

"He had more to gain than Trevor," Sharona said. "And *he's* in jail."

"Maybe the doctor's wife did it," I said. "She had to be outraged about Ellen Cole ruining her marriage."

"Wouldn't she have killed her husband or Sally instead?" Monk said.

"It was Ellen who asked for the sperm," Sharona said.

Monk cringed at the mention of the word, shook it off and continued. "But it was Sally who had the baby and ultimately stole her husband. It would be pointless to kill Ellen."

"Okay, if it was none of them, then the killer is still out there somewhere," Sharona said. "You can't leave until you've talked to the other people in Ellen Cole's life."

"What other people?" Monk asked.

"I don't know," Sharona said. "We'll have to find some."

"You find them," Monk said, "and have them call me."

Sharona turned to me. "Pull over."

It was a simple request, but not so easy to do on Wilshire Boulevard. I had to turn onto Sepulveda, which paralleled the freeway and ran alongside a vast military cemetery.

I parked at the curb, earning a few honks from angry motorists as they sped past me and flipped me off. I hope they enjoyed it because in five years, when their hands were webbed, doing that wouldn't be so easy.

"Pop the trunk," Sharona said. "I'm getting my suitcase."

"You're not seriously going to stay here," I said.

She answered me by getting out of the car. I got out and went around back with her. Monk stayed inside.

"My husband is in prison, Natalie," she said. "I don't have any choice. I'm going to find some other suspects."

"How are you going to do that?"

"I'll nose around, talk to Ellen's coworkers, her neighbors, that kind of thing," she said. "I've learned a few things about detective work from spending time with Adrian. I'll come up with something."

"What about your job?" I said. "Your son?"

"Benji will be fine with my sister," Sharona said. "I'll call in sick at work. If I get fired, well, I've always got a job with Adrian."

She saw the look on my face and shrugged. "Sorry, Natalie. That's just the way it is," she said, pulling her suitcase out of the car. "Sometimes life sucks."

Like I didn't know already. "How long will you stay here?"

"Until my money runs out," she said, "which means I'll probably be back in a few days."

"I'll nag him to keep investigating in the meantime," I said. "There must be something he can do from San Francisco."

"I hope so," she said. "For both of our sakes."

I got the subtle nudge, not that I really needed any motivation.

"Good luck," I said.

"You, too," she said. "You've still got to endure six hours in a car with Adrian Monk.

I wouldn't wish that on my worst enemy."

The drive home wasn't nearly as bad as I thought it would be. Monk moved to the front seat and kept his gas mask on until we were a hundred miles outside of Los Angeles. But he left the mask resting on the seat beside him just in case and insisted that I give him a thirty-minute warning before we neared Harris Ranch.

Monk began to browse through Ian Ludlow's books. He opened *Names Are for Tombstones,* read a page or two and slammed the book shut.

"The beekeeper did it," he said.

He picked up *Death Works Weekends* and flipped through the first few pages. "The matador did it," he said.

He closed the book and picked up another, Ludlow's latest, *Death Is the Last Word.* Once again, he gave it a couple pages before closing the book.

"The massage therapist did it," Monk said.

"You only glanced at the first couple of pages," I said.

"Ludlow is so heavy-handed, he might as well reveal the killer on the cover," Monk said. "The murderer always has a personality quirk that is his or her undoing."

"How would you know?" I said. "You haven't read to the end of any of his books."

Monk picked up a book, flipped to the end of it and nodded.

"The massage therapist is claustrophobic, so she opened the windows at the crime scene," Monk said. "That's how Detective Marshak knew it was her."

"Thanks for ruining the books for me," I said.

"They were lousy anyway," Monk said. "You live more interesting mysteries than Ludlow can make up."

"Those are work," I said. "These would have been for enjoyment."

"What's enjoyable about reading some contrived mystery where the killer is always the least obvious person who is caught the same way every time?"

"Nothing anymore," I said. "I can never read an Ian Ludlow book again."

"You'll thank me later," Monk said.

"You're always saying that and has anyone ever thanked you later?"

"I guess I surround myself with impolite people," he said. "You could thank me."

"For what?"

"For all the things I've done for you that you should have thanked me for."

"Like the time you threw out all my dishes

because one bowl was chipped?"

"That's a perfect example," Monk said.

"Yes, it is."

We drove for a few minutes in silence before he spoke up again.

"I'm not seeing your point," he said.

"Think about it some more," I said. "You'll thank me later."

He didn't.

I warned him a half hour before we got to Harris Ranch and we drove past without incident, though he kept his eyes closed the whole time and gripped the dashboard as if he were riding a roller coaster.

Not long after we passed Harris Ranch, I had to stop to use a restroom and was prepared for a layover of a couple hours while Monk cleaned a men's room so he could use it. But Monk didn't need to relieve himself.

In fact, to ensure that he wouldn't need to use a restroom at all during the drive, I learned that he hadn't had anything to drink since he awoke that morning. And he declared to me that he wasn't going to eat or drink anything for the duration of the journey.

I wasn't under any such restriction. So I had a burger, some fries and an extra-large Coke at a Wendy's while Monk sat across from me, wheezing and licking his chapped lips.

I refilled my Coke and we got back on the road. For the rest of the trip, his stomach growled and he kept making these odd choking sounds. I turned up the radio to drown him out. After a couple hours, he either fell asleep or passed out from dehydration.

We got back to San Francisco around eight p.m. I nudged him awake and helped him lug his suitcases into his apartment. He was so glad to be home that he probably would have cried if there had been any moisture left in his body.

I went to Sharona's sister's place to pick up Julie, and we went home. It was good to be back.

Julie sat down at the kitchen table. I took out two spoons and a quart of Häagen-Dazs chocolate ice cream. Then I sat down next to my daughter. We caught up on each other's lives while we ate ice cream out of the carton.

Yeah, I know, health-wise and nutrition-wise I might as well have been feeding Julie rat poison, but somehow you just can't bond with your daughter over rice cakes.

Julie had some good news for me.

"The cast-vertising is a hit," she said.

"The sales have triggered the escalator clause, so I'm going to get the fifty-dollar rate next week."

"That is great," I said. "You may end up being sorry when your arm has healed and that cast has to come off."

"Not really," Julie said. "I've decided to franchise the cast-vertising concept."

"Franchise the cast-vertising concept? What does that mean?"

My adorable daughter was beginning to sound like one of those precocious kids on bad TV sitcoms. I didn't know if I could stand that.

"Kids my age break their bones all the time," she said. "You ought to see all the kids with casts at my school. So I've contacted Sorrento's and other Noe Valley merchants about advertising on other kids."

"What do you get out of it?"

"I find the kids with the casts, arrange the cast-vertising and get a twenty-percent commission," she said. "Plus we get a ten-percent discount on any purchases we make with the advertisers. I'm incentivizing other kids by giving them referral fees for recommending people with casts to me."

"Who helped you come up with this?"

"No one," she said.

"You've never used words like 'franchising'

and 'incentivizing' before in your life."

"Did you expect me to speak ga-ga-goo-goo for the rest of my life?" she said. "I'm growing up."

"You won't be if you don't tell me who is coaching you."

She sighed. "Sharona's sister is dating an accountant. Larry and I talked a little bit about my venture."

"Your venture?" I said.

"Why do you keep repeating everything I say?"

"I'm just trying to keep up. The vocabulary is a little over my head," I said. "So what does he want out of this?"

"Nothing," she said. "At least not until we incorporate."

"I've been gone almost two days," I said. "Frankly, I'm surprised it hasn't happened yet."

"How did it go in Los Angeles?"

"Mr. Monk solved a murder and caught a shoplifter," I said. "But he hasn't figured out who really killed Ellen Cole."

"So Benji's dad is still in jail," she said.

"I'm afraid so," I said.

"I like Benji," Julie said. "We have something in common."

"Mr. Monk," I said.

She shook her head. "Overbearing mothers with control issues."

"Is that another phrase you learned from good old Larry?"

"Dr. Phil," she said.

"You are watching way too much TV," I said.

"I hope Mr. Monk finds whoever killed that lady," Julie said. "I don't want to have something else in common with Benji."

"Like what?" I asked.

"That we've both lost our fathers."

CHAPTER FIFTEEN:
MR. MONK TAKES A
BREATH

It was Thursday morning, October 20, and my horoscope in the *San Francisco Chronicle* predicted that my life was about to become unpredictable. That was a big help.

On those rare occasions when I read my horoscope, I'm looking for reassurance, some sense that I'm gaining a little edge over fate. The last thing I want is my uncertainties reinforced.

What I really needed to ease my anxieties was for Monk to solve Ellen Cole's murder and get Sharona's husband out of jail. I didn't see how Monk could do that from San Francisco. Somehow, I had to convince him to go back to Los Angeles.

It wasn't just about saving my job now. It was about seeing that justice was served and that my daughter didn't have anything more in common with Sharona's kid.

I didn't know how to pull that off except to nag Monk to go back to LA until he finally gave in. But before I could do that, I needed a day to decompress from our last trip and to do some basic household tasks, like laundry and grocery shopping.

So I called Monk and told him I wouldn't be coming by that day. He was absolutely fine with that. He needed at least a day to either clean, disinfect or burn everything that he'd taken with him to Los Angeles.

I took Julie to school, and when I came back, I saw a familiar fire engine red pickup truck parked in front of my house. It belonged to Joe Cochran, the firefighter I'd dated not so long ago. We'd met when Julie convinced Monk to investigate the killing of Joe's firehouse dog, who had been murdered while the company was away fighting a fire.

Joe and I went on only a couple dates, and just when I began to feel the chemistry between us, I dumped him.

It wasn't because I wasn't attracted to Joe. It was because I was *too* attracted to him. I couldn't risk my heart and Julie's getting involved with another man in a life-and-death profession.

But just seeing his truck made my heartbeat quicken, and I had to consciously force the smile off my face as I steered my car into my driveway.

If I'd known I was going to see him, I

would have put on something nicer than sweats, a wrinkled tank top and a hooded fleece jacket.

Joe got out of his truck to greet me, with a big, affable grin on his face. He had round, lovable cheeks that softened his natural brawniness and made him seem strong and cuddly instead of muscular and tough. His big arms looked like they could snap a tree trunk or keep a woman very snug and warm against his chest.

I did such a wonderful job of controlling my emotions that when I got out of the car all I did was give him a friendly kiss on the cheek instead of tackling him onto the grass, tearing off his clothes and having my way with him.

He put his big hands on my shoulders when he returned my kiss and I found myself yearning for him to pull me close to him.

"This is a nice surprise," I said.

"I've been thinking about you for months," Joe said. "You have no idea how many times I've driven by and thought about stopping."

"I could give you a rough estimate," I said.

"You've seen me?"

"Your truck isn't exactly subtle," I said. "And I like to sit in front of my little bay window and read magazines."

"That's why I like to drive by," he said.

"So what made you stop this time?"

"I need you and Monk again," he said. "The company got called out to put down a car fire last night, and when we got back, we discovered that someone had stolen some of our rescue equipment."

"And you want Monk to investigate," I said.

"And you, too," he said.

"This sounds like a ploy to see me again," I said.

"Of course it is," Joe said. "But we'd really also like to get our hydraulic tools back."

"Mr. Monk only investigates murders," I said, though that wasn't entirely true. "And he's already got a case, a very important homicide down in Los Angeles, that's taking his full attention."

"Oh," he said, "I'm sorry to hear that."

"You'll just have to trust the police to handle it."

"You could investigate," he said.

"I'm not a detective," I said.

"I'm sure you've picked up a few tricks from Monk."

"You just want me to hang out all day at the firehouse so you can woo me."

"That, too," he said. "You're very woo-able."

"You don't have to wait for someone to steal something from the firehouse to take me out for a cup of coffee."

"But you dumped me," he said.

"Coffee isn't dating," I said. "It's coffee."

"I'm not sure that I see the distinction," he said. "But I'm certainly not going to argue the point."

We walked down the street to my favorite little coffeehouse, which was across from Sorrento's and next door to a little independent bookstore with several copies of Ian Ludlow's latest book displayed in the window.

The coffeehouse was furnished with grungy but inviting thrift-shop couches, and we settled onto one with our coffees and cakes.

We talked for hours.

He told me about his latest firefighting exploits and his loneliness when he wasn't at the station. I told him all about Trevor's case, my fears about losing my job and my jealousy of Sharona's relationship with Monk.

It was such a relief to be able to unload all of my anxieties on someone — and Joe was a great listener. He didn't offer me a lot of advice, but that wasn't really what I was looking for. He made me feel comfortable and safe.

Afterward, he slipped his hand into mine and walked me slowly back to my house. When we got there, I impulsively and stupidly invited him in for coffee.

I knew we'd already had gallons of fresh-brewed coffee, and all I had in my kitchen was the foul instant stuff, but that wasn't the point. It was an excuse to stay together for another stolen hour or two. There was this wonderful glow between us, probably caffeine-induced, and I wasn't ready to let it go yet.

I guess you know where this story is headed, so I won't drag it out.

Yes, we made love.

Yes, we did it even though I'd dumped him and had no intention of beginning a relationship with him. But we had a natural chemistry together and I needed him. So I let my emotions, and the moment, overrule my intellect.

Besides, it was a lazy afternoon and Julie was at school, so there was none of the elaborate planning that usually went into scheduling my rare intimacies as a single mother.

It had all happened so naturally, and we

were so good together, that it felt inevitable and right. And afterward, I felt none of the guilt that I thought I would for my emotionally reckless indulgence.

Joe seemed to understand without a word between us that this wasn't the beginning of something or even the end — just a few intimate hours between two people who liked each other and needed some comfort. His kisses were warm and sincere, and I luxuriated in the safety and strength of his arms.

I stayed in bed for an hour or two after he left, cuddling the SFFD T-shirt he'd forgotten and drifting in and out of a dreamless sleep, feeling his arms around me even though he was long gone.

I guess my horoscope had been right after all.

I managed to get out of bed, shower and do a little laundry before Julie got home from school. But I didn't get around to grocery shopping. So for dinner, we took advantage of Julie's cast-vertising discount and went to Sorrento's for pizza.

As soon as we walked in, the crowd noticed Julie's cast-vertising and also took advantage of her discount. I thought the proprietor might get upset, but I was wrong. He was so pleased with the business she'd brought him that he gave us our pizza for free.

On Friday morning, my horoscope didn't say anything about unpredictability or romance. Instead, it told me I was creative and resourceful. It was nice to hear, but I like my horoscopes to tell me the future, not offer me insights into my personality. I rely on fortune cookies for that.

I was feeling centered and rested in a way I hadn't in a while. I was beginning to rethink the wisdom of keeping Firefighter Joe at a distance. Maybe my heart was telling me something my brain should pay more attention to.

But I had more pressing things to consider than romance. I had to get Monk focused on Trevor's case again. The sooner Monk solved it, the better things would be for everyone.

And then I could carefully consider the emotional perils of my sporadic love life.

Julie could tell there was something different about me that morning, but her radar wasn't so well-honed that she could tell why.

She did, however, wonder why a man's SFFD T-shirt was among the clothes that were folded and washed on the dryer.

"You've never seen this?" I said. "It was a

gift from the fire station after Mr. Monk solved the case."

In a way, it was true.

"Isn't it a little big for you?" she said.

"It keeps me warm in bed," I said. That was true, too. She seemed to sense the honesty in that, or she'd lost interest in pursuing the subject, so she let it go.

We went out to the car so I could drive her to school. But I only got the car a few feet out of the driveway before I noticed there was something very wrong with the steering. I got out, looked under the car and saw some gunky fluid all over the driveway. I didn't know anything about cars, but I knew it wasn't good when they started bleeding.

So I called another mother to pick up Julie, getting myself deeper into debt with the local moms, and then I called the auto club. While I waited for the tow truck, I called Monk to let him know I'd be late.

The repair shop told me that some doohickey or thingy had broken and that it would take a day to get the part and make the repair. They arranged for me to drive a little Toyota Corolla while my Jeep was in the shop.

Monk was standing outside his apartment building when I arrived in my compact car.

He was pacing on the sidewalk, patting his chest and taking deep, luxuriant breaths.

"What are you doing, Mr. Monk?"

"Breathing," he said. "Isn't it wonderful?"

"Yes, I hear it's really catching on," I said. "Pretty soon, everybody is going to be doing it."

"Air." He took another deep breath and let it out slowly, watching it dissipate like smoke. "I really, really like it. You should try it."

"I've had plenty," I said. "So what's our next step in the investigation?"

"Breathing," he said. "Lots of breathing."

"How does that get us closer to discovering who killed Ellen Cole?" I asked.

Monk rolled his shoulders. "I'm thinking maybe Trevor did it."

"No, you're not," I said.

"All the evidence clearly points to him."

"It's pointing in the wrong direction," I said. "You proved that."

"There's no hard evidence," Monk said.

"You saw what you saw," I said. "That's evidence enough for me. And it usually is for you, too."

"All those things I said down there, all those things I think I saw, you can't really take them seriously," Monk said. "I was under the influence."

"Of what?"

"Toxic gas," he said. "It clouded my thinking."

"Mr. Monk," I said, "you know and I know that he's innocent."

"I can't go back to Los Angeles," Monk pleaded.

"You have to," I said. "You owe it to Sharona. She saved you. Now you have the chance to save her."

"I would be saving her by staying here," Monk said. "Trevor is a bad, bad man."

"She loves him," I said. "You know what it's like to lose someone you love. We both do. Do you really want her to feel our pain, too?"

He took a deep breath, savoring it. "But I like to breathe."

"You can breathe down there," I said.

"I don't want to have webbed feet," Monk whined.

"Now you're incentivized to wrap up the case quickly."

"Incentivized?" Monk said.

"It's a common word, Mr. Monk. Even twelve-year-olds use it."

We were about to head inside and, I hoped, make arrangements to return to Los Angeles when my cell phone rang. It was Captain Stottlemeyer.

"Hey, Natalie, welcome back. I hear Monk made quite an impression down in La-La Land."

"He still has more work to do there," I said.

"It will have to wait," Stottlemeyer said. "I need him."

"He'll be back," I said.

"I need him now, Natalie."

"Mr. Monk is busy," I said. "He has another case."

"If duty calls, I have to answer," Monk said, "even if it means I can't leave San Francisco ever again."

"The other client has my sympathies," Stottlemeyer said, "but she doesn't have Monk on a retainer, which means we come first."

He was right, of course. Damn him.

"Is this a simple case?" I asked.

"Would I be calling Monk if it was?"

Chapter Sixteen:
Mr. Monk Goes to
the Beach

Baker Beach is an idyllic half-mile stretch of smooth sand beneath the Presidio's steep bluffs, which were topped with forests of cypress and pine. To the northeast was a striking view of the Golden Gate Bridge that dramatically illustrated how the span earned its name. I lived in San Francisco and I still wished I had a camera with me so I could take a picture of the bridge from this angle.

Captain Stottlemeyer was waiting for us on the sand, leaning against a brown-and-yellow sign that warned beachgoers of hazardous surf and treacherous undertow. His face seemed to carry the same warning.

Monk strode up to Stottlemeyer and rubbed his hands together eagerly. He was so eager to work he didn't even bring up the point that the sand was uneven and should be raked.

"Okay, what have we got?" Monk asked. "Let's catch us a murderer."

Stottlemeyer eyed him suspiciously. "What are you so jolly about?"

"You've given him a temporary reprieve from having to go back to LA," I said.

"You don't want to be within a one-hundred-mile radius of that place," Monk said. "You wouldn't believe what goes on down there."

"It can't be any stranger than what happens here," Stottlemeyer said.

"I sincerely doubt it," Monk said.

"You haven't seen what we've got to deal with today," Stottlemeyer said and tipped his head toward the rocks and tide pools behind him.

There was a huddle of police officers and crime-scene techs farther up the sand, presumably gathered around a corpse, but that wasn't what caught Monk's attention.

It was the sunbathers. They were all nude.

Monk immediately spun around and turned his back to the sunbathers, who were letting it all hang out. And I mean that literally. These weren't supermodels working on their tans. The full force of gravity, fatty foods and age had hammered these people.

I had to admire the sunbathers' casual confidence and their complete lack of shame. These were people who were totally comfortable with their bodies and accepted whatever imperfections they had as natural facts of life. I haven't achieved that same sense of confidence.

"You're going to have to call in reinforcements," Monk said to Stottlemeyer.

"For what?" the captain asked.

"To arrest all the perverts," Monk said.

"This is a nude beach, Monk."

"Don't these people have any sense of human decency?" Monk declared.

"It's perfectly legal," Stottlemeyer said.

Monk stared at me, aghast.

He would have stared at Stottlemeyer aghast, too, but that would have meant turning around and facing the nudity.

"The California Penal Code, section 314, clearly states that any person who willfully and lewdly exposes his or her person or private parts thereof in any public place is violating the law," Monk said. "Those are all willfully lewd persons. I've never seen such willful lewdness before."

"This beach is a state park and this is an authorized, clothing-optional area," Stottlemeyer said. "You'll just have to live with it, Monk. Let's go."

"You go," Monk said. "I'll wait here."

"The body is over there," Stottlemeyer said, pointing to the gathering of cops and crime-scene techs thirty yards away.

"They're everywhere," Monk said. "And all of them are naked."

"I was referring to the dead body," Stottlemeyer said. "You need to see it at the crime scene, if it's actually a crime scene."

"You aren't sure whether it's a murder or not?" I asked.

"Good. Call me when you find out." Monk started to go, but Stottlemeyer grabbed him by the arm.

"That's why you're here, Monk. You're the one who is going to tell us if it's a murder or not."

"Can't the medical examiner do that?" Monk asked.

"Trust me. This is a case that cries out for Adrian Monk," Stottlemeyer said and headed for the crime scene, pulling Monk along with him.

Monk looked up at the heavens as if seeking spiritual guidance, but I knew all he was really doing was trying to walk across the sand without seeing any nudity.

"If you're afraid of seeing a naked body," I said, "why don't you just close your eyes?"

"I don't want to bump into any private parts," Monk said.

"It's not like they're flung out all over the sand," I said.

He stumbled along, letting Stottlemeyer

lead the way until we reached the scene, which had been cleared of any nearby sunbathers. The forensics team, clad in jumpsuits, carefully sifted through the sand, which they'd separated into quadrants with stakes and yellow string.

"The victim's name is Ronald Webster," Stottlemeyer said. "He's single, thirty-five, and works at a shoe store. His body was found by sunbathers this morning."

"Willfully lewd persons," Monk said. "Hippies, most likely."

"The ME figures the guy died sometime last night," Stottlemeyer said. "But it's hard to tell, given the body's immersion in salt water."

We followed a staked-out path in the sand that had already been cleared by the forensics team. Disher and the medical examiner were leaning over a naked body that was floating facedown in the tide pool. The victim's midsection had been ripped open.

I turned away, sickened and repulsed.

But Adrian Monk, a man who couldn't look at a naked sunbather, had no problem staring at this mutilated corpse. In fact, he was fascinated by it.

I'm not a shrink, but I'm guessing that Monk didn't see a naked body in front of him now. Once the person was dead, he or she was no longer human to him. The victim was just an object, a puzzle piece that he had to put back into its proper place in the larger picture.

Stottlemeyer put his hand gently on my back. "Are you going to be all right? I can have an officer take you back to your car."

"I'm fine," I said.

I wasn't going to run away, even if that was exactly what I wanted to do. I didn't want to be seen as weak by the detectives I worked with. Besides, I wouldn't be much good to Monk sitting in the car.

I took a couple deep breaths, let them out slowly to calm myself and turned around again.

Monk crouched beside the medical examiner, Dr. Daniel Hetzer, a balding man who studiously maintained two day's worth of stubble on his fleshy pale cheeks.

"What do you think, Monk?" Stottlemeyer asked.

Monk rose without saying a word and held his hands up in front of himself. He tipped his head from side to side, looking at the body of the late Ronald Webster from various angles.

Then he shifted his gaze to Webster's clothes, which were neatly folded on a rock near the tide pool.

"Where was his wallet?" Monk asked.

"In his pants pocket," Disher said and held up the clear plastic evidence bag that contained the wallet. "I don't think anything has been taken. There's still a bunch of credit cards and about two hundred dollars in cash inside."

"Where are his car keys?" Monk asked.

"They were also in his pocket," Disher said, "along with his house keys."

"Where's his car?"

"The DMV told us that Webster drives a Buick Lucerne and it's not in the parking lot," Stottlemeyer said. "I have a couple of patrol cars checking the cars in the neighborhood just in case."

"If he didn't drive," Monk said, "how did he get here?"

"If this turns out to be a murder," Stottlemeyer said, "we'll call the taxi companies and talk with the bus drivers on the local lines to see if anybody remembers seeing him."

"This is a popular make-out spot at night," Disher said. "Maybe Webster came with a special friend for a late-night skinny-dip."

Monk shuddered at the thought but pressed on. "Were there any cars left overnight in the lot?"

"No," Disher said. "But maybe the friend lives nearby and they walked over."

"Or the special friend parked on the street," Stottlemeyer said. "But since we don't know who this person is, or what car we're looking for, all we can do is take down a couple of hundred license-plate numbers from cars parked in the area and work backward. That's a lot of man-hours and I'm not ready to authorize that yet, not when I don't know if a crime has even been committed."

"If Ronald Webster came with a friend," Monk said, "where is that friend now?"

"Perhaps that body hasn't washed up yet," Disher said.

"What about the friend's clothes?" Monk asked.

Disher shrugged. "They could have been washed away by the tide."

Monk rolled his head and his shoulders, as if trying to work out a kink. I knew what that kink was. There were too many could-haves, maybes and what-ifs. He hated could-haves, maybes and what-ifs.

"What's your preliminary determination on the cause of death?" Monk asked Dr. Hetzer.

The medical examiner turned the victim faceup in the water. Webster was a young man, but his hair was flecked with gray. His face was spared the brutal ravages that had been done to his body.

"Unofficially, I'd say drowning," Dr. Hetzer said. "These wounds are bad, but they don't appear to be fatal."

"What did that to him?" I asked. "Was it a shark?"

Dr. Hetzer shook his head. "I don't think so. The curvature of the bite and the amount of flesh torn away isn't consistent with a shark attack. The bite parameter is narrow and long, which suggests that whatever creature did this has a muzzle or snout."

"A wild boar," Disher said.

"There aren't any boars in the Presidio," Stottlemeyer said.

"A ravenous wolf," Disher said.

"They move in packs and they would have torn him apart," Stottlemeyer said. "There's too much of him left."

"A vicious dog," Disher said.

"A dog would have gone for the throat," Dr. Hetzer said, "not the midsection."

"A mighty seal," Disher said.

"The bite isn't consistent with a seal," Dr. Hetzer said, "mighty or otherwise."

"A gigantic clam," Disher said.

Everyone gave Disher a look. He shifted his weight.

"Do you realize how large a clam would have to be to attack a human being?" Stottlemeyer said.

"The depths of the sea are still a great mystery to mankind," Disher said.

"Is that so?" Stottlemeyer said.

"It's the last unexplored frontier on earth," Disher said. "I read that they recently discovered an entirely new species of octopus that's blind and glows in the dark."

"Maybe the octopus did it," Stottlemeyer said.

"It's possible," Disher said.

"No, it's not," Stottlemeyer said and turned to Monk. "What do you think did this?"

"It's obvious," Monk said.

"It is?" I said.

Monk nodded. "This man was attacked by an alligator."

It wasn't the strangest declaration Monk had ever made, but it was definitely among the top five.

"I see." Stottlemeyer stared at Monk for a long moment, then turned back to Disher. "Tell me more about that octopus."

"It wasn't an octopus or any other creature," Monk said. "This man was definitely bitten by an alligator."

"You're aware that alligators don't live in

the ocean," Dr. Hetzer said.

"Yes," Monk said.

"And that alligators aren't indigenous to San Francisco," Dr. Hetzer said.

"Yes," Monk said.

"Then how can you presume that an alligator did this?" Dr. Hetzer asked.

"The shape of the bite and the punctures left by the teeth," Monk said. "They are all the same."

Dr. Hetzer leaned closer to the victim and examined the wound. "I'll be damned."

You hear those words a lot when you're around Adrian Monk, especially at a crime scene.

"Unlike the teeth of other creatures, which have different sizes, shapes and functions, alligator teeth are identical," Monk said. "That's because they use their teeth primarily to grasp their prey."

"Why do you know that?" Stottlemeyer said.

The answer was obvious, at least to me. "Because there's no differences between the teeth."

"It's called uniform dentition," Monk said, "or, in a word, perfection. I'd love to have teeth like that."

"I suppose that an alligator could be responsible for these wounds," Dr. Hetzer said. "Alligators don't rip apart their prey. They grab them, twist them and hold them underwater until they drown. That's consistent with the injuries we see here and the probable cause of death. But so are a lot of other explanations."

"Like wild boars," Disher said, "or a gigantic clam."

Stottlemeyer grimaced and rubbed his temples with his thumbs. "So is this a case for homicide or animal control, Doc?"

"Ask me tomorrow," Dr. Hetzer said. "I won't have any definitive answers for you until I complete my autopsy."

"Call animal control anyway, Randy," Stottlemeyer said. "See if they've heard anything about someone losing a pet alligator. Maybe ask a few of the neighbors if some poodles and cats have started disappearing around here."

"I'll ask animal control about boars, too," Disher said, making a note to himself.

"You do that," Stottlemeyer said wearily. "Don't forget to mention the giant clam and the octopus while you're at it."

"Shouldn't I ask a marine biologist those questions?"

"I wasn't serious about the clam and the octopus," Stottlemeyer said.

"Were you serious about the alligator?"

Disher asked.

"I wish I wasn't," the captain said, "but I've learned to trust Monk's hunches."

"It's not a hunch," Monk said. "It's a fact."

"But is it murder?" Stottlemeyer asked.

Monk rolled his shoulders.

"Yes," he said, "it is."

CHAPTER SEVENTEEN:
MR. MONK AND THE
OTHER SHOE

Even though Monk had declared the case a murder, Captain Stottlemeyer wasn't prepared to commit more police resources to the Webster investigation until he got the medical examiner's official determination.

I could understand Stottlemeyer's reluctance.

He was stuck with a dead guy on a nude beach who might or might not have been killed by an alligator. While that situation raised some big questions (like "How did the guy get to the beach?" and "Where did the alligator come from?"), there wasn't actually anything pointing to murder except Adrian Monk's opinion.

Granted, Monk had never been wrong about this kind of thing before, but the powers that be at the SFPD weren't as confident in his abilities as Stottlemeyer and I were. So if Stottlemeyer wanted to keep his job, he had to play the politics and take a wait-

and-see approach until after the autopsy.

But Monk didn't have to wait.

Nor could he.

Monk would have been eager to investigate this case even if he wasn't actively avoiding the prospect of returning to Los Angeles to solve Ellen Cole's murder, though I'm sure that was an extra motivation. This particular death was just too intriguing for him to ignore.

I wasn't too happy about the way things were working out. My job security would remain uncertain as long as Trevor was in jail, Sharona was in the picture and Ellen Cole's murderer was still free. But I couldn't honestly blame Monk for the delay. The alligator attack was a legitimate case, not a stalling tactic. And getting a head start on the investigation meant he'd solve the mystery that much quicker.

Monk wanted to learn more about Ronald Webster to see if there was something in the man's life that might explain the bizarre circumstances of his death.

So we started at the shoe store where Webster worked. I was surprised to discover that the store was in my neighborhood, just two doors down from Sorrento's Pizza.

I'd never bought any shoes at the store, but I'd window-shopped there a few times.

They carried lots of fancy Italian brands and running shoes that cost more per pair than the yearly salaries of the Chinese factory workers who made them.

I wish I could say that I didn't buy the shoes as a deeply felt political statement, but it was mostly because they were way too pricey for me on my Monk salary.

Then again, so was a pack of bubble gum.

There were three customers, two salespeople and one cashier in the store when we went in.

I was never entirely comfortable in situations like this, where Monk intended to question people who didn't know who he was or his connection to the police.

The problem was that we didn't have any official standing, which meant that often the people we were meeting with had no reason to talk with us, certainly not about things that were usually intensely private matters.

So getting them to open up took a little finesse. As we walked into the store, I was still thinking about what approach to take.

There were several table displays interspersed among the chairs where people sat trying on shoes. The back wall was covered from floor to ceiling with perhaps a hundred shoes staggered on clear plastic shelves.

Monk went straight to the back wall and approached the salesman standing there, waiting to be helpful.

"May I help you, sir?" the salesman asked with a smile as synthetic as his blazer. His name tag identified him as Maurice.

Monk picked up one of the shoes on display. "Where's the other shoe?"

"We have plenty more where that came from," Maurice said, "and in several handsome styles. Would you like to see them?"

"This is the shoe for the right foot," Monk said. "Where is the shoe for the left foot?"

"I'm sure it's in the back somewhere," Maurice said.

"Why isn't it out here?"

"These are just samples, sir," Maurice said. "But it would be my pleasure to find a pair in your size."

"I want the other shoe that goes with this one," Monk said and began pointing at the individual shoes on the wall. "And that one, and that one, and that one, and that one, and —"

"You want to try on every shoe on this wall?" Maurice interrupted, giving up any attempt at sustaining his synthetic smile. But I was beginning to see an approach that I could take to get the information we wanted.

"I want to see them up on that wall," Monk said.

"Why?"

"People have two feet," Monk said.

"I'm aware of that, sir," Maurice said.

"Shoes come in pairs." Monk motioned to the wall. "Those aren't pairs."

"Like I said, sir, these are samples."

"How can you break up a pair of shoes?" Monk said.

"It's easier and more attractive to display one shoe in each style on the wall."

"But you're a shoe professional," Monk said. "You of all people should respect the rule of the unbreakable pair."

"The rule of the unbreakable pair?" Maurice asked.

"Breaking up a pair is a crime against nature," Monk replied.

"You're telling me this display of shoes is a crime against nature."

"Isn't it obvious?"

"You'll have to forgive my friend," I said, pulling the salesman aside and lowering my voice. "But Ronald Webster usually takes care of him. Ron is so good with people. Is he here today?"

"He hasn't shown up," Maurice said. "In fact, his priest called this morning looking for him."

"His priest?" I said. "Isn't that kind of odd?"

"Ronald never misses morning mass at Mission Dolores," Maurice said. "This morning he did."

"He goes to mass *every* morning?"

"Ronald is a real straight arrow," Maurice said. "Punctual, clean, extremely organized."

"You're lying," Monk said.

Maurice turned to him. "Excuse me?"

"Look at that wall." Monk motioned to the shoes again. "No organized, God-fearing man would allow that."

The salesman looked at me. "Is he off his meds?"

"Maybe Ronald is at his girlfriend's house and overslept," I said.

"Ronald doesn't have a girlfriend at the moment," Maurice said.

"I could have sworn he mentioned her to me," I said. "He said they liked to go skinny-dipping at Baker Beach."

"Ronald? Never. He won't even wear short-sleeved shirts." Maurice eyed me suspiciously. "This is a small store and I've worked here for five years. I can't recall ever seeing you or your friend here before."

"Maybe you just didn't notice us," I said.

That was when Monk whirled around and

pointed at the other salesman.

"What do you think you're doing?" Monk snapped.

The other salesman, who was easily in his twenties but still seemed to have the awkward gawkiness of an adolescent, froze in midstride with an open shoe box in his hand.

"I'm, um, returning these shoes to the back room," the other salesman squeaked.

"You can't," Monk said.

"Why not?"

"Because they were on her feet." Monk pointed accusingly at a female customer, startling the poor woman who was tugging at her loose socks. She was in her fifties and had a hairstyle that looked like it had been done in 1972 and flash-frozen on her head.

"I was only trying them on," she said meekly.

"You try, you buy," Monk said. "That's the law."

"No, it isn't," Maurice said.

"But they don't fit," the woman said.

"You should have thought of that before you put them on your feet," Monk said.

"I'm wearing socks," she said.

"You weren't wearing any when you came in," Monk said.

"They gave these to me," she said, gesturing to the other salesman, "so I could try on the shoes."

Monk turned to Maurice. "You gave her those filthy socks? How many other disgusting feet have they been on?"

"Disgusting?" she said. "My feet aren't disgusting."

"They weren't when you came in, but they certainly are now," Monk said. "Don't handle any food with them."

"I don't eat food with my feet!" she exclaimed. "I'm not a monkey."

"Then you have no excuse for sticking your feet in every shoe you see, do you?"

Like I said, finesse.

Maurice glared at us both. "That's enough. Leave immediately or I'll call the police."

"You know what, Maurice? I think that's an excellent idea." I handed him my cell phone. "You can use my phone. Ask for Captain Leland Stottlemeyer."

I know it would have been a lot easier if I'd just had the captain call the shoe store before we went there. But, technically, this wasn't an official homicide investigation yet, and if Monk went out on his own and got into a situation that was potentially embarrassing to the department, Stottlemeyer could still plausibly claim ignorance.

I didn't used to think about the politics of Stottlemeyer's job, but during the unofficial police strike a while back, Monk was reinstated as captain of homicide and I got a firsthand glimpse at how things worked in the department. I realized afterward that protecting Stottlemeyer was, in a way, simply an extension of my job protecting Monk.

But finesse hadn't worked, things were going badly, and we hadn't mined the information we needed. I had no choice. I had to bring Stottlemeyer into it.

Of course, this also meant that Stottlemeyer had to tell Maurice that his coworker was dead.

The good news, though, was that Maurice and Ronald weren't close, so while the news was surprising, it wasn't devastating. Nevertheless, Maurice closed the store for the day, politely hustled the customers out and sat down with us to answer our questions.

We should have left the store when Maurice threw us out and not bothered to bring Stottlemeyer into the situation, because, as it turned out, Maurice didn't have much to add beyond what he'd already told me.

"I worked with the guy for five years and I really don't know him any better today than

I did on the day we met," Maurice said. "He wasn't somebody who let you inside."

"What do you mean?" I asked.

"We're in the shoe business. It's awfully slow here most of the time, and when that happens, there isn't much to do except stand around and talk to each other, you know?" Maurice said. "So you talk about your girlfriends, your families, things you've done, places you've been. Ronald never talked about anything you'd remember."

"Did Ronald have any enemies?" Monk asked.

"He was a shoe salesman," Maurice said.

"Shoe salesmen don't make enemies?" I said.

"It's not a job that inflames passions," Maurice said, then glanced at Monk. "At least not usually."

"What about in his personal life?" I said.

"What personal life?" Maurice said.

"Everybody has a personal life," I said.

"Not everybody," Monk said.

Good point.

"Even so," I said, "he could have been a real rat bastard outside of this store. Maybe he slept with married women, ripped off old ladies, betrayed his friends."

"I wish he had," Maurice said. "Then at least he would have had something interesting to talk about. Ron was a nice guy but he was insanely dull. It was almost like he worked at it."

Monk cocked his head. "What do you mean by that?"

Maurice shrugged. "Nobody could actually be that boring. To be honest, I'm not surprised he had a secret life."

"What makes you think he had a secret life?" I asked.

"He was skinny-dipping at Baker Beach, wasn't he?" Maurice replied. "The guy I knew, or didn't know, wouldn't have done that."

"Maybe he didn't," Monk said.

"Did he ever mention anybody else in his life?" I asked. "Someone who might know more about him?"

"Just his priest," Maurice said.

Chapter Eighteen:
Mr. Monk Goes to
Church

Monk decided he wanted to try talking to Father Bowen at morning mass, so we called it a day. I thought that would be a good idea. It would also give Stottlemeyer a chance to call Father Bowen and warn him that we were coming. I didn't want to try finesse on a priest. I was in enough trouble with God as it was.

But I wasn't ready to let Monk off without knowing what he was thinking, not only about the Webster case but about Trevor as well. And when he was in my car, he was a captive audience. So I took the long way back to his place, which practically meant giving him a tour of downtown San Francisco.

"What makes you so sure that Ronald Webster's death was murder?" I asked.

"He was attacked by an alligator," Monk said.

"It could happen," I said.

"If he was in a bayou," he said, "not on a beach in San Francisco."

"What about the possibility that someone's pet alligator escaped and attacked him?"

"That means the alligator either had to scurry across the open sand to get him," Monk said. "Or it was waiting for prey near the tide pools and struck when he sat down on the rocks to undress. I have a hard time believing either scenario."

"Maybe Ronald took a swim, drowned and, when his body washed up on the beach, the alligator attacked it."

"I suppose that could have happened," Monk said. "But I don't believe it, either."

"Why not?"

"Because it doesn't seem to fit with his personality as the other shoe salesman described it," Monk said, "and because it's ridiculous."

"Ridiculous things happen," I said. "Imagine what people thought when they saw you walking around Los Angeles wearing a gas mask."

"What was ridiculous about that?"

There was no point trying to explain that to him, so I let it drop. "What else makes you think this was murder and not a freak accident?"

"His car wasn't there," Monk said. "My guess is that we're going to find it parked near his home or the shoe store. That whole situation at the beach was staged by whoever took him to the beach to make it look like he was skinny-dipping or nude sunbathing when he was killed."

"So you think the alligator attack was faked?"

"That's the simple explanation and the one that makes the most sense. The medical examiner should be able to determine if it's fakery or not easily enough."

"Why would someone want to make it look like Ronald Webster was killed by an alligator on a nude beach?"

"That's the mystery," Monk said.

It was certainly a far more intriguing and Monk-like puzzle than Ellen Cole's murder, which I'm sure made it a lot more compelling for Monk. That, and it was happening in San Francisco and not in the toxic environs of Los Angeles.

"It's one mystery," I said. "You still have another one to solve. Who really killed Ellen Cole? Sharona is counting on you to find out. So is Benji. And so am I."

Monk squirmed in his seat. "It's not so easy."

I gave him a look. "Someone hit Ellen

Cole on the head with a lamp. It's not nearly as complicated and bizarre as most of the cases you solve."

"In a way, it's too simple," Monk said, "which makes it complex."

"I don't understand."

"The more things that don't fit, that don't make sense, the more I have to go on in my investigation," Monk said. "Someone killed by an alligator on a nude beach is so inherently wrong that there are all kinds of questions to ask and inconsistencies I can ponder. All I know about Ellen Cole is that someone besides Trevor hit her with a lamp."

"And framed Trevor for it," I said.

"Or not," Monk said. "Trevor could be innocent of murder and still guilty of everything else he's accused of. He just made a handy fall guy. There isn't anything else out of place for me to explore."

"It's not like there's a shortage of suspects," I said.

"All of whom have solid alibis and good explanations for why they wouldn't have benefited from her death."

"That's never been an obstacle for you," I said.

"I believe them," Monk said. "I don't think either Ellen's lover or her lover's lover or her lover's lover's wife killed her."

I was getting lost following who was who, but I got his point, even if it wasn't the one he necessarily intended to make.

"So you ran away," I said.

"Of course I did," Monk said. "You saw the people down there. You saw the air. You are not supposed to be able to see air. Or chew it."

"That's not why you ran," I said.

"It's why I ran *screaming*," he said.

"You fled Los Angeles because you are afraid of failing," I said. "You have no idea who killed Ellen Cole and don't know where to start looking."

"I know I'm not going to find the answer by staying in Los Angeles and questioning everyone who was remotely involved with either Ellen Cole or Trevor Fleming."

"Isn't that how you usually investigate a crime, by asking questions, learning new information and spotting contradictions?"

Monk shook his head. "I solve it the first time I visit the crime scene. I see something that isn't right, and by trying to make things fit, I figure out how the murder was really committed."

"You saw lots of things that weren't right at Ellen Cole's house."

"But not *the* thing," he said.

"And you think you will see it here?" I said. "We're hundreds of miles away."

"I've already seen it," Monk said. "I just haven't realized it yet."

It all made sense to me now. "You're worried that you never will," I said.

"It's happened before," Monk said quietly.

He was talking about his wife, Trudy, and the car bomb that killed her. He didn't know who killed her or why.

He'd failed her.

For a while that failure crippled him. And the person who helped him through that nightmare and showed him how to reclaim his life was Sharona, and now he was terrified that he was going to fail her, too.

"You'll see the thing that isn't right," I said. "I know you will."

"How can you be so sure?" he asked.

"Because you're Adrian Monk," I said, "and I have faith in you."

"I wish you didn't," Monk said.

"You have to have faith in something," I said.

"I do," Monk said. "But I don't think Formula 409 is going to solve my problems."

Even though Julie couldn't play soccer with her broken arm, she wanted to attend the

Saturday-morning practice at Dolores Park to show her team spirit. I think she also wanted to get maximum exposure for her cast-vertising campaign. It worked out great for me, because Monk wanted to talk with the priest at Mission Dolores, which was only two blocks away from the park.

The mission was founded by the Spaniards in 1776 to proselytize the Indians, five thousand of whom succumbed to a measles epidemic brought by the same people who came to save them from their heathen ways. The adobe church that stands today was built in 1791 by the Neophytes, a fancy word for Native Americans who'd survived the epidemics and become Christians. The four-inch-thick walls had withstood the ravages of time and the 1906 earthquake, so I figured the church could withstand Adrian Monk.

I wasn't going to tell him about the measles epidemic, even though it happened hundreds of years ago, or else he wouldn't have stepped into the church. He might even have had to move out of San Francisco entirely if he learned about it.

Julie and I had an early breakfast before picking up Monk in the rental car. I dropped Julie off at the park; then Monk and I continued on to the church, getting there in the middle of morning mass.

The church was long and narrow and crowded with parishioners, all of whom faced the gilded baroque altar and the priest in his white robes and green vestments.

There was an old woman arriving ahead of us, shuffling slowly into the church. A deacon in his midthirties stood at the door and greeted us with a polite nod and a smile.

As we filed in, the old lady dabbed her fingers in the bowl of holy water at the doorway and crossed herself and kissed her fingers afterward.

Monk gasped and motioned to me for a wipe. I gave it to him and he held it out to the woman.

"Take this," Monk said. "Quick."

"What for?" she said.

"The water, of course," he said. "Didn't you see all the people who stuck their filthy hands in it?"

"It's okay, young man," she said. "It's blessed."

"But it isn't disinfected," Monk said.

"God has cleansed it," she said.

"You're old and your resistance to infection is weak," Monk said. "You should gargle immediately with a strong mouthwash before the deadly germs you slathered on your lips invade your aged body."

223

"You should be ashamed of yourself!" she exclaimed as she turned her back on him and huffed away.

"That lady has a death wish," Monk said, turning to look at me just as I dabbed my fingers in the water and crossed myself. I'm not religious, but I figure it never hurts to take whatever blessings you can get.

Monk thrust the wipe into my hands. "Are you insane, woman?"

"Mr. Monk, please," I whispered. "We're in a church."

"We're in a hot zone for disease," Monk said. "Someone's got to save these people."

"I think that's what Father Bowen is trying to do," I said, glancing past Monk to see the priest at the altar shooting us a stern, reproachful look. He might as well have been God. I felt my bowels freeze.

Monk marched past me back to the bowl of holy water, took a deep breath, then plunged his hands inside. Wincing as if he'd stuck his hands in battery acid, Monk began scooping water from the bowl and heaving it out the front door.

The deacon, shocked, stepped in front of Monk and blocked the doorway. "What are you doing?"

"Emptying this cesspool," Monk said.

"That is holy water," the deacon said. "It

sanctifies us."

"It sickens you," Monk said. "You'll thank me later."

"No, I won't," the deacon said. "This water is a remembrance of our baptism. It cleanses us of our sins and purifies our souls as we enter the presence of the Lord."

Monk was about to scoop out some more water, but I grabbed his arm and pulled him away.

"If you really want to purify people," Monk said to the deacon, "dispense hand sanitizer."

"Mr. Monk," I whispered, "people have been sanctifying themselves with holy water for thousands of years."

"That explains the black death, among other things," Monk said. "Wipe. Wipe. Wipe."

I handed him three wipes, as ordered, and he began scrubbing his hands as if he was sanding them.

"This is unbelievable," he said.

It certainly was. He was completely oblivious to the attention he'd drawn to us, but I wasn't. I smiled at everyone who was glaring at us, trying to make silent amends for Monk's disruption and disrespect.

The parishioners were filing out of the pews and lining up in the center aisle to take communion. I was suddenly jarred by a horrifying premonition of what was to come. I knew I had only a few seconds to avert disaster.

"We should go," I said to Monk, while trying to hustle him to the door. "We can come back later."

"Why should we go?" Monk said, jerking his arm free. "Father Bowen is expecting us. We have questions to ask."

"Let's wait outside until the mass is over," I said. "We'll talk to him then."

"I'm getting really tired of you yanking me around," Monk said.

"I'm sorry." I held up my hands. "Please, Mr. Monk, do it for me."

Monk shrugged and started to turn back toward the door. But as he was taking his first step, Father Bowen spoke.

"The body of Christ," Father Bowen said.

Perhaps it was the mention of a body that caught Monk's attention. Perhaps it was simply hearing someone speak.

Whatever the reason, Monk looked at the altar just as Father Bowen placed a wafer from the basket of hosts on a parishioner's tongue.

The parishioner, a young woman, swallowed it, said, "Amen," then stepped aside to the eucharistic minister, who offered her the chalice of consecrated wine. The parish-ioner took a sip. Then the minister wiped the rim with a linen cloth, rotated the chalice a tiny bit and offered it to the next person in line.

Monk stared in shocked disbelief as Father Bowen placed a wafer on a man's tongue. The man then moved to the minister with the chalice and took a sip of wine.

"Did you see that?" Monk said to me.

"We can talk about it outside," I said.

Monk watched as another person, a bald-ing man with a scraggy beard, opened his mouth for the wafer. Just as Father Bowen was about to place the wafer on the man's tongue, Monk yelled: "That's enough!"

Everyone froze. I wanted to crawl under a pew and hide. The nightmare was happen-ing just as I'd envisioned it moments earlier. Why couldn't I have foreseen this an hour ago?

"What has gotten into you people?" Monk asked the entire congregation.

"The love of God," the scraggy-bearded man said.

"First you all stick your fingers in the same bowl of water. Now you're letting this man" — Monk motioned to Father Bowen, a gray-haired man in his fifties who seemed to have aged ten years since we stepped into the church — "stick his fingers in your mouth without washing his hands first? Two seconds ago his fingers were in that other guy's mouth. Didn't you see that? Are you all *blind?*"

"This is holy communion," Father Bowen said.

"This is a public health emergency," Monk said. "How can you all sip from the same glass of wine? Who knows how many infectious diseases the people in this room are carrying?"

"We are becoming one with Jesus, who was sacrificed on the cross to atone for our sins," Father Bowen said. "Millions of people around the world do this each and every day."

"It's a miracle that there are any Catholics left," Monk said. "I'm locking down this place until the health department gets here. You're all under quarantine. We can't let the contamination spread."

Father Bowen turned to one of the ministers, handed him the basket of hosts and spoke in a whisper that we couldn't hear. Then Father Bowen faced Monk again.

"Let's talk outside," he said and motioned us to follow him out into the cemetery. "We'll still be within the mission's walls."

"I can't believe what's happening," Monk

said to me in bewilderment as we headed toward the side exit. "Ever since Sharona came back, the world just hasn't been the same."

I couldn't argue with that.

CHAPTER NINETEEN: MR. MONK HEARS A CONFESSION

Father Bowen seemed surprisingly calm, considering that he was facing the man who'd just ruined his morning mass. We stood beside the statue of Father Junipero Serra, who founded Mission Dolores and twenty others throughout California. Father Serra, who was only five feet tall, would have had to stand on a stepladder to be eye to eye with his own statue.

"I'm sorry if our religious practices are in conflict with your own personal beliefs," Father Bowen said. "But as long as you are in our church, I must insist that you respect our rituals."

"Germs don't," Monk said.

I was definitely glad I hadn't mentioned the measles thing to Monk.

"Surely you didn't come here because you're concerned about the spread of disease," Father Bowen said.

"I am always concerned about that,"

Monk said.

"We came here to talk about Ronald Webster," I said. "This is Adrian Monk."

"Ah, yes," Father Bowen said. "The police warned me you'd be coming."

"Warned?" Monk said.

"That was a poor choice of words," Father Bowen said. "They alerted me. And of course I am glad to help in any way I can."

"You can start by wearing sterile gloves when you handle those wafers," Monk said.

"I meant regarding Ronald Webster," he said. "I was shocked to hear about his death."

"What shocked you the most?" Monk said. "His death or how he died?"

"I was told that he drowned at Baker Beach," Father Bowen said. "Was there more to it than that?"

"It's a nude beach," Monk said.

"And he was attacked by an alligator," I said.

"An alligator?" Father Bowen said. Now he was really shocked — so shocked, in fact, that he had to take a seat on a bench.

"And he was nude," Monk said. "Everybody was."

"How did an alligator get on the beach?" Father Bowen asked.

"We don't know," Monk said. "Aren't you

curious about why Ronald was naked?"

"Not really," Father Bowen said.

"Was that because Ronald often liked to run around naked?" Monk said.

"No," Father Bowen said.

"Then why doesn't his nudity interest you?" Monk asked.

"Because he was killed by an alligator," Father Bowen said. "I've never heard of that happening in San Francisco before."

"What kind of person was Ronald Webster?" I asked.

"Conscientious, soft-spoken and devoted to God," Father Bowen said.

"And kind of dull," I said. "Or so we've heard."

"He wasn't the outgoing type, if that's what you're saying," Father Bowen said. "But he was a good man. He worked very hard at that."

"Why?" Monk asked.

"Why what?" Father Bowen replied.

"Why did he have to work so hard at it?"

"We all do, Mr. Monk," Father Bowen said.

"But he worked harder than most," Monk said, "didn't he?"

"Perhaps," Father Bowen said, shifting position on the bench.

"Why did he have to do that?" Monk said.

"There must have been a reason."

"Being a good person is an end in and of itself," Father Bowen said. "It allows you to be blessed in the eyes of the Lord."

"He must have wanted that blessing very badly to come to morning mass every single day," Monk said. "And you obviously knew the strength of that devotion or you wouldn't have been so worried when he didn't show up one morning that you called his shoe store looking for him."

"I'm concerned about the well-being of all my parishioners, Mr. Monk."

"If that was true," Monk said, "you wouldn't let them all drink wine from the same glass."

I spoke up, eager to change the subject. "What can you tell us, Father, about Ronald Webster's relationship with his family and friends? About his past?"

"He didn't talk about those things," Father Bowen said, shifting again in his seat. "We mostly discussed issues of faith."

I'm not a shrink or an expert on human behavior or even an astute observer of body language, but I got the distinct impression that our rather tame questions were making Father Bowen uncomfortable.

"That fits with the description of Ronald that we got from one of his fellow shoe salesmen," Monk said. "But his coworker said that it seemed as if Ronald worked at being dull. It's funny, but you used almost the same words to describe him being a good man."

"I don't see your point," Father Bowen said.

"I think that Ronald was dull on purpose. He didn't want to be noticed, which is why I don't believe he would go to a nude beach," Monk said. "I also think he was trying to overcome enormous guilt, which is why he came here every single day."

"Even if you're right," Father Bowen said, "I fail to see what that has to do with Ronald's death."

"I can think of a very good reason why a person would be guilt-ridden and desperate to remain inconspicuous."

And once Monk said that, so could I.

"Ronald Webster committed some terrible crime and got away with it," I said. "He wanted absolution."

"Did he get it?" Monk asked Father Bowen.

"Of course he did," Father Bowen said. "God forgives."

"The law doesn't," Monk said.

"Maybe someone else doesn't, either," I said.

Monk nodded. "Someone with a hungry pet alligator."

Father Bowen shuddered at the thought.

"What did Ronald do?" I asked.

Father Bowen chewed on his lower lip. I guess he was in some kind of moral or ethical turmoil.

"He's dead, Father," I said. "You aren't violating the sanctity of confession by telling us what he told you."

"It might help us catch Ronald Webster's murderer," Monk said.

"The captain didn't say that Ronald was murdered," Father Bowen said. "He said the circumstances of his death were uncertain."

"I'm certain," Monk said.

Father Bowen sighed. "Ten years ago, somewhere in the East Bay, he was speeding in his car. He hit a young woman. She was thrown up onto the windshield and, for a few seconds, looked him right in the eye before she fell off onto the side of the road. Instead of stopping to help her, he kept on driving."

"Was she killed?" I asked.

Father Bowen shook his head. "She was badly hurt. Multiple fractures and internal injuries. She may even have been left crippled. Ronald told me that the story was in all the newspapers and the police made a public plea for any information leading to the capture of the hit-and-run driver. But there were no witnesses and the poor girl didn't remember anything about the car that struck her."

"So Ronald got away with it," I said.

"On the contrary," Father Bowen said. "He saw her face every time he closed his eyes. He was tormented with guilt."

"Not enough to actually step forward and take responsibility for his actions," Monk said.

"He sent her money," Father Bowen said, "an envelope full of cash every few months. Anonymously, of course."

"How much did he send?" I asked.

"It varied," Father Bowen said. "But it amounted to tens of thousands of dollars over the years. And he gave generously to the church."

"Enough to buy your silence?" Monk said.

Father Bowen's face flushed with anger. "My silence is a given, Mr. Monk. When people confess, they do so with the understanding that I will keep what they say in complete confidence."

"Even if they've committed a crime," Monk said.

"We are all sinners, Mr. Monk."

"Not me," Monk said. "I lead a clean life."

"Nobody is that clean," Father Bowen said.

I was tempted to invite Father Bowen to see Monk's house, but I didn't want to shatter the man's beliefs.

I arranged a playdate for Julie and one of her friends with one of the other soccer moms, who agreed to take my daughter for the day. I was accumulating a lot of debts with other mothers lately, but I figured it was worth it in the long run. Even so, in the near future, I was going to be spending a lot of mornings giving rides and days playing host to other people's kids.

While I bartered that deal, Monk policed the bleachers and made sure that all the parents were observing the importance of balanced seating. They were glad to accommodate Monk's request, at least while he was present. It was the least they could do, considering he'd nailed the coach of an opposing team for murder. The Slammers were legendary now, even if they hadn't won a single game.

Then Monk and I got into the rented Corolla, which I drove back to the mechanic to swap for my fixed-up Jeep Cherokee. On the way, Monk and I discussed the case.

Although Father Bowen didn't know the name of the woman Ronald Webster hit with his car, I called Disher and told him what we knew. He said it wouldn't take long for him to identify and locate the woman. Our tax dollars at work.

"Do you think she lured Webster out to the beach and fed him to her alligator?" I asked Monk after the call.

"She certainly has a strong motive," Monk said.

"But why wait until now to kill him? And why take him to a nude beach? And why use an alligator as a murder weapon?"

"We'll have to ask her," Monk said.

"There are so many simpler ways to kill someone," I said.

"That's true," Monk said. "She could have hit him over the head with a lamp. And then where would we be?"

"Don't be too hard on yourself, Mr. Monk."

The truth was, I was glad to hear him beating himself up over the Ellen Cole case. It meant he was still thinking about it. I was thinking about Ronald Webster.

"It must be a pretty big alligator," I said.

"It must be," he said.

"You'd think people would notice if she had a pet like that."

"You'd think so," he said.

"What do you feed a pet alligator?" I asked.

Monk shrugged. "Hit-and-run drivers, I suppose."

We picked up my car from Ned, my mechanic. Monk made a point of standing far away from me when I went to the cashier to pay the bill for the repairs. I think Monk was afraid I might hit him up for a loan. He was a wise man. What I really needed were smelling salts.

I left the cashier wondering if I could get away with robbing a bank. I found Monk and the mechanic standing by my car.

"Did you take care of the tick?" Monk asked Ned.

"She didn't say anything about a tick," he said.

"You didn't?" Monk said to me.

"I never heard a tick," I said.

"Oh, there's a tick," Monk said. "A very persistent tick."

"Now this is a man who knows cars," Ned said. "Very few people realize that a tick can actually be the death rattle of the suspension bushings."

"It's not a rattle. It's a tick," Monk said. "Like this: tick, tick, tick."

"I can't afford to fix one tick," I said,

"much less three. We're taking my car and going now."

"What about the suspension bushings?" Ned asked.

"I'll be sure to bring the car in right after I win the Publishers Clearing House sweepstakes."

"But it's getting worse," Monk said. "Before the trip to Los Angeles, the tick was occurring every three seconds. Now it's every two and a half. I timed it with my stopwatch."

"Maybe that's what you heard ticking," I said.

We got in the car and left. The steering was fixed and the car was running fine as far as I was concerned. Monk complained about the tick, which I couldn't hear. I think it was only audible to Monk and dogs. But after a few minutes, he stopped whining about that so he could complain instead about my filthy car, specifically the grains of sand in the carpet, which, if you heard him describe it, made it seem like his feet were resting on a pile of gravel.

"Forgive me," I said. "I haven't had a chance to go to the car wash. Things have been a bit hectic lately."

"Things aren't hectic now," Monk said.

A trip to the car wash with Monk was, at

best, a three-hour event and I didn't see how we could spare that much time in the middle of two homicide investigations.

"You're investigating two murders," I said.

"We're in a lull," Monk said.

"We don't have to be in a lull," I said. "You could think of something to ask somebody."

"I did," Monk said. "I thought of asking you to wash your car."

My cell phone rang. It was Disher. He had the name and address of the woman Ronald Webster hit with his car. Her name was Paula Dalmas and we could find her in Walnut Creek.

"The lull is over," I said.

"What a waste of a good lull," he said.

CHAPTER TWENTY:
MR. MONK GOES TO
THE ORTHODONTIST

Walnut Creek was once a quaint little town
on the banks of a tiny creek that wound
through the walnut groves under the shadow
of Mount Diablo. In the sixties and seven-
ties, the groves were mowed down and the
creek diverted to make room for thousands
of tract-home communities with names like
Walnut Acres, Walnut Grove and Walnut
Walk.

By the new millennium, downtown Walnut
Creek had been demolished and rebuilt so
that it had become a Disneyesque shopping
center designed to evoke memories of small-
town America instead of actually *being*
small-town America.

Dr. Paula Dalmas had an orthodontics
practice in a medical complex downtown
that perfectly reflected the ethos of the new
Walnut Creek. Her practice was in a collection of offices that looked like a shopping
center and had a tract-home-community

name: Doctors' Park. The only thing missing was a Panda Express, though the panda in the logo would have needed a stethoscope around its neck to fit in.

Dr. Dalmas was open one Saturday a month for patients, most of whom were children and teenagers, who couldn't make a regular weekday appointment, probably because there wasn't a parent around to drive them.

I could appreciate that. I wished my daughter's orthodontist had weekend hours. I was thinking that it might even be worth schlepping Julie out to Walnut Creek to take advantage of Saturday appointments.

Given Monk's fear of dentists, I thought I was going to have a hard time getting him into Dr. Dalmas' office. But much to my surprise, he didn't seem at all reluctant. He practically bounded inside.

The waiting room was warm and comfortable, painted in soothing earth tones and furnished with inviting overstuffed chairs. If it weren't for the framed posters of teeth before and after orthodontics, the issues of *Highlights for Children* scattered on the coffee tables and the requisite aquarium full of tropical fish, you could have mistaken the place for someone's living room.

There were two children waiting with a

parent to see the doctor or one of her associates. Looking at those kids, and the transparent, barely perceptible braces on their teeth, filled me with bitterness and jealousy.

When I had had braces, I was stuck with a mouthful of wires, rubber bands and gleaming silver that made me ashamed to smile. I had to put wax on the wirework in my mouth so it wouldn't scratch the inside of my cheeks. You can imagine how attractive that made me. That wasn't even the worst of it. After school, I had to attach my braces to elaborate headgear from the Tower of London collection that made my face look like it was being slowly pulled off my skull.

Twenty years later, I was still feeling the shame, so much so that I resented these kids for not having to endure what I did. I'm obviously a woman with a few issues to work out.

While I presented myself to the receptionist, Monk went over and admired one of the posters. He stood in front of it, hands clasped behind his back, intently studying the vivid pictures of crooked yellow teeth and how they looked after they had been straightened and whitened. You would have thought he was in the Louvre.

"Magnificent," he said.

He took out a magnifying glass from the inside breast pocket of his jacket and examined the before-and-after pictures on the poster.

"Extraordinary," he said.

The receptionist motioned to me. "The doctor is just finishing up with a patient," she said. "You can go back and see her if you like."

"Thank you," I said.

When I turned, I saw that Monk was holding a tape measure up to the teeth in the poster. I have no idea what he was measuring, but he was nodding with approval.

"Exquisite," he said.

"Mr. Monk, the doctor can see us now," I said.

"One minute." Monk put the tape measure back in his pocket and went up to the receptionist.

"Excuse me," he said. "Do you know where I could purchase that work of art?"

"What art?" the receptionist said.

Monk gestured to the poster. "It's a marvelous piece, true genius."

"You mean the pictures of the teeth?" she asked.

"It would look fabulous in my living room," Monk said, "though I imagine it's probably way, way out of my price range."

"That thing?" she said. "I think it was some promotional junk that came with one of our orders of dental picks."

Monk smiled. "No, really. I'm serious."

"It's a freebie," she said. "They give it away."

"I get it. The doctor doesn't want everyone to know how much she paid." Monk lowered his voice to a whisper. "It wouldn't help business for her to flaunt her wealth in front of the patients. I admire your discretion."

Monk followed me back into the examination area. The hallway was decorated with candid photographs of Dr. Dalmas' smiling patients, some with braces, some without. Monk moved past them slowly, trying to look at them all. It was obvious from the expression on his face that he was impressed by what he saw.

The exam area was one big room with four dental chairs facing a large picture window overlooking the hills.

There were teenage girls in two of the chairs, one having her teeth brushed by a dental hygienist, the other having her mouth examined by a woman I presumed was Dr. Dalmas, since she was the only one wearing a lab coat.

Dr. Dalmas was tall and slender and wore her hair in a ponytail that made her look almost as young as her patients.

"Looking good, Mariska," Dr. Dalmas said. "But you have to wear your retainers more often or you'll be back where you started."

"But the retainers look so yucky," she said.

"Not as yucky as your teeth looked before," Dr. Dalmas said, peeling off her rubber gloves.

"You should listen to her, young lady," Monk said. "She's doing God's work."

Dr. Dalmas smiled at Monk. "That's quite a compliment coming from someone I've never met."

"You're turning chaos into order," Monk said. "You're saving people's lives."

"I'm only straightening their teeth," Dr. Dalmas said.

Monk shook his head and looked at me. "Can you believe this woman's modesty?"

She rose with difficulty from her stool and walked awkwardly to the counter where the hazardous waste container was kept and she stuffed her gloves inside.

I glanced at Monk and saw him watching her as she moved. I knew her uneven gait probably disturbed him. Balance and symmetry meant a lot to him. But the look on his face perplexed me. There was tenderness in his eyes but his cheeks were taut with anger.

The doctor washed her hands and turned to us and the expression on Monk's face vanished, but I saw the effort that went into accomplishing it. He didn't want her to see whatever it was that he was feeling.

"So you have a child that needs orthodontics?" she said.

"I do," I said, "but that's not why we're here."

Dr. Dalmas looked confused. "Then what can I do for you?"

"We'd like to talk with you about Ronald Webster," Monk said.

"Who is he?" she asked.

"The man who has been sending you envelopes full of cash," he said.

She looked Monk in the eye. He didn't flinch. "Let's go in my office," she said.

She hobbled past us, leading the way. Monk got that strange look on his face again as we followed her.

Her office was bright and airy. The pillows on her couch were made from a floral fabric. She had fresh flowers in vases and pictures of her husband and young son. Her degrees were framed on the wall, along with more pictures of her family. It was a very welcoming, female space. She sat down at her desk, and we took the two matching guest chairs in front of her.

"You don't look like IRS agents," she said. "Are you detectives?"

"He is," I said. "He's Adrian Monk. I'm his assistant, Natalie Teeger."

"Who are you working for?" she asked.

"I'm a consultant with the San Francisco police department," Monk said. "I'm helping them investigate Ronald Webster's murder."

She thought about that for a moment. "He was the hit-and-run driver."

Monk nodded. "How did you know?"

"I always figured it was guilt money," she said. "I could only think of one person in my life who might have that much guilt."

"When did the money start coming?" I asked.

"I can't remember exactly, maybe a year or two after he hit me," she said. "I was in and out of the hospital a lot during that time. I've lost track of all the surgeries it took to put me back together. They did an okay job."

"You look great," Monk said.

I glanced at him. I couldn't remember ever hearing him compliment a woman on her appearance. He'd certainly never complimented me.

"You can't see my scars," she said. "I hide them."

"Everybody has scars and everybody hides them," he said. "You do it better than most."

"I'm not being metaphorical," she said. "These scars are real."

"So are the other ones," he said.

"One day, when I was still living in Oakland, a fat envelope with my name handwritten on it arrived in the mail," she said. "There was no return address, just a San Rafael postmark."

"How much money was in it?" I asked.

"A couple hundred dollars," she said. "Envelopes came every month or so after that, always with a different postmark from somewhere in the Bay Area."

"He didn't want to be traced," Monk said.

"A few years after I was hurt, I left Oakland to go to school in San Diego. Not a single envelope showed up at my old address after I left," she said. "But there was one waiting for me in San Diego when I arrived. And the envelopes have continued to arrive everywhere that I've lived since then."

"So he was watching you," I said. "That must have creeped you out."

"It did," she said.

"But you never went to the police," Monk said.

"I couldn't be sure the money was from him," she said.

"Besides," I said, "you were spending it."

Her eyes flashed with anger. "There's no amount of money that could compensate me for what I lost. My face had to be reconstructed. My hips were shattered and he robbed me of my ability to have children. We had to adopt. So tell me, how could I spend a dime of his money? The thought of doing it made me sick."

"Then what did you do with all the cash?" I asked.

"After a while, I didn't even bother opening the envelopes anymore. I just tossed them all in a box as they came in," she said. "I still have every single one of them."

"What are you saving them for?" Monk asked.

She shrugged. "Today."

"What happens today?" I asked.

She shrugged again. "Where did he live?"

"San Francisco," I said. "He was a shoe salesman who went to mass every morning."

"In a way, it's good to know he was doing more than sending me cash to alleviate his guilty conscience," Dr. Dalmas said. "Did he have a family?"

"From what we can tell, he lived an intentionally solitary and dull life," Monk said. "He never stopped being afraid that he would be caught."

"Then he suffered, too," she said.

"I suppose he did," Monk said. "But someone wanted him to suffer more. He was murdered in a particularly brutal way."

"How?" she asked.

"He was attacked by an alligator," Monk said.

She stared at Monk. "Are you sure?"

"I could tell from the bite," Monk said.

"Uniform dentition," Dr. Dalmas said.

"Uniform dentition," Monk said. "It's a thing of beauty."

She cocked her head and regarded Monk in a new light. "Yes, I suppose it is."

"Where were you Thursday night?" I asked.

"Was that when he was killed?" she replied.

"That's the best guess," I said.

"You think I fed him to an alligator?" she said.

"You have the best motive," I said.

"I don't have an alligator," she said. "And even if I did, I didn't know who he was or where he was. But I've seen him."

"When?" Monk asked. "Where?"

"In a department store once, then a few years later, outside a movie theater," she said. "Another time I saw him in the bleachers at an Oakland A's game that my husband dragged me to."

"And you still didn't call the police?" I said.

"He was just a face staring at me in a crowd," she said. "It wasn't actually his face that I recognized. It was his eyes. I will never forget his eyes. It always happened so fast. I'd blink or turn away or someone would walk in front of me and then he'd be gone. Afterward, I could never be sure that I hadn't hallucinated it."

"But you knew that you hadn't," Monk said.

She nodded. "I knew."

"You still haven't told us where you were Thursday night," I said.

"My husband took my son down to San Diego this week to visit his grandmother," she said. "I enjoyed a nice long bath and a Nora Roberts novel."

"So you don't have an alibi," I said.

"I suppose I don't," she said. "What was the church he went to?"

"Mission Dolores," I said.

"Maybe I'll give them the money," she

said. "Will that be all? I have more patients to see."

"I only have one more question," Monk said. "Where can I get a poster like the one in your waiting room?"

CHAPTER
TWENTY-ONE:
MR. MONK AND THE
AUTOPSY

As we drove back to San Francisco, Monk sat with the sun visor down so he could gaze upon the framed poster depicting the transformative power of orthodontics that Dr. Dalmas gave us and that we'd wedged into the backseat.

"That work of art is going to turn my house into a showplace," Monk said.

"You'll certainly be the only house on your block with a dental poster in the living room."

"I may need to invest in a security system," he said.

"And a subscription to *Highlights for Children*," I said.

"I already have that," he said.

"You do?"

"Finding the objects in the hidden pictures keeps my powers of observation sharp," Monk said. "Plus the adventures of Goofus and Gallant are pretty exciting."

"I hope Dr. Dalmas doesn't turn out to be the killer," I said. "Or it's going to look like you took a bribe."

"She couldn't be the killer," he said.

"Ronald Webster ran her over with a car and left her crippled for life," I said. "She's the most likely suspect. Not to mention the only suspect. And best of all, she doesn't have an alibi."

"She couldn't have done it," Monk said.

"Why not?"

"Because we're kindred spirits," he said.

"You're not at all alike."

"We both fight injustice and right wrongs," Monk said.

"She straightens teeth," I said. "I don't see the injustice."

"You would if you had those crooked teeth," he said. "She restores order, just like I do."

"Maybe her idea of justice is having Ronald Webster chewed on by a creature with perfect teeth."

I saw the way she lit up when Monk mentioned uniform dentition. Then again, maybe they were kindred spirits after all.

"I was watching you when she got up from examining her patient," I said. "There was a strange look on your face. What were you thinking?"

And as I asked the question, the expression came back to his face.

"Ronald Webster broke her. The doctors tried to fix her, but didn't quite get it right. Now she's devoting her life to repairing others and she excels at it," Monk said. "What happened to her was horrible and cruel. And yet I wonder if it's because of him, and what he did to her, that she's so good at what she does."

"We'll never know," I said.

"I may," he said.

He might at that. And if he does, I'm pretty sure it will be on the day he finds his wife's killer.

We were halfway across the Bay Bridge when Captain Stottlemeyer called to tell us that the medical examiner had completed his autopsy. Stottlemeyer wanted us to meet him at the morgue to hear the results.

There are lots of things I like to do on Saturdays and visiting the morgue isn't one of them. The morgue is cold, smells bad and is filled with corpses. Other than that, it's a delightful place.

It certainly was for Monk. He was completely at home there. The morgue is clean, sterile and organized, with shiny metal and linoleum surfaces that are kept sparkling. I'm sure that he'd rather eat a meal off the floor of the morgue than on a picnic table in Golden Gate Park.

There is nothing out of place in a morgue. Nothing scattered. Nothing haphazard. The bodies are carefully tagged and lined up on autopsy tables for examination or kept in refrigerated compartments. Even the things taken out of the bodies are carefully weighed, measured, cataloged and then disposed of.

And if a mess is ever created, it's quickly and efficiently hosed down and the affected area sanitized, deodorized and probably simonized, too. That would account for the brilliant gleam.

Monk had offered many times to come over in his free time and help clean up. But the medical examiner had always politely declined the offer, much to Monk's disappointment and to my relief, since I'd probably have to be the one who drove him back and forth.

Captain Stottlemeyer was waiting down in the morgue lobby, right outside the stairwell, when we arrived. It was unusual for him to greet us there. On those occasions when we gathered at the morgue, we'd ordinarily meet around the body at the autopsy table. It was sort of like Thanksgiving, only without the meal and the fancy dishware.

"Why the welcoming committee?" I asked.

Stottlemeyer frowned. "We have a special guest today and I wanted to prepare you for it."

He meant Monk, not me.

"Who is he?" Monk asked.

"He's sort of a consultant," Stottlemeyer said. "Randy thought he might have some special insight into this case and gave him a call yesterday after we found the body."

"But *I'm* your consultant," Monk said.

"Think of him as Randy's consultant," Stottlemeyer said.

"I thought I was Randy's consultant, too," Monk said. "Why can't I be everybody's consultant?"

"Frankly, Monk, I'll take as many knowledgeable consultants as I can get, especially if they're free," Stottlemeyer said.

"I'll work for free," Monk said.

"No, you won't," I said.

"You haven't told us who this consultant is," Monk said.

"It's Ian Ludlow," Stottlemeyer said, leading us into the autopsy room. "The author."

Ludlow was standing across from Lieutenant Disher and Dr. Hetzer on the other side of the autopsy table, where Ronald Webster's body was laid out.

"Why did you call him?" Monk asked Disher.

"Randy was one of my best students and is very familiar with my work," Ludlow said, answering the question before Disher had a chance.

"I've studied every word he's ever written and it's had a huge impact on my prose," Disher said and turned to Stottlemeyer. "You've probably noticed the difference in my reports."

"I don't read your reports for the prose," Stottlemeyer said.

"Then you're cheating yourself out of the subtle thematic arcs and little touches of character," Disher said, "not to mention the raw, emotional resonance."

"Is that what it was?" Stottlemeyer said. "I thought it was my acid reflux."

"I'm surprised you didn't call me on this," Ludlow said to Monk.

"Why would I?" Monk said.

"Because of the startling similarities between this murder and an incident in my latest book," Ludlow said, shifting his gaze to me. "I signed a copy of *Death Is the Last Word* for you when we met in Los Angeles."

"I haven't had a chance to read it," I said.

"I didn't get past the first two pages," Monk said, "since it was blatantly obvious at that point who the killer was."

"I was totally taken by surprise," Disher said, almost reverently, to Ludlow. "In fact, I thought it was brilliantly done."

"The murderer in all his books is always the least-likely suspect who is undone by a personality quirk," Monk said.

"It is?" Disher said.

"I thought you'd studied his work," Monk said.

"So you've read all my books?" Ludlow asked. "I'm flattered."

"Don't be. If you've read one," Monk said, "you've read them all."

"This isn't a reading group," Stottlemeyer said impatiently. "We aren't here to discuss Mr. Ludlow's books. We're here to learn about what happened to Ronald Webster. Can we please get to it? What have you got for us, Dr. Hetzer?"

The medical examiner cleared his throat and took out a tiny, telescoping pointer, which he waved over the body like a magic wand. I don't know if he thought he was making the body appear or disappear.

"It's not as easy as you might think to determine whether a person has drowned or not," Dr. Hetzer said. "It's a best-guess situation. But I believe that is the cause of death. That said, did he drown in the ocean or somewhere else?"

As Dr. Hetzer spoke, he kept waving that pointer over Webster's naked body, drawing our attention to it. The corpse wasn't any nicer to look at than it had been before. In fact, it was worse, since in addition to the alligator bite, he'd also been vivisected and sewn back together.

And yet somehow I didn't find it so hard to look at him this time. Perhaps it was the clinical nature of the surroundings and the proceedings. Or perhaps I was just getting used to it.

"The salinity of ocean water is usually about thirty-three to thirty-seven parts per thousand," Dr. Hetzer said. "However, the salinity of the water found in the lungs may not reflect the actual salinity of the water in which the victim drowned. It has to do with the physics of osmosis, which you probably don't want me to get into."

"You're right," Stottlemeyer said. "In fact, I'd really appreciate it if you just got to the point."

But Dr. Hetzer wasn't going to do that any more than Monk would during one of his summations. This was Dr. Hetzer's chance to show off his smarts and he wasn't going to rob himself of that pleasure.

"There are microorganisms that live in

freshwater and salt water, but you find very few of them in tap water," Dr. Hetzer said. "You certainly don't find measurable traces of bath oil in an ocean tide pool."

"You're saying that Ronald Webster drowned in a bathtub and was dumped at the beach," Stottlemeyer said.

"It would appear so," Dr. Hetzer said.

"You could have saved us a lot of time by saying that to start with," Stottlemeyer groused.

"What were his stomach contents?" Ludlow asked.

"Who cares?" Monk said.

"Every fact is significant," Ludlow said.

"Two or three slices of pepperoni pizza," Dr. Hetzer said.

"See?" Monk asked. "Pointless."

"The details of what Webster ate can help us determine where he was before he died, who he might have been with and when they were together. The rate of digestion can also help us pinpoint the time of death," Ludlow said, turning to Dr. Hetzer. "And what do his stomach contents tell you, Doctor?"

"He was killed within a half hour of consuming his last meal," Dr. Hetzer said.

"Interesting," Ludlow said.

"Meaningless," Monk said.

"Were there any drugs in his bloodstream?" Ludlow asked the medical examiner.

"Nope," Dr. Hetzer said.

"So we know he wasn't drugged," Ludlow said.

"Brilliant deduction," Monk said, theatrically rolling his eyes. "Next you're going to tell us that he's dead."

"What about signs of a struggle?" Stottlemeyer said. "He looks pretty beaten up to me."

"There are bruises and abrasions on his head, arms and shoulders, but I can't determine whether he sustained them fighting an assailant before he drowned or while struggling with the alligator."

"Wait a minute," Stottlemeyer said. "You're telling me that you *still* think he was attacked by an alligator?"

Dr. Hetzer nodded. "I asked a zoologist to examine the wounds and a tooth that I found imbedded in one of his ribs. She concurred with Monk's observations."

"She concurred with me," Monk said, clearly for Ludlow's benefit, "because I saw it first."

"My official determination is that an alligator dragged Ronald Webster underwater and held him there until he drowned," Dr. Hetzer said.

"In his *bathtub?*" Stottlemeyer asked.

"I'm only telling you what the evidence indicates," Dr. Hetzer said. "Based on the size of the bite, we're looking for a big sucker. A ten footer at least."

Stottlemeyer grimaced and looked at Monk. "I knew this was a case that cried out for you."

"For me," Monk said, underscoring a self-serving point once again for Ludlow's benefit, "because I handle the tough ones."

"Couldn't the bite have been faked?" I asked.

"It's far more difficult to do than you might think," Ludlow replied.

"How would you know?" Monk asked dismissively.

"One of the characters in *Death Is the Last Word* tried to make a murder look like an alligator attack," Disher said. "That's why I called Ian last night. I thought maybe he could offer us some insight into the criminal mind."

"Oh, please," Monk said.

"I drove up from LA first thing this morning," Ludlow said. "I feel it's my civic duty as a crime novelist and as a concerned citizen to help in any way I can."

"And you just happen to have a new book out and any publicity you can get will only help your sales," Monk said. "The press is going to be all over this. You want to be sure that everyone draws the same connection between your book and this case that Lieutenant Disher did."

"I resent that, Mr. Monk. I've assisted the LAPD on many investigations," Ludlow said. "And my integrity has never been called into question."

"And it's not now. We're grateful that you're here," Stottlemeyer said. "You should be, too, Monk."

"Why?" Monk said.

"Because you're not exactly blazing a trail of discovery on your own," Stottlemeyer said, then turned back to Ludlow. "If you wanted to fake an alligator attack, where would you get the jaws?"

"Alligator heads are very easy to find," Ludlow said. "You can buy one on the Internet for as little as five dollars. That's not the hard part. It's creating the bite."

"Couldn't you just knock the guy out, hold him under water and then clamp the jaws on him?" I asked.

"An alligator champs down on his prey and then rolls, using his full weight to drag the victim under," Disher said authoritatively. "If you don't see signs of that on the body, it's a dead giveaway."

We all looked at Dr. Hetzer, who nodded.

"The wounds are consistent with the victim being pulled and rolled," Dr. Hetzer said. "It was the first thing I looked for."

Disher beamed. "I learned that reading Ian's book."

"Maybe the killer did, too," Stottlemeyer said, "and then faked the bite."

"That would be very difficult, if not impossible, to accomplish," Ludlow said. "A ten-foot alligator exerts nearly two thousand pounds of force per square inch with his bite. That's more than a ton of force. You can't fake that with your bare hands."

"Or with a bear trap," Disher said.

"A bear trap?" Stottlemeyer asked.

"That's what the character used in my book," Ludlow said. "She attached an alligator's jaws with epoxy to a bear trap and then clamped the contraption on her victim. She got everything right but the proper force per square inch."

Stottlemeyer glanced at Dr. Hetzer.

"The force exerted in this bite was easily two thousand pounds per square inch," Dr. Hetzer said. "Probably a lot more. The alligator mimics the feeding biomechanics of dinosaurs and bites harder than any animal on earth. The only creature that may have had a stronger bite is the *Tyrannosaurus rex* at three thousand pounds per square inch."

"Nearly as much force as the weight of my S-class Mercedes," Ludlow said.

"Braggart," Monk muttered.

"So we're looking for someone with a ten-foot-long alligator," Stottlemeyer said.

"Or a baby *T. rex*," Disher said.

"How hard could that be to find?" Stottlemeyer said.

CHAPTER TWENTY-TWO: MR. MONK AND THE MAN WHO WASN'T HIMSELF

Everyone except Dr. Hetzer regrouped in the morgue's windowless employee lounge to discuss the case over some cups of bad coffee instead of an eviscerated corpse. The five of us sat almost shoulder to shoulder at a tiny table, talking above the hum of vending machines and under the headache-inducing strobe of the fluorescent lights.

I preferred the ambience of the autopsy room.

"What do we know about Ronald Webster?" Ludlow asked.

"We?" Monk said. "You're just a visitor in this morgue, pal. I'm certified by the State of California in Blood and Bodily Fluid Disposal, Disinfection, Deodorization and Sterilization under the Federal Medical Waste Management Act and the Federal Health and Safety Codes."

"You *are?*" I asked.

"Want to see my card?" Monk said.

"You have a card?" I said.

"It's laminated," he said, opening his wallet and proudly displaying a certification card with the state seal on it.

"Of course it is," Stottlemeyer said. "He'd laminate himself if he could."

"I ran Webster's prints and came up with nothing," Disher said. "So I did some digging. Turns out he shares the same social security number as another Ronald Webster in Butte, Montana."

"Our dead man was living under a false identity that he stole from somebody else," Ludlow said. "He was hiding from something or someone."

"Another brilliant deduction," Monk said. "I don't know about the rest of you, but I'm impressed."

Ian Ludlow hadn't done anything to deserve Monk's nasty attitude. I admired Monk, but he could be unbelievably petty and childish when he felt threatened. When he behaved that way, I wanted to send him to his room for quiet time.

The only person who looked bad in these situations was Monk himself, but he was too busy being churlish to recognize it. Then again, he never noticed or cared how he looked to others.

Stottlemeyer glared at him. "Do you have

anything helpful to share?"

Monk frowned and crossed his arms in front of his chest. "No."

"What about everything we've learned today?" I said.

"It's not relevant," Monk said, sulking.

"Of course it is," I said.

So I told the others about our talk with Father Bowen at Mission Dolores, where Ronald Webster, or whoever he really was, attended mass every day to ease his guilt over running down Paula Dalmas and fleeing the scene. I told them that Webster had confessed his crime to Father Bowen and had been anonymously sending cash to Dalmas for years.

"I couldn't make this stuff up," Ludlow said, shaking his head with amazement.

"I wonder if Father Bowen knows more than he told," Disher said.

"We'll ask him, officially this time," Stottlemeyer said, then nodded to me. "Go on, Natalie."

I told them about Dr. Dalmas' claim that she didn't know the identity of the hit-and-run driver and that she'd never spent any of the money that he'd sent.

"But she admitted that she'd seen him stalking her a few times over the years," I said. "Her husband and her son are in San

271

Diego this week. She said she spent Thursday night at home and took a bath."

"Maybe she did," Disher said, "with Ronald Webster and an alligator."

"Get search warrants for her home and office," Stottlemeyer said.

"What do you hope to find?" I asked.

"Any evidence that she was at Baker Beach or that she might have had an alligator around."

"Maybe her husband and son aren't really in San Diego," Disher said. "Maybe they were eaten."

"This is exciting," Ludlow said.

"You're wasting your time," Monk said. "Dr. Dalmas didn't kill Ronald Webster."

"Then who did?" Ludlow asked.

"Someone else," Monk said.

"Brilliant deduction," Ludlow said.

Monk deserved that.

"We're not going to find the answers here," Stottlemeyer said, rising to his feet and bringing the meeting to an end. "I can think of only one place to start."

On the way to Ronald Webster's place, I got a call from Julie asking if she could upgrade her playdate into a sleepover at her friend's house. I said it was fine, and since her friend was on the Slammers, that meant Julie would also get a ride to the game on Sunday morning.

A sleepover worked out great for me, since it meant I wouldn't have to worry about finding someone to keep an eye on Julie if I had to work on Sunday, which was looking likely.

It also meant that I might actually have a night to myself — something rare and to be savored, perhaps with a certain firefighter, if he wasn't working.

I wasn't reconsidering my decision not to get involved with Firefighter Joe. This wouldn't be an involvement. This would be a *revolvement* — temporary involvement that revolved back to the uninvolvement.

That made perfect sense to me, or at least I was trying to convince myself that it did as we made our way across the Mission District toward the 101 Freeway and the industrial waterfront.

There's a booming market in warehouse-to-loft conversions in San Francisco, and if there is one thing there's no shortage of in our city, it's abandoned and decrepit industrial spaces. I don't really see the appeal of living in an old factory building in a decaying neighborhood, but there are people willing to spend millions for the privilege.

Ronald Webster lived in a very recent

273

warehouse-to-loft conversion, the only redevelopment in this otherwise rotting corner of the Mission District. A big billboard on the side of the building featured an artist's rendering of the luxurious lofts that were available for sale and immediate occupancy inside.

Again, I'm not quite sure what the allure is of living in a place that's gorgeous on the inside but ugly on the outside, but I'm not a rich urban sophisticate. I'm not even a poor urban sophisticate.

I didn't think Ronald Webster was, either, but that dull man was full of surprises.

There was a freight elevator up to the second-floor loft, but since Monk has elevator issues, we took the iron staircase up the narrow, grimy stairwell instead.

"There are four units in this building, two on each floor, three unoccupied and awaiting buyers," Stottlemeyer explained as we trudged up the two flights of stairs. Disher and Ludlow took the freight elevator.

"So no one would have heard anything if there was a struggle," I said.

"You could have brought an alligator, a lion and a walrus in here and nobody would have noticed," Stottlemeyer said.

On the second-floor landing, one of the two fire doors was open to a vast living room of chrome and glass and marble, which combined to make a striking contrast to the exposed beams and rough bricks of the original factory. The entire space was bathed in light from the uncurtained windows that lined one wall and the skylights above.

The rooms were essentially cubicles, set apart by rolling stainless-steel-and-frosted-glass partitions, making it possible to reconfigure the living space in a number of different ways. There was also a large rolling bookcase full of hardcovers that acted as a room divider. The only rooms that were permanently located were the kitchen and the baths, though some of their walls were on wheels, too.

It was impressive. And looked expensive.

"How does a lowly shoe salesman afford this?" I asked.

"He doesn't," Stottlemeyer said, putting on a pair of gloves. "There's a lot more to the late Ronald Webster than we think."

"This gets more incredible with each passing hour," Ludlow said. "I am always amazed at what you find when you scratch the surface of any ordinary person's life. Who would ever have thought that this shoe salesman could have so many secrets?"

Monk stopped and sniffed. "It smells like

gasoline."

Stottlemeyer sniffed. So did I, but I couldn't smell anything.

"Diesel, regular or unleaded?" Stottlemeyer asked.

"I can't tell," Monk said.

Stottlemeyer shook his head. "I'm disappointed in you, Monk."

"Me, too," Monk said. "It's that LA air. It's ruined my sense of smell."

"I was joking," Stottlemeyer said. "No one can be expected to tell the grade of gasoline from the smell."

"You're just being nice," Monk said.

Ludlow drifted toward a generic pizza box on the kitchen counter. There was a cash register receipt taped to the box. Using the tip of his pen, he lifted the lid of the box to reveal a dry, fungus-covered pizza, three slices missing.

Dr. Hetzer certainly knew his way around stomach contents.

"Now we know where he got his last meal," Ludlow said, glancing at the receipt. "Sorrento's Pizza. I wonder if he ate alone or if his murderer was with him."

Julie and I were in Sorrento's on Thursday night. Was Webster there at the same time that we were? Maybe we saw him and didn't know it.

Maybe we brushed shoulders with his killer and didn't know that, either. It gave me the shivers to realize that we'd stepped under that cloud of death.

I know that sounds overwrought and melodramatic, but think about how you'd feel if you were me. There was a killer, and there was a victim, alongside the two of us in that restaurant. There were a lot of other people, too, but still it was chilling to know that we were in close proximity of such evil and didn't sense anything more than the smell of garlic and hot cheese.

It made me think about fate and how cruel and unpredictable it could be. Of course, if it wasn't, they wouldn't call it fate. They'd call it luck.

So I guess it was fate that got Ronald Webster and luck that saved Julie and me.

Monk was browsing Webster's bookcase, as if we were guests at a dinner party instead of working a possible homicide scene.

"Webster was a fan of your books," Monk said to Ludlow. There were five or six Ludlow titles lined up on a shelf in clear plastic dust jacket protectors.

"He and millions of other readers," Ludlow said.

"How else could you afford your Mercedes?" Monk said.

"I owe a lot to my fans but they expect a lot from me in return," Ludlow said. "A good mystery every ninety days, for one thing."

"Webster doesn't have your latest book," Monk said. "He was killed before he got a chance to read it."

"Maybe if he had," Stottlemeyer said, "he would have known better than to let someone into his house with an alligator."

Disher stepped out from behind a frosted-glass partition, which I assumed walled off a portion of the bathroom.

"Check this out," Disher said.

We followed him around the partition to see a Jacuzzi on a platform tiled in travertine. It was enough to make me seriously consider switching to a career selling shoes.

Disher leaned over the rim of the tub. "I think there's some dried blood caught in the grout," he said, pointing with his gloved finger. "And a ring of salt around the drain."

"Common grocery store sea salt is my guess," Ludlow said. "The granules are larger."

Monk groaned louder than was necessary, not that he really needed to groan at all.

"I think we've just found the spot where Ronald Webster was fed to the gator," Stottlemeyer said. "Let's get a forensics team down here pronto."

Disher took out his cell phone and made the call.

Monk crouched beside a pair of parallel black smudges on the tile floor in the middle of the bathroom. There was another pair of identical smudges closer to the Jacuzzi.

"This is odd," Monk said.

"They look like scratches," Stottlemeyer said. "Maybe from the soles of someone's shoes."

"The marks are side by side," Monk said. "If they came from shoes, they'd be staggered and further apart."

"Whatever it is," Stottlemeyer said, "we'll make sure the lab guys check it out. I'm sure when they spray that tub with luminol and light it up, it's going to glow."

Luminol is a chemical that reacts to hemoglobin and makes it luminescent. Hemoglobin sticks to surfaces long after all the visible signs of blood have been washed away. I knew that less from actual experience around homicides than from watching reruns of *CSI*.

Monk squinted at a spot on the floor. "What's this?"

We all squatted around him to check out the spot.

"It looks like motor oil," Disher said.

"Or maybe brake fluid," Ludlow said.

Monk frowned to himself and stood up. "The killer was surprisingly sloppy. It seems like the only clues that he didn't leave were his name and phone number."

"Good for us," Stottlemeyer said. "Maybe we'll get some prints we can use, too."

"Do alligators leave prints?" Disher said.

I figured that was our cue to go. Besides, I wanted to get home and start enjoying my free night. I headed for the door and everyone but Disher followed.

As soon as we got outside, Monk motioned to me. I thought he wanted a wipe, but when I reached to take one from my purse, he shook his head.

"Can I borrow your phone?" he said. "I need to make a call."

I gave him the cell and stepped away to allow him some privacy. Ludlow caught up with me at my car.

"What is Monk's problem with me?" he asked.

"This is his turf," I said. "He feels threatened by another expert."

"But I'm not an expert," Ludlow said, "as he keeps reminding me."

I smiled. "You're a rich, famous author of crime novels. He can't help but feel a little overshadowed."

Ludlow nodded and glanced at my Jeep. "These cars are real warhorses. How does she run?"

"Not bad for a car with 177,000 miles on the odometer," I said.

"That's how I feel about myself sometimes," Ludlow said.

Monk joined us and gave me the phone. "Have you solved the case yet?" he asked Ludlow.

"I'm working on it," Ludlow said. "But I have no illusions that I can make sense out of it all before you do, not that it's any kind of competition."

"Of course not," Monk said.

"The last thing I want to do is invade your turf or rob you of any glory," Ludlow said. "I'm not a detective and I'm certainly not as gifted as you are. I'm just a writer looking for a good story to tell. When this is over, I'll go away and write another book."

"I understand," Monk said. "I apologize if I was rude."

I couldn't believe what I was hearing. Monk was actually acknowledging he was at fault and apologizing for it. This was a first.

I might have pressed him on that point, but my cell phone rang. I glanced at the display and recognized the number. It was Firefighter Joe. If his impeccable timing kept up, I'd have to start calling him Mind Reader Joe.

"Excuse me," I said to Monk. "It's Firefighter Joe."

I stepped away so I'd have some privacy when I took the call.

"I hope I'm not calling you too soon," Joe said.

"I was just thinking about you," I said.

"You have no idea how good that makes me feel," he said.

"As it turns out," I said, "I have a free night."

"As it turns out," he said, "so do I."

"Would you like to be free together?"

"I had the same thought, but I don't think I could have expressed it any better than you did."

"I'll call you after I've dropped off Mr. Monk," I said, told him good-bye and returned to my car, where Monk now stood alone. Ludlow was farther down the street, making a call on his cell phone.

"I thought you and Joe weren't seeing each other anymore," Monk said.

"So did I," I said. "But then he came by my house on Thursday looking for you, or so he claimed, and —"

"On Thursday?" Monk interrupted.

"He wanted you to investigate a burglary that happened at the fire station on Wednesday night," I said. "But it was really just an excuse to —"

"Call him back," Monk interrupted me again. "Tell him we'll meet him there."

"*We* will?" I said sadly, feeling my wonderful night slipping away. "But he's got the night off."

"I want to investigate," Monk said.

"Can't you investigate tomorrow?"

"I'm two days late already," he said and got into my car.

CHAPTER TWENTY-THREE: MR. MONK GOES TO THE FIREHOUSE

It was like déjà vu. Once again Monk and I were at the firehouse atop a hill in North Beach, investigating a crime that occurred there while the company was out fighting a blaze. Only this time neither man nor beast had been hurt.

The firehouse had a multimillion-dollar view of Coit Tower and the Transamerica Pyramid, but only if you were standing out front. Inside the firehouse, the few windows looked directly into the building next door. It was almost as if the architect intentionally wanted to deprive the firefighters of the view.

Fog was rolling in off the bay and lapping up against the tall buildings like waves in the encroaching darkness.

Firefighter Joe didn't seem any happier about being at the station that evening than I was, but our shared frustration created a nice tension between us that was going to be fun to burn off.

Captain Mantooth was pleased to see Monk again, probably because it meant that they were likely to recover what had been stolen and get the chrome on their fire trucks thoroughly shined as well.

Before we came in, Monk pinned a junior firefighter badge onto his lapel. The children's badge was a red helmet atop an emblem of a fire truck encircled with a golden firehouse. I found the gesture both endearing and amazing. He had no idea when he got dressed that morning that we'd be visiting a fire station, so that meant he must have carried the badge around with him at all times.

I wondered what else he had in his pockets.

"Tell me exactly what happened," Monk said to Mantooth, a man in his fifties who looked like he'd been chiseled from stone.

"We got called to a car fire at approximately eight fifty-two p.m.," Mantooth said. "It took about two hours to contain the fire and do the necessary cleanup before we got back."

"Tell me more about the fire," Monk said.

"Someone stuffed a rag soaked with gasoline into the fuel tank of a painter's van parked down by Washington Square," Joe said. "It made quite a blast."

"And created a lot of attention," Monk said.

"That's usually why arsonists do it," Joe said.

"When we got back at approximately eleven p.m., we commenced cleaning our rig, replenishing supplies and unloading our stuff," Mantooth said. "That's when one of the guys discovered that we were missing one of our small hydraulic cutter/spreaders and a lightweight power unit from the firehouse."

"Why didn't you take it with you?" Monk asked.

"We've got a couple of them," Joe said. "Different sizes for different jobs. And we keep backups here."

"Can you show me what one of these tools looks like?" Monk said.

"Sure," Joe said and led us over to what looked like a giant bolt cutter. "We use this mostly in car accidents to free the people who are trapped inside their crushed vehicles."

Mantooth pointed to the blades. "The tips of those aluminum-alloy pincers are heat-treated steel and can tear through just about anything."

"Or we can close the blades, jam this into

a tight spot and, instead of cutting," Joe said, "we can spread an object apart or lift it off of somebody."

"Can I see what the power unit looks like?" Monk asked.

Joe motioned to something that looked sort of like an outboard motor without the propellers. It fit into a square iron frame, the bottom two bars serving as feet for the unit.

"The one that was stolen was a smaller version of this," Joe said. "It's basically a Honda 2.5-horsepower, four-stroke engine."

Monk nodded as if he knew what those stats actually meant. "What does it use for fuel?"

"The same as any engine," Joe said. "Gasoline."

That was when I got my first shiver of realization — one Monk probably had back at Webster's place when I told him why Joe had stopped by my place on Thursday.

Monk squatted beside the motor and examined its feet. "Could one person carry both the power unit and the rescue tool?"

"Sure," Joe said. "It's only about forty pounds nowadays. We call the package the 'Jaws of Life.' "

Monk rolled his shoulders and tilted his head from side to side. A new clue was rolling around in his brain. It was almost as if he was using his body motion to make the clue hit different synapses like a pinball. I hoped he was scoring lots of points.

"How much pressure would one of these jaws exert on an object?" Monk asked, standing up.

"Depends on the size of the tool," Mantooth said. "I'd say the one that was stolen probably had a maximum cutting force of about eighteen thousand pounds per square inch."

Monk glanced at me. I looked back at him. And in that moment, I knew why Monk had smelled gasoline in Webster's loft. I knew what had made those marks on Webster's bathroom floor. I knew how the killer had solved the problem of mimicking an alligator's bite. And I knew that my date with Joe wasn't going to happen tonight. One way or another, I would still be working on the case.

Joe studied Monk. "You know why someone stole our stuff."

"Yes, I do," he said.

So did I. It was nice to be in the know for a change.

"Do you think you can get it back for us?" Mantooth asked.

"Probably not," Monk said. "My guess is

that it's probably at the bottom of the bay by now."

"How about whoever did it?" Joe said. "Can you at least get him?"

"Definitely," Monk said.

"Well," Mantooth said, "at least that's something."

The captain thanked us for our help and asked Monk if he wanted to check the fire truck for spots and smudges. Monk almost skipped away.

That left Joe and me alone for the moment.

"We aren't having an intimate interlude tonight, are we?" Joe said.

"I'm sorry," I said.

"Another time, I hope."

I gave him a polite kiss. Maybe too polite.

"There's always hope," I said and walked away.

I found Monk shining the grille on the fire truck. If it shined any brighter, it would have qualified as a star.

"Let me see if I understand things right," I said. "On Wednesday night, someone firebombed a car down in Washington Park to draw the firefighters out of the station long enough so he could steal the Jaws of Life, which he needed to replicate the biting force of an alligator."

"He glued a set of alligator jaws onto the blades," Monk said.

"Somehow the killer got into Ronald Webster's loft, knocked him out, stripped off his clothes and tossed him in the bathtub, which he filled with water and sprinkled with table sea salt," I said. "Then the killer brought in the Jaws of Life and chomped on Webster with them. Webster must have regained consciousness and struggled, causing the power unit to drag across the floor, leaving the streaks on the tiles."

"Obviously," Monk said. "Too obviously, if you ask me."

He got up and dropped his rag in a laundry basket. Together we started walking out to my car. He took his junior firefighter pin off and put it in his pocket.

"The killer then lugged the body and the Jaws of Life down to his car, drove to Baker Beach and dumped Webster there," I said, "along with his neatly folded clothes."

"You left out a few things," Monk said.

"Like why the killer bothered with the whole alligator thing at all," I said.

"Like who the killer is," Monk said.

I stopped walking and stared at him. "You *know* who the killer is?"

"You don't?"

"No, of course I don't," I said. "Because

if I did, I would have said, 'Hot damn, the killer is Mr. X and here's what he did.' That's what a normal person would do."

"Are you saying I'm not normal?"

He looked genuinely hurt. I took a deep breath and tried to fight the urge to strangle him to death right there on the street. He was my employer, after all.

"What I'm saying, Mr. Monk, is that most people would start by sharing the most important news first. The identity of the killer is probably the most important thing we don't know right now."

"I know it," Monk said.

Hot damn, I thought.

"Then perhaps you would be kind enough to share it with me," I said. "Who killed Ronald Webster?"

"The same person who killed Ellen Cole."

I blinked hard and probably even did a double take. It seemed like an enormous leap of logic to make, even for Adrian Monk.

"But these two murders have absolutely nothing in common," I said.

"They are practically identical," Monk said.

"The victims weren't the same sex, they weren't even in the same city and they were killed in entirely different ways," I said. "Ellen Cole was clobbered with a lamp by an intruder. Ronald Webster was murdered in a ridiculously elaborate way to make it seem like he was attacked by an alligator on a nude beach."

"Exactly," Monk said. "Now do you see the similarities?"

I rubbed my temples. I was getting a Monk-ache.

"No," I said, "I don't."

"It's me."

"You're the killer?" I said.

"I'm what they have in common," Monk said.

I opened my purse and began searching madly for some Advil to relieve my misery. Or a gun. Unfortunately, I didn't have either.

"I am very confused and my head feels like it's being split open by the Jaws of Life," I said. "I think you could really clear things up and relieve some of my blinding pain by telling me straight out who the killer is."

"I will be glad to," Monk said.

"Great," I said.

"Tomorrow morning," Monk said. "Sharona will be back by then."

"You talked to Sharona?"

"That's who I called on your cell phone," Monk said. "She's going to check out something for me and then take the first flight to San Francisco that she can get."

"Did you tell her who killed Ellen Cole and framed her husband for the murder?" I said.

"I told her she'd find out tomorrow," Monk said.

"How did she take it?" I asked.

Monk cleared his throat. "If you come to my house tomorrow morning and discover that I've been strangled with some part of my own anatomy, she's the first person you should suspect."

"Only if I don't get to you first," I said.

CHAPTER
TWENTY-FOUR:
MR. MONK TELLS
ALL

Monk was always doing that, dangling the solution to a mystery in front of my face and then not revealing it to me.

I used to think he did it just to torture me, creating suspense the way a writer might to hold a reader between chapters.

But I don't really think that was why he did it. I think he only held back like that when he wasn't entirely convinced that he was right. He needed more time to ponder the clues and double-check his own reasoning. He also wanted to hone his presentation. Telling us what he knew, and how he figured it out, was ninety percent of the fun for him and he didn't want to blow it.

Perhaps more important, he didn't want to waste his performance on me and have to tell the same story twice. Tomorrow he'd have an audience of at least two.

So Monk's delay wasn't cruelty. It was a combination of insecurity, a flair for drama and sheer laziness.

Understanding that, however, didn't make the wait any easier to endure and completely ruined my free night.

After I dropped Monk off at his place, I went home, heated up a Lean Cuisine meal, paid some bills and browsed eBay for cheap clothes. But I couldn't stop thinking about the murders of Ellen Cole and Ronald Webster.

I'm what they have in common.

That was what Monk had said. What did he mean by that?

It was easy to see Monk's connection to Ellen Cole. She was supposedly murdered by the husband of Monk's ex-assistant. But Monk didn't know Ronald Webster and neither did I, though it was kind of strange that the shoe salesman worked in my neighborhood and ate at the same pizza place I did, and that the Jaws of Life used to kill him was stolen from Joe's firehouse.

Was *I* the connection to Monk?

I went to bed trying to follow that line of reasoning and the only place it took me was to a dream about an alligator sitting in a hot tub like a person and eating a slice of pizza, bits of cheese and pepperoni getting stuck in the wires of the braces on his pointy teeth.

Rick Springfield climbed into the hot tub at some point, too, and sang a rousing rendition of "Jessie's Girl" but I was pretty sure that he had nothing to do with the murders.

I arrived at Monk's door at nine a.m. sharp — at the same time as Sharona. She looked tired and angry. It seemed like it had been months since I'd last seen her.

"How did it go in Los Angeles?" I asked her as we walked in without knocking, like it was our home. In a way, I guess it was.

"The only thing I discovered was that I don't have what it takes to be a detective," she said.

"Not everyone can be Adrian Monk," I said.

"And humanity is worse off for it," Monk said as he came in from the kitchen. "Imagine how clean and orderly the world would be."

"You're not going to be part of this world much longer, Adrian, if you don't spit out the name of the killer right now," Sharona said.

But before he could, Captain Stottlemeyer came in behind us, looking a bit disheveled. He was wearing the same clothes that he'd worn the day before.

Either he'd worked all night, which I doubted, or Monk had called him on his cell at his girlfriend's place, catching the captain before he had a chance to go home, shower and change.

Stottlemeyer probably would have given Monk hell the moment he walked in but he was caught off guard by the surprise of seeing Sharona.

"Hey, Sharona," he said and gave her a hug. "It's real good to see you."

"You, too, Captain," she said.

"How's Benji?" he asked.

"He's doing fine," Sharona said. "He'd be doing a lot better if his father wasn't in prison."

"I was sorry to hear about that," Stottlemeyer said.

"Don't be," Sharona said, turning her gaze to Monk. "Adrian is going to correct that injustice right now, aren't you? You're going to tell us who really killed Ellen Cole."

"Yes," Monk said, "I am."

"Wait a minute," Stottlemeyer said, glaring at Monk. "You got me out of bed on my day off because you said you'd solved the Webster homicide."

"I have," Monk said.

"Well, which case are we talking about

here?" Stottlemeyer said. "Her case or mine?"

"Both," Monk said. "The same killer is responsible."

"Who is he?" the three of us demanded in unison. We sounded like the Rolling Stones.

"Ian Ludlow," Monk said.

He smiled triumphantly, but his declaration didn't feel like a revelation. It felt like petty vindictiveness.

"Oh for God's sake, Monk," the captain said. "I know you hate that he's helping us out, and you aren't getting our complete attention, but this is over the top, even for you."

"He's the guy," Monk insisted.

"How could he possibly be the guy?" Stottlemeyer said.

"Ludlow helped the police investigate the Ellen Cole murder and led them to Trevor," Monk said. "Now he's up here, consulting on the Webster investigation."

"The only reason he's here is because Randy called him," Stottlemeyer said.

"Which Lieutenant Disher did because the murder was reminiscent of a scene from Ludlow's new book," Monk said.

"So what?" Stottlemeyer said.

"That's only one of the coincidences," Monk said. "There's more. The shoe store where Webster worked is in Natalie's neighborhood and so is the restaurant where he bought his pizza."

"That's nothing, Monk. No, it's *less* than nothing," Stottlemeyer said. "You must really feel threatened by this guy to be seeing connections where none exist. It's not just sad — it's pathetic." Stottlemeyer started for the door.

"Wait, there's more," Monk said. "I know how he faked the alligator attack."

"What alligator attack?" Sharona said.

"It's a long story," I said.

"Okay, Monk," Stottlemeyer said, turning back, "how was it done?"

"Ludlow glued an alligator's jaws to a hydraulic cutter and used the rescue tool to replicate the thousands of pounds of force in the creature's grip," Monk said. "There was no way Webster could free himself, no matter how much he struggled, which is what caused the streaks on the bathroom floor."

"Webster was killed by somebody using the Jaws of Life," Stottlemeyer said, mulling it over for a moment. "That explains all of it except why he was killed and who did it."

"Ludlow did it," Monk said.

"Your jealousy and insecurity are pathological but at least you figured out the alligator thing. I've got to hand that to you," Stottlemeyer said. "So here's the deal. I'm just going to forget all the Ludlow stuff. You get yourself some help from Dr. Kroger and we'll pretend like the rest never happened."

"It was Ludlow," Monk said.

"Because Webster sells shoes and had a pizza in the same city where we *all* live?" Stottlemeyer fumed.

"Because on Wednesday night someone stole the Jaws of Life from the same firehouse where Natalie's lover works," Monk said.

I felt my face flush with embarrassment. I don't know why. I was an adult. I was allowed to have sex.

"He's not my lover. We aren't involved," I said. "Much."

"Much?" Sharona said.

"We're revolved," I said.

"Revolved?" Sharona said.

"You know," I said, "the typical involved-then-not-involved-then-involved-and-not-involved-again thing. Revolved."

It was just getting worse. Luckily, Stottlemeyer saved me.

"It's a weird coincidence. I'll grant you that, Monk," Stottlemeyer said, kindly ignoring my love life. "But there's a reason why somebody created a word for coincidences. *Because they happen.* You have nothing that actually links Ian Ludlow to any of this."

"Or to Ellen Cole's murder," Sharona said, "which is all I really care about."

"There's more," Monk said. "Show them, Sharona."

"Show them what?" she said.

"The picture I asked you to take last night in Ellen Cole's house," Monk said.

Sharona took out her cell phone, which had a camera feature on it, and pulled up a close-up image of a row of books. She showed it to us. We looked over her shoulder. I recognized the titles on the spines of the books. They were Ian Ludlow mysteries.

"Ellen Cole owned almost all of Ian Ludlow's books," Monk said. "So did Ronald Webster."

"I do, too," Stottlemeyer said. "So do millions of other people."

"*That's* your link between the two murders?" Sharona said angrily. "That's nothing, Adrian!"

"You aren't much of a detective. You said so yourself and I must agree," Monk said. "You're obviously missing the intricate ways these clues fit together."

"*I'm* a detective," Stottlemeyer said. "And I think she's right. Worse, I think you're having some kind of mental meltdown."

I was inclined to agree.

"There's more," Monk said.

"You keep saying that," Stottlemeyer said. "And there really isn't."

"Ludlow confessed to us," Monk said. "Three times."

"I don't remember that," I said.

"Neither do I," Sharona said.

"He only confessed to you once," Monk said to her.

"If he confessed to killing Ellen Cole," Sharona said, "I would remember it."

"Ludlow writes four books a year," Monk said. "When we were at his book signing in Los Angeles, a fan asked him if he was ever afraid of running out of ideas. Ludlow said no, saying he gets his stories from real people."

"I don't see what that has to do with Ellen Cole," Sharona said.

"When he finishes a book, he does book signings, then hangs out with Lieutenant Dozier, waiting until a murder comes along that interests him. But I don't think he waits."

"You believe he killed Ellen Cole for a book?" Sharona said.

"He picked her at random, maybe from a crowd at one of his book signings, followed her for a time, then killed her," Monk said. "He hung around with the police, watched how the case developed and who the people were in her life, then created his own ending by framing Trevor, the least likely suspect, for the crime."

"You came up with all of this just from Ludlow saying he was inspired by real cases?" Stottlemeyer said.

"There's more," Monk said.

"I wish you'd stop saying that," Stottlemeyer said.

"That's how he gets his stories. He said he couldn't make up anything as good as the real conflicts in Cole's life. And then yesterday, at the morgue, Ludlow said virtually the same thing again," Monk said. "Later, at Webster's house, he said he's always amazed at what he finds when he scratches the surface of an ordinary person's life. He had no idea that an ordinary shoe salesman's life could be so complicated."

"Not as complicated as the way he was killed," I said.

"Exactly," Monk said, turning to Stottlemeyer. "You said Ronald Webster's murder was a case that cried out for me. You were right. That was the whole point."

"You were the point," Stottlemeyer said.

"Ludlow murdered Webster in this outrageous way for two reasons," Monk said. "To make sure you'd bring me in to investigate and so Disher would see the similarity to Ludlow's book and call the author in to help."

"So this is all about you," Stottlemeyer said.

"Yes, yes, now you're getting it," Monk said. "When I showed up to investigate Ellen's murder, Ludlow saw a way to add a twist to his story. So he came up here and murdered Ronald Webster, another one of his fans."

"All so you could be the star of his new book," Stottlemeyer said.

"Not necessarily the star," Monk said, "but certainly a major character."

"Certainly," Stottlemeyer said. "I wouldn't expect anything less." He sighed wearily and headed for the door.

"Are you leaving to arrest Ludlow?" Monk said.

"Nope," Stottlemeyer said. "I'm just leaving."

And that was that. The captain walked out.

Monk stared at the door for a long moment after Stottlemeyer left, then turned to the two of us.

"What is his problem?" he said.

"You, Adrian," Sharona said.

"I just solved two murders," Monk said. "He should be thanking me and arresting that phony."

"You're selfish, self-centered, and completely self-involved," Sharona said. "The whole world has to revolve around you, and when it doesn't, you freak out."

He looked at me. "What's her problem?"

"Mr. Monk, you know that I have enormous faith in your abilities as a detective," I said.

"As you should," Monk said. "I'm always right."

Sharona groaned. I tried not to do the same myself.

"But it looks to me like your thinking on

this case is heavily influenced by your animosity toward Ian Ludlow," I said. "Listening to you today, it seems that you're determined to put yourself front and center, even if it means twisting things to make Ludlow the villain."

"Do you really think that about me?"

I double-checked with myself. Monk was never wrong about murder, but there was always a first time, and this seemed like it could be it. His conclusions required a bigger jump than any conclusions he'd ever jumped to before.

"Yes, Mr. Monk, I do," I said. "I don't think you're doing it intentionally. It's just how you're choosing to interpret the facts."

"The facts are what they are," Monk said. "There is only one way to interpret them."

"That's your problem, Adrian. It's always got to be your way," Sharona said. "Everybody has to see things the way you do, arrange things the way you do, act the way you do, or they're committing a crime against nature. God forbid that *you* should ever change for anyone."

"Ian Ludlow is a fraud. Can't you see that? A know-nothing blowhard," Monk said. "He's the murderer who framed your husband."

"What hurts the most isn't that you're

wrong and that the real murderer is still out there. It's that you can't see past your own selfishness to help me," Sharona said. "I needed you, Adrian, more than I've ever needed anyone. You let me down." She walked out, slamming the door behind her, and leaving me alone with Monk.

"I'm right," Monk said. "You know that I am. In your heart of hearts, you know."

"If you're right, Mr. Monk, why does Ludlow care so much about you?"

"Because I'm brilliant," Monk said. "And he's not."

I was glad that Sharona wasn't there to hear him say that. "I rest my case," I said.

"You haven't made a case to rest," Monk said.

"You're letting your ego and insecurity blind you to other possible explanations."

"I don't think so," Monk said.

"Of course you don't," I said.

Arguing with him was pointless. Sharona was right. He would never change. I turned to leave.

"You can't go," Monk said.

"It's my day off," I said.

"But I need you," he said quietly.

"Now you know how Sharona feels," I said. I was almost at the door when Captain

Stottlemeyer walked in, a grim look on his face.

Monk burst into a big smile. "I knew you'd see reason. You've come to get me for the big arrest."

"I'm afraid not, Monk," Stottlemeyer said. "Natalie, you need to come with me."

I felt a pang of terror. "Is Julie okay? Has something happened to Julie?"

"No, she's fine," Stottlemeyer said. "You'd better come, too, Monk."

"What's going on, Captain?" I asked as we followed him outside. "Where are we going?"

"Back to your house," Stottlemeyer said.

"Why?"

But just as I asked that question, I noticed to my great surprise that my Jeep Cherokee wasn't parked in front of Monk's place anymore. It was gone. Stottlemeyer's car was parked right where my car used to be.

"Somebody stole my car," I said.

"It wasn't stolen," Stottlemeyer said. "It was towed away."

"Who towed it?" I said. "I wasn't parked illegally and I don't have any unpaid parking tickets."

"That's not why we towed it," Stottlemeyer said.

"We?" I said.

But Stottlemeyer didn't say another word. I didn't like the sound of that.

The street in front of my house was clogged with official police vehicles — black-and-white cruisers, unmarked detective sedans and a couple vans from the crime-scene investigation unit.

The last time I had a party like that at my house was when I killed an intruder who tried to kill me. That was how I met Monk.

Now my house was a crime scene again. That meant that a crime had been committed in the house or items related to a crime could be found there. I didn't like the implications of either scenario. Regardless of the explanation, I was sure my neighbors were already circulating a petition demanding that I move.

Captain Stottlemeyer had remained silent during the short drive but when we pulled up to the curb in front of my house, he looked over his shoulder at me in the back-seat and finally spoke.

"I didn't know anything about this," Stottlemeyer said. "Neither did Randy. I heard about it after I left Monk's place. Ludlow went over our heads."

"Ludlow?" Monk said. "What's he got to do with this?"

"It's his show," Stottlemeyer said as we all got out of the car.

Ian Ludlow, Disher and Sharona were waiting for us in my living room. There were other uniformed cops, plainclothes detectives and forensics guys scurrying around. I didn't know what they were doing that was keeping them so busy or why they were doing it.

I'd left the house locked. Now all these people were in my house, going through my stuff, without asking me first. It pissed me off. I was sure they had a warrant, but that still didn't make it right.

Disher looked as grim as his boss, and Sharona was radiating anger. I couldn't figure out why she'd been dragged to my place. Then again, I didn't know why I was there, either.

"Thanks for coming down," Ludlow said.

"I live here," I said testily.

"Indeed you do," Ludlow said.

"Another brilliant deduction," Monk said.

"What are we doing here?" Sharona asked.

"I thought you'd like to know who killed Ellen Cole," Ludlow said.

"You were the one who said it was my husband," Sharona said.

"I was wrong," Ludlow said. "When I heard what Monk told Lieutenant Dozier, I realized I'd been misled by the evidence and I immediately resolved to let nothing stop me from getting to the truth."

"And you've found the truth in my living room?" I said.

"As a matter of fact," Ludlow said, "I have."

"So spit it out," Sharona asked. "Who killed Ellen Cole?"

Ludlow smiled at Sharona. "You already know the answer to that."

"If I did," Sharona said, "I wouldn't be asking."

"*You* killed Ellen Cole," Ludlow said to her.

I glanced at Monk. He seemed perplexed, his features all scrunched up as he grappled with this new concept.

Stottlemeyer and Disher were both looking at Sharona.

"You're lucky there are two cops standing here," Sharona said, glaring furiously at Ludlow. "Or you'd be flat on the floor, looking for your teeth."

"That's your best argument?" Ludlow said. "More violence?"

"First you say my husband killed her," Sharona said. "Now you're saying that I did. What have you got against us? Did we run over your cat or something?"

"I've known Sharona for years," Stottle-meyer said. "I just don't believe she's capable of murder."

"It's exactly that predisposition that provoked me to go over your head to the deputy commissioner to arrange for this search warrant and for Captain Toplyn to serve it," Ludlow said, motioning across the room to a stocky man, who I presumed was Toplyn.

Toplyn acknowledged our glances with an expressionless nod. He was within earshot but outside our circle, standing beside a cardboard box full of bags of collected evidence.

But evidence of *what?*

"I knew that you'd be too biased to see things in an objective light," Ludlow said.

"Convince me that I'm wrong," Stottle-meyer said.

If Ludlow thought Sharona was a killer, why were the cops crawling all over *my* house and *my* car instead of hers? What did I have to do with any of this?

"Sharona killed Ellen Cole and framed her husband for the murder," Ludlow said. "She did it to get out of an abusive marriage."

"If I wanted out of my marriage, I wouldn't have had to kill anyone," Sharona said. "I would have just walked out. I've done it before."

"Yes, you have. You did it because Trevor is a creep, a loser and a lousy father. But what happened? He came back. You got sucked into the marriage again, even though you know he's the same loser that he's always been," Ludlow said. "You are helpless against his charms and you know it."

Monk nodded in agreement. Sharona glared at him.

"What are you nodding for, Adrian? He's accusing me of murder here," Sharona said. "Aren't you going to do anything about it?"

"I'm listening," Monk said.

"You're listening and nodding," Sharona said.

"Only to the part about Trevor," Monk said, "not the part about you murdering someone."

"I didn't murder anyone," Sharona said. "That's the point, Adrian. You have to tell him he's wrong."

"You knew that there was only one way to save yourself and your son," Ludlow said. "You had to find a way to get Trevor out of your life for good."

"So why wouldn't she just kill him?" Stottlemeyer said.

"Because she would have been the most

obvious suspect," Ludlow said. "It made far more sense to kill a complete stranger who couldn't be connected to her, frame her husband for the crime and get him locked away forever."

"Oh, yeah, that makes a lot of sense," Sharona said, "if you're insane." She looked at Monk again for support, but he seemed distracted, lost in his own thoughts.

"Is that going to be your defense?" Ludlow said. "Temporary insanity?"

"She's not going to need a defense, because you've got nothing on her," Stottlemeyer said. "It's all wild speculation. Where's your proof?"

"All the evidence against Trevor, for one thing," Ludlow said, turning to Sharona. "It points right back at you."

"How do you figure that?" Stottlemeyer asked.

"The person in the best position to set up an eBay account in his name using his checking-account number and to plant the stolen goods in his truck was you," Ludlow said. "You had unfettered access. And in your most brazen act, you told Lieutenant Dozier how you did it."

"I told him how *somebody* could do it," Sharona said.

"Perhaps the most revealing thing of all is

that you never called your old employer, Adrian Monk, to help you," Ludlow said. "He's one of the best detectives on Earth, and yet you didn't seek his help. Why? Because you knew he'd discover the truth, that you killed Ellen Cole."

"I didn't go to Adrian for help because I thought he hated me for leaving him and because I thought Trevor was guilty," Sharona said. "I was wrong on both counts."

"But in a cruel twist of fate, you encountered Monk and his new assistant, Natalie, anyway," Ludlow said. "And your carefully plotted scheme began to unravel."

I realized that Ludlow wasn't so much speaking as he was writing aloud. Everything he was saying would be coming out of his hero Detective Marshak's mouth by the time the book was written.

"There are a thousand ways a reasonable person could interpret everything you've told us," Stottlemeyer said, "and reach an entirely different conclusion."

"For instance," I said, looking at Ludlow, "maybe you killed Ellen Cole."

I turned to Monk, waiting for him to run with that, but he remained silent. I was shocked. Stottlemeyer was probably relieved. I was sure that the last thing the captain wanted to deal with were two absurd theories about the murder from two bullheaded egotists at once.

Even so, I wish Monk had stepped up. I wish he had done it for Sharona. But once again, he was letting her down when she needed him most. And I didn't know why.

"C'mon, that's just stupid," Disher said to me. "We're talking about Ian Ludlow here. He's the man."

"What about me, Randy?" Sharona said. "Do you really think that I'd kill a woman I don't even know and frame my husband for it?"

"You're more likely to do it than the greatest crime writer of our generation," Disher said, then turned to Ludlow. "But I just don't think you're right about this. You don't have any evidence to support your charges."

"Three days ago I didn't," Ludlow said. "But then you called and asked me to come up here to figure out how someone was killed on a nude beach by an alligator."

"How does Ronald Webster's murder prove that Sharona killed Ellen Cole?" I asked.

Ludlow smiled at me. "Because *you* murdered him, Natalie."

CHAPTER TWENTY-SIX:
MR. MONK LOSES AN ASSISTANT

Ludlow might as well have punched me in the stomach. I couldn't breathe. I couldn't find the air to speak. His accusation was so wrong, so unfair, so terrifying that it left me numb.

I didn't know where to begin. How do you argue against something that goes against all logic and everything you know to be true?

It was surreal. At first, I thought he was just getting back at me for my crack about him being the killer. But I could tell by the way he was studying me for telltale signs of guilt that he meant it.

The best I could muster, once I found air in my lungs again, was to say with all the moral conviction, truthfulness and outrage that I could muster: "That's not true!"

I don't think it was very convincing, at least not to Ludlow, who had this smug, self-satisfied look on his face, not unlike the look Monk gets during his summations, only minus the smugness.

I turned to Monk, expecting him to leap to my defense, but he said nothing, which was the scariest thing of all to me. He hadn't spoken since Ludlow started making his crazy accusations. It was like he was a member of the audience watching the show instead of a member of the cast of characters.

"Adrian, speak up," Sharona said. "Are you just going to stand there and let this happen?"

Monk shrugged and looked away. He was abandoning me, too.

"You should be ashamed of yourself," she said to him, then turned to Stottlemeyer and Disher. "What about you two? The next thing Ludlow is going to do is accuse one of you of murder."

"It wouldn't surprise me," Stottlemeyer said, "considering the way things have been going."

Ludlow faced Sharona and pointed to me. "Natalie knew how much you meant to Monk. She was terrified that Monk would fire her and rehire you. So you simply had to go, and the best way to accomplish that was to get Monk to prove that Trevor was innocent. If Trevor was freed, you'd go back to LA, and her job would be safe again."

That much was true, but I didn't want to acknowledge it because I was afraid it would add credibility to whatever idiotic thing he was going to say next.

But unfortunately, Stottlemeyer and Disher already knew that Ludlow was right about that. I had owned up to it, no matter how embarrassing it was.

"Being petty and selfish isn't a crime, though it's pretty humiliating," I said. "But once I met Trevor, it stopped being about me or what I wanted. I knew he was innocent. I believed him."

"Of course you did, because he was telling the truth," Ludlow said. "But this created a huge problem for Sharona. Your meddling could send her to prison. She had to stop you. But how? This part is where I've had to do a little guesswork."

"Just this part," Stottlemeyer said, "because everything else you've said has been so firmly grounded in fact."

Ludlow ignored the captain's sarcasm and plowed ahead. "Somehow Sharona convinced you that even if Trevor was innocent, he was an abusive husband who would make her life, and her son's, a living hell. She made you a deal: She agreed to disappear from Monk's life forever if you helped her keep Trevor behind bars."

"You're guessing wrong," Sharona said.

"That conversation never happened," I said. "None of this did. It's fiction, something you're very good at."

"You concocted a brilliant scheme," Ludlow said to me. "You committed another murder in San Francisco, one so bizarre you knew Monk wouldn't be able to resist it, one that even the police would agree 'cried out for him.' And while you did that, Sharona remained in LA to establish an alibi and erase whatever tracks she'd left behind when she killed Ellen Cole."

His theory was so ridiculous, and his reasoning so flawed, that I actually felt relieved. Nobody would ever believe that he was right.

"You think that I murdered a complete stranger just so I could keep my job with Mr. Monk?" I said. "Do you have any idea what this job pays?"

"You didn't do it for the money," Ludlow said. "You did it because you're in love with him."

The surprises never stopped coming from Ludlow. Of all his accusations, that was by far the stupidest.

Disher gasped and looked at me. "You *are?*"

"Of course not," I said. "I don't love him."

I regretted it the instant the words were out of my mouth.

I'd hurt Monk. I could see that. His whole body seemed to sag with the pain of it. I'd broken his heart, even though I knew he didn't love me either. Not like that. Not like he loved Trudy or I loved Mitch.

"That's not what I meant," I said. "You know that I want you in my life, Mr. Monk, and that I care deeply for you, but not the way Ludlow is making it seem."

I felt terrible and hated Ludlow for having made me say something so cruel and hurtful to someone I was close to. It was a crime and I wished there was some way I could punish him for it.

But at the moment, it was all I could do to hold my own against the wave of accusations that were coming at me. And he wasn't done yet.

"Your protestations would be a lot easier to believe if there wasn't so much irrefutable evidence to the contrary," Ludlow said. "I suppose I'm somewhat to blame for what happened. On Tuesday, you bought a signed copy of my novel *Death Is the Last Word,* which gave you the inspiration for your fiendish plot."

"I didn't read your book," I said.

"Of course you did. I asked Lieutenant

Dozier to do some checking for me," Ludlow said. "He discovered that on Tuesday night, you visited a Web site called Cassidy's Curios, where you used your credit card to buy a set of alligator's jaws and have them sent overnight priority to your home in San Francisco."

"That's not true," I said. I kept saying that and it sounded hollow, even to me. I needed to refute what he was saying with facts and reason, but I couldn't. I didn't have the facts and I was too overwhelmed to reason.

"We found the packaging in your trash can," Ludlow said, motioning to Captain Toplyn, who I'd forgotten was even there.

Toplyn reached into a box at his feet and pulled out an evidence bag containing a torn-up FedEx carton and stuffing. The label on the carton said CASSIDY'S CURIOS.

"Anybody could have ordered that using my credit card, had it sent here and swiped it off my porch that morning," I said. "I didn't get back from LA until Wednesday."

"Which is when you set fire to a car in Washington Park and stole the Jaws of Life from the firehouse where your lover works," Ludlow said. "That's how you knew where to find it. I bet you even had a key to the building."

"I was home with my daughter that night," I said.

"You crept out when she was asleep," Ludlow said. "You probably made sure she'd be out cold by slipping her a sleeping pill with her painkillers."

"I didn't drug my daughter, I don't have a key to the firehouse and Joe Cochran is not my boyfriend!"

I was yelling. I couldn't help myself. My heart was pounding with terror, pumping adrenaline into my veins and making me shake.

"If he's not, perhaps you can explain why you have Joe's T-shirt," Ludlow said, motioning to Captain Toplyn again, who held up an evidence bag containing Joe's SFPD T-shirt, "and why he spent the morning here with you on Thursday. Don't bother lying. We have statements from your neighbors who saw him here."

Stottlemeyer and Disher were looking at me with doubt and disappointment. Even Monk was looking at me sadly. The only person looking at me with any sympathy was Sharona, but she was in the same fix that I was in.

"It was the first time I'd seen Joe in months," I said. "He came over because he wanted Mr. Monk to recover their stolen rescue equipment."

"And did you tell Monk about it?" Ludlow asked, pointing his finger accusingly at me. "No, you didn't. Why? Because you knew Monk would be getting the Webster case soon. You didn't want him to have the stolen Jaws of Life already on his mind. Because you knew that if he did, he'd quickly put the facts together and follow the trail of coincidences straight to you instead of spinning around in circles of futility for months."

Circles of futility. I'd become a character in a badly written book and I wanted out.

"That's not why I didn't tell him," I said, turning to the others, hoping one of them would say something or do something to end this ordeal.

Couldn't they see how Ludlow was twisting things?

Why was Monk just standing there? Why wasn't he cutting Ludlow down, deftly refuting each one of his unbelievable accusations?

Was it because Monk *believed* them?

I looked Monk in the eye, or at least I tried to. He wouldn't meet my gaze.

"I didn't want you to be distracted from the Ellen Cole investigation," I said. "The sooner you found out who really killed her, the sooner Trevor would be freed from jail, and the sooner I'd have my life back the way it was."

I needed him to believe me. If he didn't, then I was lost. Julie was lost. Everything was lost.

"Please, Mr. Monk, say something," I said.

But Monk didn't.

"That's what this has all been about," Ludlow said, "keeping your life intact and sending Sharona away again. For that, a man had to die. For that, you turned the Jaws of Life into the Jaws of Death."

"The Jaws of Death," Disher repeated, almost reverently. "It's going to make a great title for the book."

"There isn't going to be a book," I said, "because none of this is true."

"It was Joe's fateful call to you last night that was your undoing, and ultimately Sharona's as well," Ludlow said. "When I overheard that you were talking to a firefighter, everything fell into place for me. In one exhilarating moment, I realized how the alligator attack was faked. Once I discovered that the Jaws of Life were stolen from your lover's firehouse, I knew that you were the killer. After that, the rest was easy."

"What rest?" I said. "There is no rest."

"Ronald Webster worked in the same

neighborhood where you live," Ludlow said. "That's how you picked him at random on Thursday night to be your victim."

"Until I arrived at the Baker Beach crime scene, I'd never seen Ronald Webster before in my life," I said.

"That's a lie and I can prove it." Ludlow glanced at Captain Toplyn, the man with all the damn evidence bags.

This time, Toplyn held up a bag containing a tiny slip of paper.

"What's that?" Disher asked.

"The cash-register receipt that was taped to the pizza box in Webster's kitchen," Ludlow said. "He went to Sorrento's for pizza on Thursday night and so did you, Natalie. That's when you saw him there."

"I didn't see him," I said.

"The time-stamped receipt shows he got a ten-percent discount on his pizza, because he was there the same time you and your daughter were," Ludlow said. "We know that because he asked for and received the discount offered on Julie's cast. That's when you chose him as your random victim."

"There were lots of people in the restaurant," I said.

"But he was the one you hit on," Ludlow said. "He was the one you went to visit at his home after your daughter was asleep.

He was the one you murdered."

"Just because I may have been in the same restaurant at the same time as Webster doesn't make me a killer," I said.

"No, it doesn't," Ludlow said. "But this does."

Oh hell, I thought.

We all looked at Toplyn this time without waiting for Ludlow to gesture to him. He was holding an evidence vial containing some kind of green goop.

"What you didn't know when you stole the Jaws of Life was that there was a small leak in the hydraulic line," Ludlow said. "We found phosphate ester fluid in your car, the same greenish liquid that Monk discovered on Webster's bathroom floor."

So that was why they towed my Jeep. They wanted to give it a forensics once-over.

"It must have been planted in my car by someone," I said. My explanation sounded desperate and pathetic, which I most certainly was. I could feel myself getting boxed in by the false impression he was creating about me, about my actions, about what I had and hadn't done.

"But that's not the only leak that's sinking your plot," Toplyn said, startling me. So far, the man had simply been Ludlow's silent Vanna White, if Vanna were a middle-aged man who favored off-the-rack suits from Wal-Mart. "We found steering fluid in your driveway and it matched steering fluid we found in the parking lot outside Webster's loft."

I'd been framed. As neatly and efficiently as Trevor had been. The evidence was so compelling, I was almost persuaded that I *had* killed Webster.

If only I'd listened to Monk and gone to the car wash when he'd suggested it, there would be no evidence linking me to the murder. I was doomed by my own slovenly ways.

I looked again at Monk, expecting him to rub it in. But he didn't. He wouldn't even meet my gaze.

Toplyn stepped forward, taking out a pair of handcuffs. "Natalie Teeger, you are under arrest for the murder of Ronald Webster."

Toplyn glanced at Disher and motioned to Sharona. The silent command was clear. Disher hesitated, but as he started to step forward to do his duty, Stottlemeyer cut him off.

"No, Randy, I'll do it." Stottlemeyer faced Sharona and sighed wearily. "I'm sorry about this. I really am. Sharona Fleming, you're under arrest for the murder of Ellen Cole."

Ludlow smiled triumphantly and clicked off the tiny dictation machine he'd had hidden in his pocket. He'd solved another case and simultaneously finished what would be the closing chapter of his next bestseller.

Monk didn't say anything. He wouldn't even look at us. He lowered his head and walked away while we were still being read our rights.

CHAPTER
TWENTY-SEVEN:
MR. MONK AND THE
JAILBIRDS

Sharona and I shared a cell with a couple women, who I assumed were prostitutes or drug addicts. They looked haggard, wrung-out, and desiccated.

I thought maybe that was how I would look in a few months.

Before we were put in the cell, we were fingerprinted and booked. Sharona used her one phone call to reach her sister, who agreed to take care of Benji and Julie, which relieved my biggest worry. I hadn't figured out how I was going to explain to Julie what had happened or ease her fears about what was to come. Mainly because I didn't know the answers myself.

I used my call to contact my parents in Monterey. I don't have much money, but I come from a wealthy family. I knew my parents would hire the best criminal attorney in San Francisco to defend us — as soon as they got my message on their answering machine. They were away for the weekend.

At least I hoped it was only for the weekend and not some monthlong Caribbean cruise.

Wherever they were, they were sure in for a shock when they listened to their messages. It's not every day that your kid is arrested for murder. I tried to imagine how I'd feel if I got a call like that from Julie.

No matter where my parents were, or when they were getting back, one thing was certain: Sharona and I would be spending Sunday night in jail. And, if we were unlucky, the rest of our lives.

I wasn't scared. I wasn't even angry anymore. I was too tired. Declaring your innocence loudly and strongly in the face of mountains of contrary evidence is exhausting work.

I was so tired that the concrete bench I was sitting on actually felt comfortable and inviting to me. Sharona sat beside me, almost shoulder to shoulder.

For a long time, neither of us spoke. We just stared at nothing, the situation slowly sinking in and, with it, a certain resignation. We were caught up in something now that we had very little control over. All we could do was wait and see what happened next.

In a way, I was sort of thankful for the quiet. My ears were no longer ringing with accusations and lies.

"This is payback," Sharona said softly.

"From who?"

"From God," she said. "This is what I get for not believing Trevor. I'm being made to suffer the same way he is."

"If we go to prison," I said, "both of our kids are going to be orphans."

"They are going to be screwed up for life," Sharona said.

"Totally," I said.

"They'll have one bad relationship after another, searching for the stability they never had as children."

"They'll probably become alcoholics or drug addicts," I said, "if they're lucky."

"I guess this means we're both out of the running for the mother-of-the-year award," she said.

"I was disqualified from consideration long before I was arrested for murder," I said.

"Come to think of it," Sharona said, "so was I."

We were silent for a time. We were only joking, but not by much. We were both genuinely afraid that we'd failed our children.

"I'm sorry," I said.

"For what?" Sharona said.

"For all the nasty things I thought about you and every selfish thing I did because I was worried about losing my job."

"I'm sorry, too," Sharona said.

"For what?"

"For leaving Adrian and forcing him to find a new assistant," Sharona said, "because if I hadn't done that, you wouldn't be in this mess."

"I'd be in another one," I said.

"You're probably right," she said. "But would there be a murder involved?"

"I guess you never heard about how I met Mr. Monk."

"No, I haven't," she said.

"I caught a guy stealing a rock from my daughter's fish tank," I said. "He tried to kill me, but I killed him first. Captain Stottlemeyer brought Mr. Monk in to help figure out what was going on."

"What was so special about this rock?"

"It was from the moon," I said.

"You've been to the moon?"

"Not since Thursday," I said.

"The firefighter?" she asked.

I nodded. "The thing is, there's enough truth to the things Ludlow said about me, my life and the things I've done to make the untruths look truthful."

"And the only reason for you to do what he's charged you with doing is if I murdered Ellen Cole," Sharona said, "which I didn't do."

"I know that," I said.

"Just making sure," she said. "The case against you is being used as a case against me."

"And it's all speculation," I said. "There isn't half as much evidence against you."

"There's *no* evidence against me," she said. "If we can prove Ludlow wrong about Ronald Webster's murder, then his case against me falls apart, too."

"How are we going to do that?" I said. "Not even Mr. Monk could do it."

"Adrian didn't even try," Sharona said. "He froze up."

"After everything we've done for him," I said, "how could he do that to us?"

"Because he doesn't know," Sharona said.

"He doesn't know if we're guilty?"

She shook her head. "He doesn't know who is."

As tired as I was, I didn't sleep much that night. I only had catnaps. During those periods of wakefulness, when I was cold and scared, I thought about everything that had happened and everything that was said.

I thought about Sharona's comment that Monk froze because he didn't know who the real killer was. It made a lot of sense. Not knowing who killed Trudy had frozen Monk for years. He was completely unable to function. Now the two people who were closest to him were in trouble, their freedom depending on the solutions to two murders that he couldn't solve.

We'd be lucky if Monk didn't go back to the way he was before Sharona saved him.

Or become catatonic.

It did make me wonder, though.

Who would save Monk this time?

And who would save us?

I'd drifted off again — I didn't know for how long — and woke up suddenly in a panic, unsure where I was. It took me a moment to slip back into place. I was in jail, accused of a murder I didn't commit. I wished I had a mysterious one-armed man I could claim was the real felon. Maybe I would anyway.

I was drifting off into sleep again, counting one-armed men instead of sheep, when Sharona spoke up.

"I love him, too," she said.

"I didn't say that I did," I said.

"You didn't have to," she said.

We were silent for a time. I thought about what she'd said. "Then how could you leave him?" I asked.

"I got back together with Trevor," she said.

"That doesn't answer my question," I said. "If Trevor wanted you so badly, he would have stayed with you in San Francisco. You can't lay this on him. *You* decided to leave Mr. Monk."

"Working for Adrian isn't a job," she said. "It becomes your life. It starts with him needing you, demanding all of your time and attention. And then, somewhere along the way, you discover that you need him almost as much as he needs you."

She was right. Why else would I have become so fiercely protective of my job? I'd moved from job to job before. But this was more than that. I knew it, Sharona knew it and I bet even Julie knew it.

"All the more reason not to go," I said.

"What if you fall in love with someone again?" she asked me. "What if you want to get married?"

"I don't think that's going to happen," I said.

"It will," Sharona said. "And when it does, where is Adrian going to fit in to that?"

"I'd keep working for him," I said.

"You couldn't give Adrian the attention he needs," Sharona said, "not without sacrificing your marriage."

"Then I'd quit," I said. "We could remain friends and a part of each other's lives."

"That would never work. Adrian wouldn't acknowledge the change. He would keep making the same unreasonable demands on you and your time," she said. "I wanted to give this marriage my best shot. I owed Trevor and Benji that. I knew I couldn't do it with Adrian Monk in my life."

"So in order to be happy," I said, "it means that someday I will have to hurt Mr. Monk."

"You won't hurt him," Sharona said. "You'll break him."

Sharona fell back to sleep but I wasn't able to manage the same feat. Every time I started to nod off, a snore from one of the prostitutes jarred me back into wakefulness. I didn't want to be awake alone, so I nudged Sharona.

"Was there ever anything between you and Disher?" I asked.

"Like what?"

"Erotic tension," I said.

"Maybe for him," she said. "I have that effect on men."

"Me, too," the prostitute said.

We both looked at her, but she closed her eyes and started snoring again.

"He seems to think you had something," I said.

"There may have been an innocent flirtation," Sharona said, "but not more than I have with the cashier at the grocery store or the mechanic who fixes my car."

"I wouldn't even call that flirtation," I said. "It's friendliness. It's attentiveness. It's showing an interest in people. But men misinterpret that basic social courtesy as erotic tension."

"I think men are born erotically tense," Sharona said. "That's why they do most of the stupid things that they do."

"It's a good thing," the prostitute said, "or I'd be out of a job."

When I woke up again, it was Monday morning, though I wasn't sure of the time. Sharona, the hookers and the drug addicts were awake, too.

"I mean no offense by this," Sharona said, "but do you ever wonder why Adrian hired you?"

"All the time," I said, "though he might be asking himself the same question now that I've turned out to be a sociopathic killer."

"So am I, remember?" Sharona said.

"Mr. Monk clearly has terrible instincts when it comes to hiring assistants."

"He didn't hire me as an assistant," she said. "I was brought on as his nurse. Adrian called me his assistant so he could feel better about the situation and himself."

"I can understand that," I said.

"You have no nursing or professional caregiving experience."

"Nope," I said.

"So what were you doing before you got this job?"

"I was a bartender," I said. "A lousy one."

Sharona nodded, mulling that over.

"I'm sure Adrian interviewed a lot of qualified nurses before he met you," Sharona said. "But he didn't hire them. He hired a bartender who'd just killed a man in her living room."

"That's because having experience mixing drinks and stabbing men was listed as required qualifications for the job."

"I think I know why he hired you," she said.

"You mean it wasn't my vivacious personality and irrepressible charm?"

"You're me," Sharona said.

"You just got done telling me all the ways that I'm *not* you."

"But you are in the ways that count," she said. "You're a single mother with a twelve-year-old kid. So was I. He wasn't looking for a new assistant with nursing or even secretarial skills. He was looking for a new actress to play the same part."

"My relationship with Monk is entirely different from yours," I said.

"Of course it is," Sharona said, "because as much as Monk tried to keep things the same, you made the role your own. You may resemble me on the surface but you aren't me. We really aren't alike at all."

"Except that we both love him," I said, "despite his many faults."

"Yes," she said, "we do."

"Do you think he loves us?" I said.

"In his own way," she said.

"He gave me a bottle of disinfectant and a scrub brush for my birthday," I said.

"That's his way," she said.

CHAPTER
TWENTY-EIGHT:
MR. MONK AND THE
THIRD SUMMATION

It was late Monday morning when the guards came to our cell, put Sharona and me in handcuffs and led us out to see some visitors. I hoped that meant my parents had arrived with a high-powered criminal lawyer who'd make Perry Mason look incompetent by comparison.

We were led into a windowless conference room, where Stottlemeyer, Disher, Ludlow and Monk were waiting for us. I would have preferred to see my parents and the lawyer.

"You can remove the cuffs," Stottlemeyer said to the guards.

"That's against policy," the stockiest of the guards said.

"I'll take responsibility," Stottlemeyer said.

"You're putting yourselves in danger," the guard said.

"I don't think so," Stottlemeyer said.

The guards unlocked our cuffs.

"We'll be right outside the door," the

stocky guard said.

"I feel safer already," Stottlemeyer said.

"What do you want, Leland?" Sharona said. "Because unless it's an apology, I don't want to hear it."

"Monk called this meeting," Stottlemeyer said. "He says there are some new developments."

I looked at Monk, who was standing at the end of the table, a grocery bag in his hand. He broke into a happy grin. No, it was more than that. He was practically breaking out in song.

I knew what that meant. Either he'd finally found two perfectly identical potato chips (a freak occurrence rarely found in nature, or so he'd told me) or he'd solved the murders.

I glanced at Sharona, Stottlemeyer and Disher, and I could see that they knew it, too. The only one who wasn't getting the message was Ludlow. But he would soon.

"So what's the news that's got you so excited?" Ludlow asked him. "Have you found some leverage to make one of these two turn against the other?"

"It won't happen," Monk said.

"You'd be surprised what people will do when they're looking at life in prison," Ludlow said.

"They're innocent," Monk said.

"I think I've proved quite conclusively that they aren't," Ludlow said.

"You proved the opposite," Monk said, setting the grocery bag on the tabletop. "But I couldn't demonstrate that yesterday. It was a Sunday."

"You were taking the day off?" Sharona said.

"I couldn't get the final piece of evidence until today. I could have found it a lot earlier if I'd only seen what was right in front of me all along," Monk said. "If I hadn't been so self-absorbed, I would have realized what was going on in time to stop this from happening. I owe you both an apology."

"What is he talking about?" Ludlow asked Stottlemeyer.

"I think he's getting ready to tell us who killed Ellen Cole and Ronald Webster," Stottlemeyer said.

"We already know," Ludlow said, tipping his head toward Sharona and me. "It was the two of them."

"It was you," Monk said.

Ludlow laughed. Stottlemeyer groaned.

"It sure would be nice if you and Monk could expand your list of suspects beyond the people in this room," Stottlemeyer said. "There's a whole city of possible killers out there. Pick one of them."

"At least Monk didn't say it was you or me, sir," Disher said. "Isn't it our turn?"

"The day is just getting started," Stottlemeyer said. "There's still time."

I wanted to believe that it was Ludlow because I needed it to be true. But I have to admit my heart sank just a little. What if I had been right before? What if this was the first time that Monk was wrong? I glanced at Sharona, who was expressionless, so I assumed she felt the same ambivalence that I did.

"Monk is joking, Captain," Ludlow said. "Don't you have a sense of humor?"

"I do," Stottlemeyer said. "But Monk doesn't."

"It's just that my sense of humor is very refined," Monk said. "Almost antiseptic."

"I'm not sure what that means," Ludlow said.

"You'll have plenty of time to think about it in prison," Monk said.

Ludlow laughed again. "Okay, I get it now. It's a very dry wit."

"I really mean it. You killed Ellen Cole and Ronald Webster," Monk said. "You can't come up with stories to meet all your deadlines, so you murder someone you've met at a book signing, observe how events unfold, then pick the least likely suspect to frame for the crime."

Monk detailed the evidence again, laying it out exactly as he had for us at his house on Sunday. I could be mistaken, but I think he even used the same words.

Ludlow listened to it all with amusement.

"That could make a pretty good plot in a novel. In fact, I might use it," he said. "But don't worry. I'll be sure to credit you in the acknowledgments."

"So far, Monk, you haven't told us anything you didn't tell us yesterday," Stottlemeyer said. "And it hasn't become any more convincing since then."

I hated to admit it to myself, but the captain was right. My hopes were fading fast, and from the look on Sharona's face, so were hers.

"The only thing I got wrong yesterday was thinking that Ludlow's scheme was all about me," Monk said. "It never was. I'm not sure he even knew I was involved until we showed up at his book signing in Los Angeles. But at that moment, he set out to frame Natalie and add another twist to the plot of his book."

"How can you say that?" Disher said.

"Because all the events leading up to Ronald Webster's murder began at that point," Monk said. "That's when Natalie used her credit card to buy Ludlow's book, the one with the fake alligator killing in it."

"Death Is the Last Word," Disher said, "which, if I may say, is destined to enter the pantheon of classic crime novels."

"Thank you," Ludlow said.

"Stop sucking up, Randy," Sharona said. "It's revolting."

"Here's what happened," Monk said. "Ludlow looked over her shoulder and got her credit card number and, for good measure, stole her credit-card receipt when he signed her book. He used the number to order the alligator jaws and have them sent overnight to her in San Francisco."

"Let's say you're right about that," Stottlemeyer said. "How did he know about Natalie and her relationship with the firefighter?"

"He didn't," Monk said.

"He didn't," Stottlemeyer said. "Doesn't that pretty much torpedo your whole theory?"

"Ludlow was teaching in Berkeley when I solved the Golden Gate Strangler case," Monk said. "He told us that he'd thought about turning it into a book."

"Too late," Disher said. "I'm already into the first draft. Only I've made some changes."

"Let me guess," I said. "Now the foot-crazy killer is caught single-handedly by a dashing lieutenant on the San Francisco police force."

"And the killer is called the Foot Fiend," Disher said, "as he should have been all along."

"Ludlow must have done some preliminary research into me and probably learned about the firehouse-dog murder investigation," Monk said. "Natalie's relationship with Joe was one of those nice surprises that Ludlow hopes for when he does these random killings."

"Meaning you can't prove that Ludlow knew anything at all about Natalie and the firefighter," Stottlemeyer said.

"The proof is that she's accused of murder," Monk said. "If Ludlow didn't know about them, then she wouldn't be here."

Stottlemeyer sighed wearily. "He told you how he knew about them. Ludlow found out after she got the phone call from the guy."

"That's not how he knew," Monk said. "Forget his story. Follow mine."

"Your story is inventive," Ludlow said. "But the plotting is weak. It's simply not believable."

"Don't take the criticism personally, Monk," Disher said. "He gave me the same notes on my first story."

"I'm having a hard time following the plot myself," Stottlemeyer said. "What's missing is evidence."

"On the contrary, there's evidence all over the place," Monk said. "The streaks on Webster's bathroom floor. The salt in the bathtub. The drop of blood in the grout. The drop of hydraulic fluid on the floor. The pizza box. The FedEx packaging. The drops of steering fluid in the parking lot and Natalie's driveway. Joe's fire department T-shirt. It's way over the top."

I raised my hand. "The T-shirt was me."

"It was *all* you," Ludlow said.

"Why would a killer who'd supposedly concocted such a clever and complicated method of murdering someone suddenly become so sloppy?" Monk asked.

"Killers make mistakes," Ludlow said.

"Not this many," Monk said. "You left an obvious trail of clues that would lead straight to Natalie and, by extension, incriminate Sharona."

"Let's forget for the moment that your imaginative scenario lacks evidence to support it," Ludlow said.

"I haven't," Stottlemeyer said.

"There's one glaringly fatal flaw in your creative thinking," Ludlow said. "Everything you described had to happen on Wednesday and Thursday. But Randy didn't call me until Friday."

"He's right," Disher said.

"I was in Los Angeles all that time," Ludlow said. "I didn't get here until Saturday. I couldn't have done any of the things you've suggested."

Monk smiled.

And what a smile it was. It was the grin you'd get if you came up with three cherries in a row on a slot machine.

It was a winning smile.

Sharona looked at me and I could see the excitement in her eyes.

"You called Ludlow on his cell phone, didn't you?" Monk asked Disher.

"Yes," Disher said. "So?"

"So you don't actually know where he was when he got the call," Monk said. "He could have been anywhere."

"I was in Los Angeles," Ludlow said.

"I can prove that you weren't. Like most bad mystery writers, you have your murderers dropping clues all over the place so that your detective can wrap everything up nice and tight," Monk said. "And you did the same thing when you framed Natalie. But you added one clue too many."

Monk reached into the grocery bag on the table and pulled out a piece of paper.

"This is a copy of the register receipt that was conveniently taped to the Sorrento's pizza box in Webster's kitchen," Monk said.

"The one that shows, without a shadow of a doubt, that Natalie was in the restaurant on Thursday night," Ludlow said.

"That's right," Monk said. "Why is that again?"

"Because of the ten-percent discount Webster got for mentioning the advertising on Julie's cast," Ludlow said. "That proves he was there at the same time that she was."

"How do you know?" Monk said.

"It's right there on the receipt," Ludlow said, pointing at it.

"Yes, it is," Monk said. "But how do you know?"

"Because I can see it," Ludlow said.

"But you had to have seen Julie to know about the discount advertised on her cast," Monk said. "And you've never met her. So how would you know about the discount unless you were here and saw them go into the restaurant?"

Ludlow sighed. "Someone at the pizza place told me about it during my investigation. I'm very thorough."

"That explanation might have worked, but like the killers in your books, you've been betrayed by a personality quirk," Monk said. "There's a bookstore across the street from Sorrento's. Unfortunately, it's closed on Sundays, so I had to wait until it opened this morning to buy this."

Monk reached into the grocery bag again and pulled out a copy of *Death Is the Last Word.*

"Would you like me to sign it for you?" Ludlow said.

"It's already signed," Monk said. "And dated."

Monk opened the book to reveal Ludlow's signature on the title page and the date below it.

October nineteenth.

Wednesday.

"The bookseller in Los Angeles told us that you had a compulsion," Monk said. "You can't pass a bookstore without signing your books. She was right."

Disher stared at Ludlow in stunned disbelief. Stottlemeyer looked pretty stunned, too.

I had to stop myself from raising my fists into the air and yelling *"Yes"* at the top of my lungs.

It was only a moment later that I realized that I hadn't stopped myself.

I'd done it.

Sharona broke into a big grin and gave me a hug.

Ludlow took a deep breath, let it out slowly and took a seat.

"You were watching Natalie and waiting to pick just the right person to kill," Monk said. "You saw Ronald Webster go into the pizza parlor while they were there. You befriended him afterward and, well, we know what happened next, don't we?"

Ludlow had lost and he knew it.

"This is going to make a much better ending for my book," Ludlow said with a rueful grin. "No one will ever suspect the author."

CHAPTER
TWENTY-NINE:
MR. MONK AND THE
HAPPY ENDING

Monk, Sharona and I walked out of the jail together. I took a deep breath. San Francisco had never smelled so good. I couldn't wait to get home and give my daughter a great big hug. And then I wanted a hot, bubbly bath and a long nap in my own bed.

Stottlemeyer and Disher both apologized to us. Disher almost got on his knees to beg forgiveness, but it didn't seem good enough, at least not the way I was feeling.

Monk apologized and he'd saved us. But there was still one thing neither Sharona nor I understood about the way he'd acted on Sunday.

"Why didn't you say anything yesterday when Ludlow was making his case against us?" Sharona asked him.

"At first, it was because I was ashamed of myself for my mistakes," Monk said. "Later it was because I didn't want to say anything that might tip him off that I was on to him.

I didn't want him going back and buying all of his signed books. But it turns out that I shouldn't have worried."

"Why not?" I asked.

Monk showed me what else was in his grocery bag. It was full of Ludlow books.

"It wasn't the only bookstore where he signed stock on Wednesday and Thursday," Monk said. "He also stopped at bookstores in Union Square and out near Baker Beach."

"What a moron," Sharona said.

"He didn't expect anyone to ever consider him as a suspect," Monk said. "So he didn't think he was taking a chance. Not that he could have stopped himself anyway."

"I would say that arrogance was another personality quirk that betrayed him," I said.

"Imagine having a compulsion like that," Monk said. "How did he manage to function in life?"

Sharona gave him a look. "You have a thousand compulsions like that."

"Yes," Monk said. "But I have you two to help me."

He had a point.

In the weeks immediately following Ian Ludlow's arrest, Trevor was released from prison and so were the five inmates who'd

354

been convicted of the murders that had "inspired" Ludlow's last five books.

Monk was able to show prosecutors how Ludlow had framed those others in the same way that he'd framed Sharona and me. The pattern of evidence against all of the wrongly convicted people was strikingly similar, mirroring the structure of the mystery novels Ludlow wrote before he started killing people for his plots and to make his draconian deadlines.

Lieutenant Dozier also pointed out exactly how Ludlow had steered the investigations in the direction he wanted them to go. Aiding the prosecutors was a selfless act on Lieutenant Dozier's part, because it meant conceding his role in the injustices that occurred. He resigned from the force rather than be made a scapegoat by the LAPD and the city, which was facing the likelihood of paying out millions of dollars in settlements to the people who'd been falsely imprisoned.

All six of the people framed by Ludlow were immediately offered book deals, of course. And so was Ludlow, for the story behind the murders he'd committed.

Trevor was the only one who declined the offers from publishers. He also turned away all the lawyers who wanted to sue the city for him.

For the first time in Trevor's life, not just one but two surefire get-rich-quick schemes had come his way and he'd ignored them both.

And Sharona loved him for it.

Trevor told me it was an easy decision. Pursuing the book or the lawsuit would have made a career out of reliving the nightmare his family and he had endured, and there was no amount of money that was worth that.

If Sharona didn't know it before, she knew it then: Trevor really had changed. I had a feeling that this time, the marriage was going to last.

There was still one mystery that Monk hadn't solved, and that was who Ronald Webster really was and where all his money had come from.

Monk wasn't interested. He'd found Webster's killer. His job was done.

I wondered why the mystery didn't eat at him in the same way that a murder or a robbery might. And after some thought, I think I've figured it out.

Ronald Webster's life wasn't a mystery. It was secret. Finding the answer wouldn't restore order, right an injustice or reestablish some kind of balance. It would simply satisfy Stottlemeyer's curiosity. And mine. And probably yours.

But Monk didn't care.

I wish I could tell you that I knew the answer to Webster's secret, but so far, nobody has found out.

If you figure it out, let me know.

It took Monk a full week to hang his dental poster. First, he had to pick the right spot on the wall in the right room. Then he had to center the poster and make sure that it was level and that the rest of the room was balanced around it. That's no easy feat.

Take it from me, feng shui is nothing compared to Monk shui.

He finished hanging his poster just in time for the pizza party we threw at his house in honor of Sharona, Trevor and Benji on their last day in San Francisco. They were going back to Los Angeles, where Trevor was going to relaunch his landscaping business.

The only other guests at the party were me, Julie and Monk. Stottlemeyer and Disher weren't invited. Sharona and I still hadn't quite forgiven them for arresting us. We knew they had to do it, but they could have fought against it a little harder.

The pizza was courtesy of Sorrento's, which was enjoying a lot of publicity and business in the wake of Ian Ludlow's highly publicized arrest. Julie was out of her cast, but her cast-vertising concept had really taken off. Every kid with a cast in her school was advertising something and Julie was getting her percentage. She even wore her Velcro cast now and then to make a few extra dollars.

Monk insisted on ordering the pizza "uncut" from Sorrento's so he could measure and cut the slices himself to assure they were each the same size and true triangles.

He almost returned the whole pie, though, when his measurements indicated that it wasn't a perfect circle.

Sharona and I managed to talk him out of ditching the pizza by reminding him that it was free.

"That's because it's defective," Monk said.

"Probably," I said, "but it still tastes good."

"It doesn't taste very circular," Monk said.

"You can taste that?" Trevor asked.

"Can't you?" Monk said.

"No, but I suppose it's just one more way I can't compare to you," Trevor said. "You've taken real good care of my family. Better than me."

"That's not true," Sharona said.

Trevor held up his hand to stop her. "I want you to know, Mr. Monk, that's one area where I intend to outshine you. I'm going to make it my lifework."

"It sounds like a good job to me," Monk said.

Trevor shook Monk's hand and went outside, where Julie and Benji were kicking around a soccer ball.

Sharona gave Monk a wipe before he even asked for it. "I guess this is good-bye again."

"This is good-bye for the first time," Monk said. "You skipped that part before."

"I wish I hadn't," Sharona said. "Thank you for giving me my life back, Adrian."

"You did it for me once," Monk said.

Sharona nodded. "I guess this makes us even."

Monk's eyes lit up. "Even. I like that."

"It's the way everything should be," Sharona said.

She kissed him on each cheek, just to keep things even, and walked away to join her husband and son outside.

I offered him a wipe for his cheeks but he declined it. That was progress.

Or maybe it was love.

"I'm going to miss her," I said.

"Me, too," Monk said. "All over again."

I nodded. "I have to admit, though, that it's sure nice to have my job back."

"You never lost it," Monk said. "It's yours

for life."

"That long?" I said.

"Whether you like it or not," Monk answered me.

ABOUT THE AUTHOR

Lee Goldberg has written episodes for the USA Network television series *Monk,* as well as many other programs. He is a two-time Edgar® Award nominee and the author of the acclaimed *Diagnosis Murder* novels, based on the TV series for which he was a writer and executive producer. His previous Monk novels, available in paperback, are *Mr. Monk Goes to the Firehouse, Mr. Monk Goes to Hawaii,* and *Mr. Monk and the Blue Flu.*

We hope you have enjoyed this Large Print book. Other Thorndike, Wheeler, and Chivers Press Large Print books are available at your library or directly from the publishers.

For information about current and upcoming titles, please call or write, without obligation, to:

Publisher
Thorndike Press
295 Kennedy Memorial Drive
Waterville, ME 04901
Tel. (800) 223-1244

or visit our Web site at:

www.gale.com/thorndike
www.gale.com/wheeler

OR

Chivers Large Print
published by BBC Audiobooks Ltd
St James House, The Square
Lower Bristol Road
Bath BA2 3SB
England
Tel. +44(0) 800 136919
email: bbcaudiobooks@bbc.co.uk
www.bbcaudiobooks.co.uk

All our Large Print titles are designed for easy reading, and all our books are made to last.